The Melo'
Following Phish a

Carl

Also available by Carl Cole:

Feasting on the Breeze:
A Memoir of Hitchhiking America at the Turn of the Century

Purchase this and other books directly from the author online at:

www.lulu.com/spotlight/carlcole

Contact the author through Facebook. You can easily find me through my band:

STIMULUS
www.facebook.com/stimulus69 or
www.stimulusmusic.com

Part One:
You Can Feel Good

~1~

Some things in life happen so effortlessly we call them destiny. Melody's destiny was woven with music. When she was just five years old, Melody was constantly pestering her mother for something to do. She said, "There's nothing going on at all."

"Melody, you can't expect a parade to go by every day."

Her life was saved by rock and roll.

It was alright.

July of 1999, like every July in the Northeast, was hot and muggy. The sun was down, but the humidity kept the temperature up. Why were 70,000 people camped out on the tarmac of Oswego County Airport in upstate New York?

Just to see one band?

The place was huge. It had been an Air Force Base at one time. Black tarmac and mowed grass covered with tents, cars, and people stretched in all directions. It seemed ridiculous to Melody.

Here it was, Friday night, all these people were camped out, and the band wasn't even playing until tomorrow night. It was the biggest party Melody had ever seen in her eighteen years of life. A lot of people had beer to drink and to share. Melody had smoked more weed that evening than she had in the last month. Pretty much everyone she met was friendly, smiled at her, and invited her in for a conversation.

She couldn't believe some of the people. They were so different from people she'd met anywhere else. Imagining some of them walking down the street in a city made her laugh. Instantly she noticed how many of these people had dreadlocks.

Long ropes of hair fell down their backs. The women looked like goddesses, and the men like heroes. Undoubtedly, their hair and their dress drew stares in the outside world, but here they were at home.

She soon realized, after a few discussions, that some of these people passed for normal in the outside world. They had haircuts and regular jobs: some in offices or restaurants, some as schoolteachers. Here they were someone else. To the complete bafflement of their friends, family, and co-workers, they would disappear for days, weeks, or months at a time to follow this band, or one like them, around the country. Some people she met numbered the shows they've been to in the hundreds.

The lights of more and more cars kept coming in.

"Hey, beautiful girl." Melody is beautiful. Flowing blonde hair goes past her shoulders and bright green eyes shine from sharp features that soften as she smiles.

The random, middle-aged shirtless dude calling out to her seemed nice enough. She smiled back. He was obviously a little weird, but he certainly didn't seem dangerous. He smiled from behind the dirty stubble on his face to reveal a missing tooth.

"Have you ever seen Phish before?" He asked.

"No, but I'm super excited," Melody replied.

"You should be. You're in for the best time of your life. Seriously," he got a strange look in his eyes and leaned in on her. He looked at her as if he were telling her the most important secret ever.

"Once those lights go down tomorrow night, life is going to change for you in every way, shape, and form possible. I know. I can tell."

"Oh yeah. How can you tell?"

"It's my job to be able to tell."

"Uh-huh."

"No, really. I've got a government grant to write a report on what happens to people when they start moving around as a tribe. You know, living beyond the grasp of mainstream society. It's top secret. You can read it."

It seemed, even to an eighteen year old girl, that every other thing this guy was saying was bullshit.

"Hey, Melody! Come help us with this tank." She was glad to hear Phillip calling her away from this strange person.

"I gotta go." She turned and walked over to Phillip's van. Lucy was sitting in the van with a bag of balloons on the seat next to her. She was counting through a wad of cash.

"Thanks for saving me from that guy," Melody said. "He was kind of creepy."

"Is that the guy who says he's working for the government?"

Melody nodded.

"I know that guy. He's alright. No worries, Melody. You're rolling with us now. We got your back." Phillip put his arm around her and she relaxed. Lucy finished counting through the wad of bills and said to Phillip: "You did pretty well in Jersey, huh?"

"Yeah. It was off the hook. Can one of you help me with this tank?"

Phillip was at the back of the van. He opened the door and Melody saw eight metal cylinders shoved under the backseat. Phillip smiled over at her, "I stopped in Philly on the way up here."

Melody nodded, even though she had no idea what was in the tanks or what Philadelphia had to do with it.

"Hey, keep a lookout, okay. If you see any security guards or cops coming let us know. Okay Melody?" Melody nodded

"You ready, baby?" Phillip asked Lucy.

"You know I am," she hopped out of the van, shut the door, and gave Phillip a kiss. Phillip kissed her back. "I missed you in Jersey. It's good to have my girl back."

He drug the tank between cars and towards the main street where dozens of people were walking by. Melody and Lucy followed close behind. When Phillip got to the main street he set the tank up and looked over his shoulder. Lucy was right there to hand him an empty balloon. As soon as he turned the valve to fill it people walking by heard the sound, stopped walking, and turned towards them.

"How much for a balloon?" A guy in his twenties with short hair and a ball-cap asked.

"Five bucks," Lucy said flatly.

Already she had two balloons in her hand and Phillip was blowing up a third.

"Whatever happened to one for $3 and two for $5?" The college kid asked.

From behind him, swerving with a handle of Jim

Beam in one hand, a drunken man with dreadlocks to his knees stumbled up. He had a cardboard sign on a string around his neck with blocky magic marker writing that read "Friend for life, 25 cents."

He passed the handle of Jim Beam to the college kid in the ball cap and said, "Shit kid, I remember when it was one for $2 and three for $5."

"Five bucks, no deals." Already Lucy had sold the two balloons in her hand and Phillip was handing her two more. As the hiss of the tank echoed through their section of the parking lot, people gravitated towards the sound. Melody had never seen anything like it. Phillip was blowing balloons as fast as he could, handing them to Lucy, who was taking money and passing them out as fast as she could.

Whenever someone got a balloon they sucked in the air and a glassy expression came over their face. Most people shared them with friends and generally they smiled and laughed together. But Melody noticed one guy in the back who had bought three balloons and then snubbed his friends when they tried to get one from him.

He huffed on the first balloon and glazed over. He hardly waited before he got into the second. After a huge hit from the balloon he fell flat on the ground. The third balloon fluttered away and he went into convulsions. Melody felt her stomach drop as she wondered what to do for the guy twitching on the ground. He looked like he was dying, but his friends were laughing as they sucked on their own balloons. In a few seconds he got up, a sheepish grin on his bloody face, and made his way back through the crowd to get more gas out of the tank.

Melody watched all this for about forty-five minutes. The crowd gathered. The same people emptied their pockets to get more balloons. Eventually she saw some flashlights coming through the crowd and some angry looking guys in black.

"Hey, Phillip! Lucy!"

They looked up expectantly from the tank. Melody

caught their eyes and said, "Security!"

Instantly Phillip and Lucy dropped the tank and took off back through the cars. Melody watched for a second longer then followed them. The security came through the crowd of people sucking on balloons, where they found the unclaimed tank on the ground. They took it away and only glanced for a minute at the crowd. They didn't seem to care too much about finding out whose it was.

Back in the van Lucy was counting money again. It was in a huge pile between the seats. Bills were scattered and crumpled. Lucy was trying to make sense out of it. "Tens here, twenties there, fives in this pile, and ones over here," she said to Melody.

"Hey, what do I do with this hundred?" Melody asked.

"Keep it," Phillip said. "Good job on the lookout."

They finished stacking the money. "Okay, guess," Lucy
said.

"Well, we probably got most of the tank blown off, so I'd say about $3,000," Phillip calculated the pile of money for a minute. He came up with $3,684 dollars, not counting the hundred Melody had in her pocket.

"How does it always come to an odd number when we do balloons for $5?" Phillip laughed. "Whatever. We've got enough money now to play all day tomorrow. We won't have to work again until after the show. Security probably won't be around so much tomorrow night, anyway. They'll be busy."

"What's in those balloons?" Melody asked

"Medical grade nitrous oxide." Phillip said.

"What's nitrous oxide?"

Phillip and Lucy looked at each other.

"Laughing gas, silly" Lucy giggled.

"Hippie crack," Phillip chimed in.

"What does it do?"

"Let's find out," Phillip said. He blew up three balloons,
and handed one to each of the girls.

3

Yesterday Melody was working as a checkout girl at the grocery store down the street from her grandparent's house. She had just graduated high school and had no idea what she wanted to do with her life. She did, however, have some notions of what she didn't want to do. She didn't want to get stuck checking out groceries forever. She didn't want to be like her mother. She didn't want children, and she didn't want to go to college. She wanted to live everyday like a parade, but most of her days were the same boring thing over and over again.

June slipped by and nothing happened. July began and it seemed as if another month would pass into oblivion and more of Melody's young life would slip away as well. She was eighteen years old and beautiful. Her big green eyes glowed whenever she smiled; though she didn't smile enough. She had a vulnerable appeal to her, like she really wanted someone to hold her, but didn't really know how to accept it.

Unlike her mother, who was short and borderline obese, Melody was shapely and tall. She had luckily inherited her father's genes. Since she was fourteen, men had been looking at her in a way that made her a little uncomfortable.

Unfortunately for Melody, the way she wore this discomfort somehow only added to her appeal. All day men came through her checkout line and flirted with her. She would be uncomfortable with their advances, turn away, and it only made them want her more.

She spent so much of her youth moving from one bad situation her mother created to another that she never made any close friends. There was some uncomfortable sex with a few boys along the line, but nothing like love had ever entered her life. She was pretty sure she didn't even love her mother or her father, though it made her feel awful to think such a thought.

"Melody, is that really you?"

Melody looked up from weighing broccoli to see a beautiful young woman with long dark hair that flowed as smoothly as the bright purple dress she was wearing.

"Holy shit, "Melody said, suddenly ignoring the old lady who was waiting patiently with her stack of coupons.

"Lucy, I can't believe it's you. I haven't seen you since..."

"Graduation. I mean, we went to that party together, but remember I said I was leaving. Well, I did. I went to Oregon, of all places, and now I'm on tour."

Melody was confused, what did she mean on tour?

"Are you in a band or something?"

"No, I've been going to Phish shows all summer. Just living, you know? They played in Boston for two nights, but I decided to skip the two nights in Jersey to come see mom for a minute and now I'm going up to Oswego, New York for a festival. Oh Melody, it's so amazing. The music is just beautiful and I've been all over the country with the greatest people. I'm loving my life. How are you? You still work here, huh?"

Melody looked around the grocery store, dingy orange and brown in that bewildering color scheme popular in the seventies and early eighties. Melody wondered how long they would let it go without a remodel. The colors made her sick. The fluorescent lights made her dizzy. The old lady with her broccoli and coupons frustrated her. Her life felt like a disease from which she had no cure. She couldn't stay here any longer.

A strange thought entered her head and Melody just went with it. She had no idea this simple decision would effect the entire destiny of her life. "Could I come with you?" she asked.

Melody was reaching out for anything to have

more value than this crappy existence.

"Umm, sure. But I'm on my way out like right now. What time do you get off?"

Melody was supposed to close and it was only 5:30 in the afternoon. She'd only been there an hour and a half. She'd be here for another five hours at least.　She couldn't wait that long.

She took off her apron, rolled it up on her register, and left the old lady staring at her broccoli on the scale.

"I'm ready to go right now. Can we stop by my grandparent's house? I need to get some things."

Melody had just cashed last weeks paycheck for $280 so she figured she could afford to go on a little vacation. She'd leave the $300 she had in a coffee can and be just fine when she got back. She could find another job at another grocery store, a newer one.

Lucy parked down the road while Melody snuck into the travel trailer she lived in outside her grandparent's house. She filled a backpack with her summer clothes. She left her grandparents a simple note. She didn't want to confront them. Melody generally avoided confrontation.

--Something came up and I'm leaving town
for the weekend to have some fun.
Don't worry, I'll be back next week.
I love you, Melody-

"So you just quit that job, huh?" Lucy said when she got back in the car.
"Fuck that job. I don't know why I kept working there except that I couldn't think of anything else to do. I mean, I guess I've been waiting for something to happen to take me out of here. Then you came along."

"Oh Melody, I'm so glad you're here. You're so going to love this."

"Are there any cute boys on tour?"

Lucy smiled, "The cutest."

The two girls laughed rolling down the highway in Lucy's two-door Oldsmobile. The car was a wreck, but it made it down the highway alright. Lucy told Melody stories about the west coast, a little about her boyfriend Phillip, and about Phish.

Melody had heard of Phish, but had never really listened to them. Lucy popped a tape in the cassette deck. "They're the most amazing musicians, and the places they can take you with their music…ahh….there's nothing like it. When I first saw them out in California it was like something happened inside of me. It's so hard to explain, but seeing them live is like having reality open up and show you her mysteries. Especially if you're on some good drugs," Lucy winked.

The music started and Melody, even though she was skeptical, found herself closing her eyes and being taken along like she always was with good music. There was something different about this, though. She grew up listening to Nine Inch Nails, Jane's Addiction, The Smashing Pumpkins, Pearl Jam, The Cure, Nirvana, and a whole slew of other musicians who were able to tap into the frustration Melody and a million other teenagers were feeling just before the turn of the century. Melody could listen to music and it would take her somewhere else; beyond her mundane life.

Almost everything Melody listened to before Phish had some feeling of despair or anger tied into it. This band was singing about a dog that took the rent money and hit the road. It was nonsense. Melody smiled to herself and listened to the guitar. She felt like she was running away from home herself.

There were dozens of songs she'd listened to her whole life that were about running away and leaving. They were all sad. This was a happy song about leaving. She could listen to this music, relate it to her life, and not have to feel anguish at being alive. She turned up the volume and sang along with the background refrain, "Runaway, run away, run away.

4

They pulled into the campground of Oswego the day before the show listening to the Grateful Dead.

"I always thought they were a heavy metal band. You know, all the skulls and skeletons," Melody shook her head.

Lucy laughed, "There's a lot you don't know, yet." They got out of the car and Lucy screamed and ran over to Melody. She almost tackled her giving her a hug. "I'm so glad we're here. I'm so glad you're here!" Lucy shouted. Melody felt a little bashful at the display, noticing all the other people near them. No one seemed to mind and Melody just let go. Fuck it. She was here to have a good time. She screamed as well, at the top of her lungs: "I'm so glad I'm here!"

A few of the people next to her started cheering at her outburst of joy. The people next to them picked it up and soon a wave of applause and yells rolled through the thousands of people gathered.

The girls laughed and fell into each other's arms again.

"Okay," Lucy said. "Getting down to business we need to find some tickets and find Phillip."

"Phillip?"

"My boyfriend, silly. He said he'd meet me on Shakedown today or tomorrow."

Lucy locked up the car and started skipping through the crowd, a spirit of light as she made her way. She still wore the same purple dress and seemed to float through the air. There's was something almost exotic about Lucy that made her stand out.

She was constantly happy.

Melody watched her and saw how truly beautiful she was. All the women Melody saw on lot were just so beautiful and so happy. They waved and smiled at Melody. She wished she could feel the same way, but somewhere in the hunch of her shoulders she was worried about losing her job, leaving her grandparents, and especially worried about Rachel, her mother.

For most of her life Melody had done her best to squeeze her almost six-foot frame into something shorter and less conspicuous. She'd made a career out of being invisible, hiding from her mother's boyfriends, hiding from the abuse of negligence, and hiding from herself. Now, as she watched Lucy singing through the crowd, hugging strangers and smiling at everyone, Melody was forced to wonder exactly why she'd spent so much time cultivating her isolation.

She was surrounded by smiling, half-clothed people; a lot of them very cute boys. This was like nothing she ever expected to see in her life. There was music coming from everywhere, and Melody was hearing a refrain from the Phish they'd been listening to, "Can't I live while I'm young?" She had arrived at the everyday parade.

The sensation associated with this understanding arced up her spine like electricity and she let out a yell. Lucy stopped skipping and looked at Melody. She visibly saw Melody shed the years of frustration, anger, and inhibition with that yell. Her back straightened up, the lines on her young face smoothed out and a real natural smile crossed her lips. She let out her yell, took in a breathe, and became an almost entirely new person. Melody had this unmistakable feeling she was born to do this.

Lucy couldn't help it. She gave Melody another hug, and now the two girls skipped arm in arm towards "Shakedown Street." There was nowhere else in the world to be.

When they got to Shakedown (the row of vendors in the parking lot; named after a Grateful Dead song) Melody came face to face with the center of this "town." An entire row of the parking lot was devoted to pirate merchants. Set up out of the backs of cars and vans was a staggering array of products being offered up. It was like a flea market and everything was available the traveling kid could possibly want. There were crystals and rocks, handmade clothing, unique T-shirts, stickers, glass pipes, and all kinds of food; amongst other things.

Melody stopped in front of a crystal and gemstone display under a pop-up tent. The display was complete with glass cases that apparently fit into the Chevy van along with the young guy behind the display, his long dreadlocks, and his smiling and pretty dreadlocked girlfriend. Melody couldn't help staring at a smoky quartz that stood a full three feet tall.

"Hey Melody, you know what's dumber than a box of rocks?" Lucy said. Melody shook her head. "I know this one," the guy smiled at them from behind the counter. He was angelic to Melody with his genuine and caring face.

"The hippie carrying them," he smiled at Lucy. The girls laughed as did the guy. "Take it easy," he waved to them as they walked away.

"This is amazing! Do these people have vending licenses?" Melody asked.

Lucy laughed, "I don't know. Maybe? I don't think so." Melody walked down Shakedown just lost in the frenzy of it all. People were pressed against her, laughing and smiling. The amount of exposed flesh made her feel a little uncomfortable, but in a good, sexy kind of way. Then Lucy grabbed her arm, "Oh shit, we need to work on getting some tickets."

"Okay. Where is the box office."

Lucy laughed and laughed, she was always laughing, smiling and getting smiled at. "Two beautiful young girls like us don't need to buy tickets. We get them for free."

"How?"

"Like this," Lucy stuck her hand up into the sky with just her index finger raised. "I need a miracle. Who's got my ticket!?" she shouted. "Just do like I do and this won't take very long," she said to Melody.

Melody copied her, lifting her index finger high

into the air, but was a little shy about yelling.

"Ticket, anyone got a ticket," she mumbled.

"You gotta holler, girl!" Lucy egged her on.

They strolled down Shakedown, their fingers high in the air and calling out for tickets. Suddenly Lucy put her finger down, let out another scream (Melody was getting used to the fact that Lucy was one of the loudest girls on the lot) and took off running through the crowd.

Melody saw her jump into the arms of a shirtless boy in his early twenties. He lifted her off the ground and they spun around in happy, loud circles for a moment. He was shorter than Melody, but taller than Lucy. He had dark dreadlocks slinking down his stout and muscular frame. His beard was scruffy, but his brown eyes were bright, and soft. He looked a little like a puppy to Melody.

"Phillip, you've got to meet Melody," Lucy was saying.

He put down Lucy, gave her another kiss, and turned to Melody. He smiled. His brown eyes lit up from behind his scruffy young beard. "I'm Phillip," he held out his hand.

"Hi, I'm Melody," she shook his hand. It was rough and sweaty.

"It's Melody's first show," Lucy said.

"I thought you looked a little wild-eyed. It's fun, isn't it?"

He raised his eyebrows as he was looking at her and she felt a flutter in her chest. She tried to look away from his dark brown eyes. "He's so cute, isn't he?" Lucy jumped in and wrapped her arms around Phillip.

"Yeah," Melody said before Lucy was quite finished, still answering Phillip's previous question. Suddenly she felt very awkward and tried to regain some of her footing. "I mean, it's fun here. That's what I was saying 'yeah' to."

"Oh, so you don't think I'm cute," Phillip said.

"No, you are...I mean, for Lucy. Oh my god!"

And all three of them started laughing.

"You girls wanna smoke a bowl?" Phillip asked.

"Of course! I haven't had any herb since the Boston shows," Lucy said.

"C'mon, then." They followed Phillip through the cars. He led them rows and rows away. They ended up somewhere out in the campground that even though it was kind of isolated was just a few rows away from one of the main thoroughfares leading through the airport.

And that's what this place was: an airport. It took a space as big as an airport to hold all the fans coming together for this show. Melody was finally getting a grasp on the sheer scale of what was going on here. 70,000 people were camped in an impromptu city for the purpose of getting together, listening to music, dancing, and enjoying life for no other reason than because they were alive.

"So, do you girls have tickets yet?" Phillip asked.

"Not yet," Lucy answered.

"Well, I got you covered. I picked up a few extras for this down in Jersey. So, here." He handed Melody and Lucy each a ticket, which made Lucy jump up, scream, and give Phillip another kiss.

"So, there," Phillip said. "Now that's out of the way, and there's no show until tomorrow night, maybe you ladies can help me work."

"What kind of work do you do?" Melody asked.

Phillip just laughed.

5

Phillip's first show was the Grateful Dead at Deer Creek in 1992. He was 16 yrs old and he flew in on a helicopter. Backstage, before the show, he got to shake Jerry Garcia's hand. There wasn't a conversation, Jerry was just walking slowly down the hall by himself while Phillip and the helicopter pilot were walking the other way. Phillip's friend, the helicopter pilot said, "Hey Jerry!"

"Hey, Tom," Jerry said.

"This is Phillip."

Phillip shook Jerry Garcia's hand, noticing his missing finger, but not even really knowing who he was, except that he was in the band. Jerry said to him, "Hey, man."

Phillip nodded. His knowledge of the Grateful Dead was strictly from a box of tapes he'd heard a week ago. Was this the drummer or the guitar player? Phillip was just super-stoked Jerry had called him "man," instead of "kid."

"Gotta run," Jerry said, and he was off, though not exactly like a shot. He kind of ambled away.

Later in life, Phillip would play the scene over and over in his head and kind of wish he'd had something to say. At that point, he knew nothing of the Grateful Dead's history, except that they were somehow involved with the Hell's Angels; or else Phillip wouldn't even be here.

Jerry seemed like a nice enough guy. He was pretty wasted, really, at that point. Two months later he would collapse and the fall tour would be cancelled. But Phillip didn't know any of this. All he knew was he liked the music he'd heard on the tapes and a golden opportunity presented itself almost instantly for him to be flown in backstage on a helicopter. Why not?

What Phillip didn't expect was an event that formed his future life. For one thing, he didn't even know hippies existed to this magnitude in 1992. Didn't they all die off or get jobs sometime around 1975? He looked out into the crowd, but was afraid of going out there. He wasn't sure he would fit in even though there were thousands of other young people. He stayed backstage and nibbled off the catering table. He got a beer out of one of the coolers.

Eventually the band started playing. It was mid summer, so the sun was still shining when they took the stage. Phillip chuckled to himself at the goofy old men out there. The bass player, in particular, looked like such a dork. Not to mention the guitar player in his short shorts. Up close, from the side of the stage, they didn't seem like much.

They kicked off the show with "Help>Slipknot>Franklin's": a trio of songs that blend together in a groove that puts the crowd to dancing instantly. Before Jerry was singing "Roll away the dew," Phillip had closed his eyes, forgotten what the band looked like, started dancing, started feeling awkward backstage, and jumped the fence into the crowd.

He weave-danced his way through the crowd. His gaze locked with a fiercely beautiful blonde woman with green eyes and dreadlocks. She smiled at him. He smiled back and his heart filled with something. His eyes began to tear up. He turned away and danced through the crowd some more. He didn't think it was possible that he could smile any bigger. It was amazing to him how everyone could be moving together, and never really touch at the same time. Even the guy who looked like he was fucking nuts, with hair down to his ass, gold sparkles on his bare chest, and wearing a skirt; even that guy spinning out of control never seemed to crash into anyone.

Phillip spent that first set dancing through the crowd in the sunshine up front. His smile was infectious, and everyone who saw this kind of goofy, kind of cool little sixteen year old kid dance up and smile at them, well they had to smile back.

It also didn't hurt that Phillip sparked up joint after joint (from the stash he'd brought in) with almost everyone who did smile.

At one point, there was a guy scribbling on a notepad. "Watcha writing?" Phillip asked.

"'To Lay Me Down.' They haven't played this in a long time."

"Is that the name of the song? You write down what they play?"

"Yeah, man. I keep a setlist. Wanna see?"

He handed Phillip his notebook. "Oh shit, there goes Jerry," the guy said as Jerry went into singing the lyrics. He closed his eyes and started swaying, staring up at the sky. Phillip flipped through the notebook, there wasn't much he could make out. It was a well-handled three subject binder, with hundreds of pages. The thing was nearly half full of scribbled lists of songs; little notes next to them.

Phillip had a hard time handing the notebook back to the guy. He didn't want to open his eyes and stop swaying. Phillip felt bad for tapping him on the shoulder, but the guy stopped dancing, took the notebook and smiled at Phillip.

"Have a good show, brother," the guy said.

Phillip walked away while Jerry was singing "To Lay Me Down," for what would be the last time. Phillip hiked to the top of the hill at Deer Creek and sat down. He lit another joint. Looking out over the crowd swaying from side to side, the people didn't look like individual people. They looked like a field of grass blowing in the wind.

Phillip couldn't believe he'd shaken the man's hand who was up there crying his soul into the microphone and through his guitar. It was almost too much for Phillip. Everything had happened so perfectly for him to be here. Now, as he looked out over Deer Creek at sunset, with The Grateful Dead in perfect harmony for one more last time, Phillip went to lay down in the grass, very content, and smoke his joint. He felt the music pulsing through him, through the grass beneath him, through the field of people blowing in the wind. Everything was intertwined and Phillip, for that instant, felt perfectly as one with it all.

There is a harmony between all things. Sometimes, somewhere, people get struck by the lightning of feeling this harmony.

WhaWhaWhaWhaWhaWha

Melody lost control of herself. Her eyes went into the back of her head. Her body felt like it was lifting up out of itself. Everything tingled. She could kind of see people, flashes of them. Lucy was laughing. Melody saw her and started laughing. She couldn't hear anything, though. Nothing except:

WhaWhaWhaWhaWhaWha

Then she came to, a little. She was still giggling. "So this is nitrous. This is fun!" Phillip took a big hit off his balloon. He laughed and his voice was comical it was so deep.

"HuhHuhHuh." He laughed.

Nitrous is always accompanied by strange sounds.

Melody took another hit. She went away again. When she came back she was sprawled in Lucy's lap. Now they had three empty balloons.

"Let's do some more balloons," Melody said.

"No, let's smoke a bowl first," Phillip said.

Phillip packed some of the weed he'd brought from Oregon, weed that he'd grown, into his pipe. He offered the first hit to Melody. She pulled on it and coughed, burning up every bit of green on top. Lucy took a hit and passed it to Phillip.

He held the pipe for a minute before hitting it, then passed the bowl to Melody. "So, Melody, what are you thinking of doing now? I'm just saying because Lucy and I have talked about it and if you want to ride out the rest of tour with us, we'd be down with that."

"Really? I haven't even thought about it. Do you think I could? Go on tour, you mean."

"Yeah, go on tour," Lucy said, mocking the words. Then she giggled, "You should come with us. We can have so much fun together. We were always really good friends who just weren't able to spend much time together. I really think that's because this is our time now. We finally get to be best friends. Please come."

"How many more shows are there?"

"Well, there's two nights here, then we're skipping the show in Canada. We don't want to be crossing any borders. Then there's a night in PA, a night in Ohio, a night at Alpine Valley, then 2 nights at Deer Creek. After that, they're off to Japan. We're heading back to Eugene after that. You can even come with us to Eugene if you want."

"You mean all the way to Oregon?"

"Sure, why not." The calmness in Phillip's voice kind of unnerved her. He was talking about crossing the entire country, leaving everything behind, and jumping into a life she had almost no clue about. She'd never been further west than Chicago.

"What would I do in Oregon?" Melody laughed.

"I'd give you a job," Phillip said.

"Oh yeah, doing what?"

He smiled, "Secret agent for the ganja team."

His family was well connected. His father and uncles were Hell's Angels. They moved cocaine and weed through Cincinnati and Cleveland.

Phillip was brought into the scene at an early age. It was only natural. He was his mother's son. She was the only sister in a family of six children. All five of her brother's were older and no more than 2 years separated each of them. They grew up as a gang, intimidating every other kid in their neighborhood, and being viciously protective of their little sister. The oldest brother, Dean, was the first to get a motorcycle and start running cocaine from Chicago to Cincinnati for the Hell's Angels.

As Dean moved up in seniority his younger brothers each took their turn at the bottom of the hierarchy. Phillip's father was another Hell's Angel who met his mom, impregnated her almost instantly, married her, and stayed married to her. His secret to a happy family was being gone as much as possible. Phillip never knew exactly what it was he did, except that it took almost all of his time. Phillip's uncles were the main contributors to his education and influence.

He was born into a world of motorcycles, loud parties, occasional beatings, and drug trafficking. He loved music that was loud, fast, and hard. When he got old enough to find his own music, he left his father's AC/DC and ZZ-Top and listened instead to Suicidal Tendencies, Anthrax, Nirvana, and was in love with something new a friend had just given him called Rage Against The Machine.

It was a Saturday in Mid-June of 1992 that Phillip heard the Grateful Dead for the first time. He was helping his uncle Curtis trim weed. They'd just begun harvesting 35 mature plants from underneath five 1,000 watt lights. Curtis had a basement that ran the entire length of his three bedroom house. The only way down was through a door that Curtis had made to look like a bookshelf.

The smell of fresh skunk sticking to everything was the only indication aboveground that something was going on below ground. That, and the outrageous power bill. But Curtis was smart. Before he started growing here, he had an electric sauna installed in the basement. He had a certified electrician run heavy-gauge wire down to the basement, had the city come inspect it, had the sauna and a breaker box installed, had the power company gauge his new bill for using his new electric sauna, had the city inspect it all again, then unplugged the whole thing and plugged in his electric marijuana farm.

All the expensive redwood sauna was used for anymore was chemical and fertilizer storage.

Each of Phillip's uncles eventually found their own specialty within the underworld. Curtis went from being really good at smoking weed, to being really good at selling it, to being really good at growing it. He grew his weed in a special soil mix he taught to Phillip. Curtis was into crossbreeding rare strains he found and consistently grew some of the best weed available in the state of Ohio. He was hoping to yield as much as ten pounds from this harvest that he could easily sell for at least $3,500 a pound and as much as $4,800, depending on the buyer and the circumstances.

"Those little girls are going to be ready to move in here and get put on flower pretty soon." Curtis said to Phillip.

"Probably veg 'em out for another week or two, though. Wouldn't you say?" Phillip asked.

"Ten days outta be about right. That'll give us enough time to take down the other room next week and get it trimmed, cured, and sold. Should be another ten pounds or so. I think it'll be a little more than this room, because those plants look bulkier."

Phillip was Curtis's protégé in the marijuana farming business. They spoke a language few outsiders could understood. It's not an easy job being a marijuana farmer, but Phillip had an excellent education in the field.

At fourteen he was sent over to help with his uncle's burgeoning, but profitable and relatively safe, new business. At first he helped hang lights and plastic sheeting. Then he helped maintain the operation by scrubbing buckets, washing everything, watering, and learning how to mix the soil. When the time came he was trimming the harvest with Curtis.

Curtis showed him everything he knew about growing weed..

Today they were trimming. Tomorrow they'd be trimming, and the next day they'd still be trimming. It's tedious work. The ganja plant grows it's flowers with leaves sticking out all over the place. People don't want to smoke the leaves, so those have to be cut off before the herb can be sold. The only way to do it is with a pair of scissors, some patience, and maybe some cocaine.

Curtis didn't approve of cocaine in his sister's son, but was sure to have plenty on hand for himself whenever a trim session came along. Phillip snuck bumps when Curtis wasn't looking.

The hours ticked by as they snipped their way through the plants. "Got any music to listen to?" Phillip asked.

"Actually, there's a box of tapes I snagged from this hippie guy. He owes me some money. I coulda beat his ass, but it's just no fun beating up on a hippie. Too easy. So I grabbed his box of tapes instead. If there's anything a hippie really loves, it's his music. He'll pay up."

Phillip put down the scissors, stretched his back, and walked over to check out the tapes. Every single one of them had "GD" on the label. Beyond that, the only difference was a date.

"What's GD?" Phillip asked.

"I don't know. They're from a hippie, so Grateful Dead probably."

"They're the band that does that cocaine song, right?"

"Which one? There's a lot of cocaine songs? Speaking off..." Curtis laid himself out another rail.

"Something about driving a train."

"Yeah, (snorrrrt) they do that one. Hey, you know how many hippies it takes to screw in a light bulb?"

Phillip shook his head.

"None, they just let it burn out, then maybe follow it around the country for a few years."

The joke was lost on Phillip and Curtis could tell. He shook his head.

They put in a tape and Phillip actually liked the music.

The guitar player was really good and the band had a crazy synchronicity to their playing. Since they were stuck in the basement for a few days, Phillip had time to really explore the music. They went all through the box of tapes over the next few days. The last day of trimming, when they were the most strung out and the basement was in the worst shape, the doorbell rang. Curtis went a little crazy trying to clean all the little weed trimmings off himself before he went upstairs. Phillip just stayed put.

In a few minutes Curtis came patiently back downstairs with some hippie guy in tow.

"There's your tapes, man. Thanks for paying me. I really didn't want to kick your ass, did I Phillip?"

"Nah, he said it wouldn't be any fun. Hey, I really like that band, the Grateful Dead."

"Yeah, they're playing in a few days over at Deer Creek. I actually fly the helicopter for them when they're in the Midwest. In and out of places like Deer Creek, Alpine Valley, and Soldier Field."

"So you're flying for them at this show coming up?" Curtis asked.

"Yeah, man. I am."

"So, for the inconvenience to me, by you not paying me what you owed me when you owed it to me, I'm willing to forget any interest or have any bad feelings that might affect our future business if you'd be willing to fly my nephew here into the show as well."

Phillip spent the next three years on Dead tour. He got by selling weed, selling LSD, selling ecstasy, selling whatever he get a hold of (which was a lot for a kid with legitimate Hell's Angels connections).

After Jerry Garcia died, and the Grateful Dead stopped touring, Phillip moved to Eugene, Oregon, to live with Alice, a girl he'd fallen in love with on tour.

Things didn't exactly work out with Alice, but Phillip liked Oregon a lot better than Ohio. With some startup capital from tour he bought enough equipment to get going. Then he made one more trip to Ohio to get genetics from his uncle Curtis. Phillip rented a house with a basement and went to work. He made pretty good money, but he missed the tour scene and started experimenting with Phish shows. He found his groove again, got a partner to watch his house while he was gone, and went back on tour. On Phish tour, he was up to his old tricks again. On lot, Philip never sold herb. He sold everything else instead.

And that was how Phillip lived his life. He grew marijuana, dabbled in growing mushrooms, was trying to learn how to make LSD, and spent the rest of his time hustling the lot with whatever drugs he could find. He was really good at it. He was 23 years old and had $30,000 in cash buried in a lockbox in his backyard.

Just in case.

8

"What's with the dreadlocks?" Melody asked Phillip.

Phillip stirred in his seat. He hated any kind of questions about his dreadlocks. It was something very personal, even though he wore them in public view. He ignored the question for as long as he could, blowing up three more balloons.

"I've seen so many people with dreadlocks today. It's amazing, but what's it mean? You all seem so proud. Are you Rastafarian? Like Bob Marley?"

Phillip was sucking on a balloon as Melody asked him the last part. He bust out laughing, partly from the nitrous, and partly from the question. To Phillip, it seemed he was caught in that laughter for half-an-hour. In reality, it was about twelve seconds.

The question, however, was forgotten for a few more seconds as Phillip and the girls sucked down the balloons and just laughed at each other. What were they laughing about? They didn't know. It didn't matter. Melody inhaled the gas from the balloon and held it in her lungs. Her feet began to tingle. As she breathed out waves ran over her body. The tingling spread over her entire body, the waves coming faster. She was twisting and falling.

Her eyes closed and the outside world ceased to exist. A strange kind of serenity enveloped her. She washed away from everything into the spin cycle of reality. Everything made sense in the wash. She had been here before. She knew it.

Her eyes opened and still she saw nothing and knew everything. Then a tunnel opened up and she heard Phillip laughing before she saw his distorted face. The spinning stopped and Melody got off. Vertigo still churned in her stomach. She smiled.

What a strange feeling? For seventeen seconds she felt completely connected to the thread of cosmic understanding. Coming back to her regular unsure self was kind of a disappointment. It seemed to her that she should have just turned into profound light and transcended instantly.

She wanted another.

Before her head even stopped spinning she was holding her hand out for Phillip to pass her another balloon. She didn't even want to catch her breath. She just wanted to go again.

This is where the dangers of nitrous lie. Breathing nitrous oxide can be entertaining, but isn't necessary for supporting life, like breathing oxygen is. Too much NO_2 and not enough O_2 and a person starts fishing out. So named for the similarity in action between the nitrous user and a goldfish flopping on the floor.

Phillip saw the hungry look in her eyes. He didn't need Melody turning into a crackhead.

"Wanna smoke a bowl?" He asked.

"Sure," Lucy said. Phillip looked over at her and smiled. She'd already learned about nitrous and how addicting it can be; and how shitty it can make you feel the next day. Not just sick, but worthless as a person with nothing to look forward to. It's really an awful trade for some empty laughs.

Phillip packed the bowl and smiled as he handed it to Melody.

"You know, these nights when there's not a show, but we're already where we're supposed to be are almost as good as the show nights. There's no running around, there's nothing we gotta do but hang out. It's relaxing."

Melody passed the bowl to Phillip at her left.

"So how is your mom?" Lucy asked Melody. "Is she still? You know?"

Melody hesitated, she didn't even want to think about Rachel, much less talk about her. Phillip pulled the smoke into his lungs, pretending to focus on the lighter and the pipe, but looking past them all to Melody. So this was Melody's uncomfortable subject.

It made him feel better to know her weak spot. Already she was making her way into his plans. Phillip always had plans for people.

Melody let the question float through the air, hoping it would go away. Phillip grabbed it. "Alright," he said. "You tell me about your mom, and I'll tell you about my locks."

"Oooooh," Lucy said. "This should be good."

They both turned and glared at her.

"Geez, sorry you two. Should I blow up a few more balloons?"

"Nah," Phillip said. "Save that shit for the custies. I wanna talk to Melody for a minute, and I want to talk to you, too. It's something really important."

Phillip packed another bowl and they passed it around in silence. It was a strange counterpoint to the frenzied laughter of a few minutes ago. Everyone felt a little empty and spent. Melody was the first to break the silence. Phillip had been waiting for this.

"I'm so scared of turning into her," Melody said.

"Who?" Phillip asked.

"Rachel, my mom. She's a crackhead, you know."

Lucy nodded. When they were growing up everyone knew. Melody was in Lucy's class for kindergarten, third grade, part of seventh, all of eighth, half of ninth grade, and the last half of their senior year. Everyone knew that Melody had to move whenever her mother let things get out of control, whether it be one of Rachel's boyfriend's becoming obsessed and abusive, or just plain leaving; or the crack dealer wouldn't give Rachel anymore crack because she owed too much money. Rachel moved them to some other small town in western Massachusetts.

"She was never really a mother to me. She never hugged me. I remember that. Never. There were times, like when I fell down or something, and I'd come crying to her. She would just look at me with this glazed look like she didn't care. She was high. She was always drunk or high."

"Where was your dad?" Phillip asked.

"Oh, he's not much help. He's crazy himself. He only married my mom because she got pregnant. He told me that once. He never wanted to have a kid with her. She told him she couldn't get pregnant. Well she did, and here I am."

Melody held out her arms as if presenting herself to the world. She was ashamed of herself, but what else could she do? Where she came from wasn't a place that felt anything like home. In thinking of her family, the only people she loved were her grandparents. No matter where Rachel moved them to, they were never very far from Bill and Betty.

They were Melody's solid rock. Whenever Rachel couldn't make rent or Melody needed new school clothes, it was grandma and grandpa who paid. They weren't rich. In fact, quite the opposite. The only thing they had going for them was that Bill had built Betty a house as a wedding present when they were married in their early twenties. They were pushing eighty now and wouldn't be around much longer.

Her mother and her sisters were hovering over the house like vultures, waiting to get their piece of the pie when one or both of their parents died.

"My family was never really a family except for grandma and grandpa. Mom and Dad got divorced before I was a year old and dad moved into the forest in Maine. He got a little cabin up there where he doesn't have to deal with the world and lives off government disability from the army for being crazy."

"Was he around at all when you were a kid?" Phillip asked.

Lucy already knew the answer to this. In the summers, when Lucy was playing with the other kids in their hometown, Melody got shipped off to Maine for 2 months to be in the woods alone with her father.

"A little. He's a good man, but he has his problems. When I was with him he did his best to be good to me, but I could tell just having me around made him nervous. We laughed and played sometimes, but he usually got a headache afterwards and had to lie down for hours. He'd sleep a lot during the day and stay up late at night. He tried to teach me some things, but he doesn't really know anything about how to live. Asking him for advice was ridiculous. He can't grasp how to deal with people and social situations. He eats a lot of pills."

"So mostly, you were raised by your mom?"

"No. Mostly I was taking care of my mom, but sometimes, for a few months in the summer, or a week here and there, I rode the Greyhound for a day and took care of my antisocial dad way up in Maine. Mom is on Food Stamps, but she doesn't eat. Which is strange because she's pretty fat. I guess it's the beer."

"Anyway. I made grocery lists of things for my mom to buy and made dinner for myself. Sometimes I made her breakfast or dinner, trying to cheer her up or make her feel better when she was sick, but nothing I ever did made her happy."

"When I turned 18, halfway through my senior year in high school, I moved in with my grandparents."

"That's when you came back to school with me, right?" Lucy said.

"Yeah. I just couldn't stand to be around her anymore. I wanted to get away from everything, but I figured I had to finish high school first."

"So you moved during your senior year? That must have sucked," Phillip said.

"It makes it kind of hard to find friends. Everyone's already known each other forever and has a history and it's almost over and here's this new girl."

"Only you weren't the new girl," Lucy cut in. "We went to kindergarten together. I always knew you."

"No, you're right, Lucy. You were always a good friend. You were always nice to me and I liked hanging out with you, but you were a cheerleader and knew everybody and never had time for me."

"I always wished I did."

Melody felt her eyes water and Lucy the same. Lucy's lip trembled and she bawled a strange sound that made Phillip jump. Then she leaped across the van and gave Melody a hug that made Melody feel both protected and vulnerable at the same time.

Before either of them could say anything, Phillip chimed in, "I didn't know you were a cheerleader, Lucy."

They all laughed together, a deep and soulful laugh that mingled with the tears and somehow made it all okay.

"I never knew your mom didn't hug you," Lucy said. "Never, really?"

Melody couldn't talk. She was crying and laughing in Lucy's arms. Unlike Lucy, Melody was mostly quiet. She hardly ever complained about anything even though her young life bordered on child abuse. Too many nights were long nights of random men coming over for sex and bringing drugs while Melody hid in the other room. Sometimes it was an insane drunken car trip that Melody felt lucky to survive.

In the end, she would see her mother, crumpled on the couch, crying by herself and alone, and all Melody wanted to do was hug her. If she came near, Rachel told her to go away. Melody didn't know how to feel. Any emotions resembling love were met with cold indifference or ignored altogether.

Tears were soaking Lucy's purple dress, she held Melody tighter. Melody made hardly a sound, just a squeak or a sob here and there. Lucy held her tighter.

"I love you sister," Lucy said softly, stroking Melody's hair.

Melody laughed a little through the tears and took a breath. Those words were so unfamiliar to her. It always made her flinch a little when Bill or Betty would say 'I love you.' They were the only people in her life to regularly say so. She didn't know what to say back to them. Usually, she just said, "Okay, bye."

This time, in a van in a field next to an airport in upstate New York, where 70,000 strangers were gathered together like family, Melody knew exactly what to say.

"I love you, too."

9

Phillip packed another bowl while the girls were crying and hugging each other. He couldn't believe his luck. These two were perfect. They trusted each other completely and he needed that. Now he needed them to trust him.

He passed the bowl to Melody first, as she was wiping tears from her cheeks. She pushed her wet blonde hair out of her face, and even with her eyes puffy from crying and being high they were still a cheerful shade of green. Melody glowed with a kind of light that wasn't born from the circumstances of her life. There was something innate about her beauty.

"I'm sorry," she said, blew her nose into a tissue, laughed a hollow laugh, and shook herself.

"Don't be. It's fine. Most of us have a fucked up family. That's why we're out here, creating our own family." Phillip reassured her as Lucy nodded and patted her on the shoulder.

"Welcome home, sister."

Melody hit the pipe, this time she noticed how Phillip and Lucy both started a bowl by not burning all the green off the top. She passed the bowl with most of the green left to Phillip. He took in the smoke, closed his eyes and touched the pipe to his forehead. Melody had noticed him doing this before. "Why do you do that?"

"It reminds me that this herb is kind of like a sacred medicine. I put it to my head and my third eye." Phillip figured this was as good an opportunity as any to get started telling these girls what he needed and wanted them to know.

"You want to know why I grew my locks, well, it all kind of connects to the herb for me. See, I've been involved with herb for a long time. My family isn't really the normal suburban family. My uncle started teaching me to grow weed when I was 14. When other kids had after school jobs at McDonald's, I was selling them weed and taking their paychecks."

"I've always been different, you know? Not just from my friends, but from my family also, even my uncle. I used to do my best to blend in and keep myself as inconspicuous as possible. But I didn't feel right. I wanted to do something so that people would know the minute they saw me that I was different from them, living a different kind of life, you know?"

"What's different about your life?" Melody asked.

"Well, for one thing I've never had what you would call a 'real job.' I'm really conscious of what I put into my body. I don't eat meat at all or anything from an animal. I don't smoke cigarettes. I may use drugs, but I think of it as a way towards enlightenment and the herb is just daily medicine for me."

"When did you start growing your locks?" Melody asked.

Lucy sat back listening, Phillip hadn't opened up to her like this
before.

"Five years, now. I had long hair before that, but I didn't let it lock up until after Jerry died and I moved to Oregon." Phillip had to get away from everything. Dead tour got really crazy in the last years; the only years Phillip knew. There were the usual drugs: LSD, mushrooms, ecstasy, and cocaine, but new things were popping up. Ketamine, a powerful animal tranquilizer was particularly appealing to Phillip. It sent him into another world, like DMT did. Anything that opened up another world was appealing to Phillip. He smoked heroin, though he never shot it up. Some of his friends were shooting needles. Just like Jerry was.

When Jerry died it all came to a grinding halt. Everyone had lost their drive. People were left wondering what to do with their lives. Phillip was actually glad. It was the first time he'd ever wondered about what to do with his life.

If Jerry hadn't died, Phillip probably would have. He was on his way to either killing himself or winding up in prison for a very long time. He was deeply involved in bringing drugs like Ketamine and DMT and Heroin to the lot. His family connections gave him the product and his marketplace devoured it.

Everyone could tell he was strung out, but no one could argue with the kind of money he was bringing in. When Jerry died, he reluctantly told his family he wouldn't be bringing so much work home anymore. To his surprise, they were glad as well. Any fool could see where Phillip was heading. What his family didn't expect was that he wouldn't be coming home to Ohio. Instead he was going to live with Alice in Oregon. Phillip wanted to do his own thing, and he'd never be on his own living anywhere near his family.

He couldn't tell Melody or Lucy any of this. They couldn't know about his family. It was time to change the subject.

"See, my locks are kind of like a filter. Certain people don't even talk to me. Those people are generally bigots, or close-minded assholes and who wants to talk to them anyway? They can go right ahead thinking they're better than me. But I know I'm healthier and I make more money in a month than most of them make in a year."

He hated bragging about himself and loved it at the same time. He told himself he was justified letting Lucy and Melody know a little about his real operation because he needed them involved. Lucy was in, though she didn't know to what extent. Melody was still in question.

"See, In my business, you have to make a decision on who you can trust in a split second. The locks give me a little credibility with the people I deal with. They know I'm for real. My locks are my roots."

"See, this nitrous," he slapped one of the metal tanks. "This is just bullshit to get us around on tour. I do it because, technically, it's not illegal. I'd get in more trouble selling weed out here than this hippie crack and it's way harder to sell weed. People want to look at it, try and talk you down in price, while the cops are prowling around looking for guys ducked between cars. With nitrous, all I gotta do is turn on the tank and heads come running. I make as much on a tank of nitrous in an hour as I would working out a whole pound of herb in eighths."

"But herb is my real business," Phillip hit the pipe again and held it to his head. "I've got an indoor growing operation and I pull down up to 20 pounds of herb every time I cycle it; and I cycle it every ninety days. I get $4,000 a pound and sell it all at once. Do the math."

Lucy did the math and liked the numbers she came up with.

~10~

July 17, 1999 was a night that Melody would never forget and never quite remember at the same time. She woke up that morning and the van was an oven in the sun. She threw open the doors to find something to breathe. The air outside was thick and humid. The sun was glaring down. She shielded her eyes and looked around.

Phillip was sitting with his shirt off under a pop-up canopy in a camp chair. In his hand he held a bottle of Corona with a lime in it. A pimply guy of about eighteen was sitting under the shade on a blue cooler strapped to a skateboard.

"You want a Corona with lime?" He asked Melody.

"Oh my God, is it cold?"

"Ice cold. One for $3 or two for $5." He smiled at Melody.

Normally this kind of guy might have repulsed her. His shaggy brown hair was unkempt and jutted out from under his dirty ball cap. His clothes were too big and needed to be washed. But his smile was bright and sincere. He was at home with his cooler full of Corona's, his skateboard, a ticket, and a few dollars.

Melody bought two beers, one for Lucy who was still asleep in the van, and sat back in the empty camp chair next to Phillip.

She sipped the very cold beer and watched the kid roll away on his cooler. He had the cooler strapped to his skateboard and just coasted down the blacktop. A few cars later he pulled over, opened up his cooler, and made another five bucks. From where she sat Melody could still see his smile and hear his genuine laugh.

"That guy was cute," she said to Phillip.

He laughed and took another drink of his beer.

There was a hum in the air. Melody could feel it. She sat back in the shade, sipped her beer, and rested deep inside of herself. The crowd was a tranquil murmur in the background, punctuated by occasional laughing or a happy yell.

The world is generally such a bustling place. Phones are ringing, bills are coming in, and there's work to be done. A person rarely finds the time or the space to reflect on themselves, their inner heart, and how it relates to the world at large. In the crowd at a Phish show, especially one that camps out for a few days, those moments come with frequency.

As Melody sat under the pop-up, occasionally sipping her beer, she had time for this.

No matter what was going to happen, she was glad she was here. No matter where she ended up after this, she felt if she could just hold onto a piece of this tranquility, everything would work out well for her. The stillness was finally broken by Lucy yelling from inside the van.

"Holy shit! It's so fucking hot!"

"C'mon, girl. I got you a cold beer," Melody called to her friend.

Lucy emerged from the van, her dark hair leaping from her head. She'd changed some time during the night into pajamas and one of Phillip's T-shirt's that said, "Play Mound, Dammit!" Phillip couldn't help but to stare at Lucy. No matter the situation, Lucy was young and beautiful and perfectly at home in her shapely body. So many of the women on tour have an internal glow and a beauty that doesn't fade against such a mundane backdrop as a hangover.

Lucy had her reasons for being here as well. Her life appeared normal on the outside. She lived in a happy home in the suburbs with her three older sisters. Her father was an engineer in an office and her mother worked evenings as a yoga instructor.

Over the years her fathered sexually molested each of Lucy's sisters in turn. Lucy's mom finally admitted the situation and divorced the foul man when he got to Lucy. No one in town knew why they had divorced and Lucy had never spoken of it to anyone.

"You look beautiful this morning," Phillip smiled at

her.

That was why she liked him. He gave her constant attention.

"I feel ugly," she frowned and he got out of his chair to hug and comfort her and bring her the cold beer Melody was holding.

They spent the day under the shade canopy, it was too hot to do anything else. The kid with his cooler of Corona's kept coming by. They smoked a few bowls. At one point Lucy and Melody ventured off to Shakedown wearing as little as possible. They bought a couple grilled cheese sandwiches and a bowl of veggie stir fry. Phillip had some of the stir-fry.

The heat was ridiculous. It was even hotter than yesterday. They spent the entire day under the shade, drinking Coronas, smoking bowls, and phasing in and out of consciousness. Luckily Phillip had brought plenty of water along so they didn't have to wait in the extremely long water lines.

Sometime in the late afternoon they ventured out again.

On Shakedown they bought a large, deep fried egg-roll called a Jerry roll. It was okay, vegan, but a little heavy with grease.

After dinner Phillip pulled out a bag of mushrooms. "Who wants to go to the moon?" he asked.

The girls both held out their hands. Phillip laughed and split the bag 3 ways.

"If anyone gets lost, just meet at the van afterwards. Later tonight we're going to blow a few tanks."

They drifted into the show. They passed through a field of teepees, a giant roasting marshmallow, and a field of rocks that people were stacking and arranging in whatever way they deemed fit. It was like nothing Melody had ever seen before. They wandered through a grove of trees spider webbed with masking tape. Someone was on hand to pass out the masking tape.

As they walked past the Ferris wheel, Lucy turned to Melody and a goofy grin crossed her face. "The mushrooms are starting to kick in," she said.

"Uh-huh," said Melody. The sun was still up, but it was starting to descend. The heat was stifling. The twisting in Melody's stomach from the mushrooms added to her feeling uncomfortable. She'd never done mushrooms around such a large group of people before. She wondered if she'd be able to handle it.

Mushrooms usually have a feeling of anxiousness associated with them, especially as the trip starts to come on. Melody was feeling this anxiousness. She looked around the crowd of unfamiliar faces and felt out of place. What was she doing here? What was going to happen to her? She forced a smile, but it didn't help.

Suddenly there was a sound from the stage, a loud whump. Then the song started instantly. Melody felt her hips start to shake and her head start to rock back and forth. She couldn't make out the words to the song, something about science and knocking on a door.

"For fun, he knocked on it some more." Melody caught that lyric.

Then something really happened. Something stupendous. Melody floated outside of herself. She wasn't held by her reservations, or inhibited by her shortcomings. This music, the thumping bass, the hypnotic drums, and the gliding notes from the guitar and piano, elevated her above herself.

"Woooo!" she screamed. She lost sight of Lucy and Phillip out of the corner of her eye and started dancing through the crowd, closer and closer to the stage. She shook her body through the crowd, in time with the music. People moved out of her way, smiled, and she smiled back. For a minute she caught the eyes of a woman with long blonde dreadlocks cascading down her back. She and Melody danced together for the second solo section during Tube.

Eventually Melody found herself at the front of the

concert. The mushrooms were really doing a number on her now. They were strong and they churned in her stomach. The music felt like a warm blanket wrapped snugly around her body. She'd made it all the way onto the front row when Phish went into their second song for the evening. This would blow her mind wide open.

Right up front, the rest of the world disappeared. It was just Melody and Phish alone together in the world. Phish was singing "Boggie on Reggae Woman," just for her; as far as she could tell.

One song flowed into the next and the sound filled every empty space. She got lost. Then she found herself, and let go again because being lost was more fun. Revelations about herself and her life flowed in through the music, the lights, the crowd, and the mushrooms. The whole experience could possibly be explained by saying it was directly caused by the drugs, but that's just not right. In the past, medicine men from around the world have used different types of hallucinogens to induce visions. None of them mistake the agent as the source of the vision, only as a facilitator to discovery. Living in today's world, there are no medicine men left, so we each do our own soul searching.

Melody reached a level of acceptance with herself as she shook her body to the music. She knew without a doubt after that night her life wouldn't be lived along ordinary lines. She usually felt out of place, never quite at home in herself or her world. But right here, right now, she hears the lyric "What is wrong with you?" and has no answer. For the first time ever, Melody doesn't feel that anything is wrong.

Instead, everything is perfectly right. For the rest of the night she dances through the crowd, from up close to way in the back. People pass her joints, she smokes them without stopping from her dance. She gets passed water bottles. She takes a drink, smiles, and passes it back. For the rest of the show she moves. Her body shakes and struts with the music.

Whenever the mushrooms seem like they might get too intense, Melody just closes her eyes and listens to the music and everything is all right again.

After the sun sets, the lights come up, and Melody's visuals amplify. The band settles into their space, and the music just flows. For the next two and a half hours there is absolutely nothing wrong in the world, at least as far as Melody and most of the 70,000 other people in attendance are concerned.

When the last notes of "Tweezer Reprise" fade into the nighttime air, and the band walks off the stage, Melody just falls down in the grass: exhausted, happy, laughing, and content.

From now on, her life will be measured against a different ruler.

She was still laughing to herself and lying in the grass when Jessica found her.

"Hey girl, how you doing down there?"

Melody was stunned. Her eyes were wide. She was completely drained. Eventually she had gravitated to a place to her left, towards the side of the stage the keyboard player was on, and found enough room to dance about halfway back.

She just closed her eyes and flew through the last hour of the show in that place and perfectly in tune with the music. When it was over she just collapsed, completely drained. She was lying there, looking up at the girl with long dreadlocks standing over her: Jessica.

"It got away," Melody whispered up to Jessica and no one in particular. The refrain from "The Squirming Coil" was replaying itself over and over in her head. It was the last song before the "Tweezer Reprise" and the end of the show.

Jessica laughed. She'd seen Melody dancing near where she and her friends usually posted up, on Paige's side. There was something about the girl that appealed to the mothering nature inside of Jessica.

"It's okay," she said. "They'll be playing again tomorrow night, right here. Let me help you up."

Melody and Jessica burst into laughter together. "I've never seen anything like that," Melody said.

"Was that your first show?" Jessica asked. Melody just nodded.

Jessica laughed and clapped her hands, "Seriously!?! Oh goodie. I love meeting virgins."

Jessica was 26, born and raised out on Long Island. She'd been on tour now for a couple of years, starting out small, catching a few Phish shows here and there in 92-94. The Grateful Dead were still playing at the time, but she'd never really been into the Grateful Dead. During those days, Phish didn't draw a crowd of 70,000 people, but that would all change. It happened right after Jerry died.

In 1995 Jessica went on tour. She was seeing every show that Phish would perform. Over the next two years she would watch the band go from playing medium-sized auditoriums to playing fields and stadiums and complexes and airports. She loved it and hated it at the same time.

Jessica had dreadlocks that trailed down almost to the back of her knees. They were dark and straight and clean. Her face was stern, which really didn't match with the kind person she was inside. She was still young and pretty, but compared to Melody, her age was beginning to show. Years of smiling and laughter had worn grooves along the corners of her mouth and eyes.

She held out her hand and helped Melody up off the ground. "C'mon girl. You look like you need a babysitter. Where are your friends?"

"I lost them at the beginning. I went dancing up front. They're in the parking lot, I think. By the van."

"Oh, that should be helpful. Come with me. You'll be alright."

Melody had some trouble getting her legs under her, and the ground wobbled beneath her as she stood. But once she was walking, she felt lighter than air again. Jessica led Melody through the parking lot to Shakedown Street. Jessica was moving kind of fast. She held Melody's hand and pulled her along.

On Shakedown they weaved through the crowd. Jessica kept looking back, assuring herself that Melody was still in tow.

In front of a maroon Dodge minivan was a kitchen. The kitchen had a ceiling. It was tent, a white EZ-Up bought at Sam's club for $300. The kitchen had burners. Three propane camp stoves from Wal-Mart at $35 each. The stoves were on a table. A white plastic fold out for $60. The stoves had flat grills laid across them, $12 each. On the flat grills were quesadillas. Cheese melted between the tortillas, combining with broccoli and salsa to create the menu.

The kitchen had a chef. He was tall, about 6'3". His dreadlocks were longer than Jessica's. A full, shaggy beard grew from his face and fell down the front of the white apron he had tied around his waist. He held a spatula in his hand, paused from his cooking, and belted out the menu.

"Veggie Quesadillas, one for $3, two for $5."

Then he saw Jessica. "Hey, Jess! What's going on? Where have you been? I'm slammed."

Jessica directed Melody to a fold-out camp chair behind the kitchen and reached to tie an apron on herself. "Sorry. I found this girl all spun inside the show and I wanted to help her out."

"That's cool," the chef put down his spatula and turned around. He smiled and reached out to shake Melody's hand where she sat. "I'm Kale. What's up?"

"Melody," She wanly smiled back and shook his hand. The camp chair she sat in felt as if it were twisting and turning beneath her, so she decided it was best not to move.

Jessica and Kale, on the other hand, were constantly moving. Jess was taking orders from the long line of people in front of the table and collecting money. Kale was flipping quesadillas, wrapping them in paper plates to be sold, and starting new ones on the flat grills. They twirled and danced around each other in the makeshift kitchen as gracefully as any dancers.

It was the blowout. The time after the show when everyone returns to the parking lot hungry, high, and spent. It was the time Jessica and Kale did most of their business. For an hour Melody sat in the chair watching Jessica and Kale dance with each other. A permanent grin was fixed to her face. Jess and Kale laughed with the crowd, made some deals on quesadillas, but mostly stuck to their price. Jessica was fond of the saying, "No Deals!," as was Kale. They called this phrase out enough that they were known on lot as the "No Deals Café."

At one point, Jessica passed a quesadilla back to

Melody, waiving off any money. Even the "No Deals Café" bends the rules from time to time. Melody saw a hundred smiling faces approach the table. There was the nervous young couple, with the girlfriend who looked slightly disgusted at eating this food. There were the drunk college guys, all laughs and hifive's. There was the shady hippie guy in a patchwork hoodie, and the middle-agers who kind of looked out of place, but actually fit right in. The bearded, aging, grey hippie really liked the food and came back for seconds.

Then the spunion showed up. He was sweating profusely. His T-shirt stuck to his body. His face was red and puffy. He leaned against the table, putting his entire weight against it.

"I'm so hungry," he said to Jessica.

"Here have a quesadilla."

She passed him the cheesy tortilla and veggies wrapped in a paper plate. He looked at it as if it were a foreign object, something he'd never seen before. He swayed a little in front of the table, and took a bite from the quesadilla.

"It's good," he smiled, his mouth full of food.

"It's also three bucks."

He looked confused and dejected. In his mind, wherever his mind was, this food was supposed to be complimentary. Kale was laughing his ass off at the exchange, and the spunion glared at him for a minute. Kale slipped another quesadilla into a paper plate and Jessica cleared her throat at the spunion. She held up three fingers and smiled at him, the line behind him was growing again and the people just behind him looked as if they might leave. He fished some crumpled bills out of his pocket, threw them at Jessica and walked off.

"Hey, man," she called out after him as she uncrumpled the bills. "This is too much."

"Fuck it. Just keep it." He called back from between bites.

Jessica laughed a full and healthy laugh. "That

guy just gave me two twenties and a five for that quesadilla."

"Fucking cool," Kale went back to flipping tortillas.

"Can you believe this?" Jessica held out the money for Melody to see and laughed .

Melody smiled back. "Whatever. You tried to tell him."

"I know. Fucking spunion," she laughed again.

~12~

The Ferris Wheel was still open and Lucy and Phillip were sitting together on top of it. The wheel was stopped to load some laughing passengers at the bottom and Lucy and Phillip had the view from the top.

"Look at all these people," Lucy swept her hand in front of her. "They're all so beautiful."

Phillip had been to a few more shows and seen some of the underbelly and darkness that also lives on the lot. Still, he couldn't disagree with Lucy.

"They're just pilgrims trying to find their way. Like us."

"Like us," Lucy said and held his hand. She looked him in the eye and they kissed.

Phillip felt his heart flutter. He hadn't felt like this for a woman since Alice. But Lucy was so young. It didn't seem like she should have the kind of wisdom and freedom she possessed at such a young age. When he met her in Eugene, Oregon, he was instantly impressed with her.

He was sitting in front of the Out of the Fog coffee house, sipping on a bottle of green life smoothie from Genesis juice. Genesis juice was a local bottler in Eugene, and they made the best juice Phillip had ever tasted. He was completely addicted to it, as much as the coffee drinkers around him were to the black caffeine. Lucy walked right up to him and asked him what he was drinking.

He told her.

"Can I try some?" she asked.

She took a drink, unabashed, right from his bottle. He kind of flinched, concerned about her germs, but then decided he wanted her germs all over him anyway. They talked away the afternoon. Phillip had nowhere to go and Lucy was just traveling the west coast in her Oldsmobile.

She'd wound up in Eugene after going to Cougar Hot Springs. She'd been through San Francisco, the redwoods of Northern California, and up the Cascade Range of Oregon. She didn't really know where she was going, but had enough money form graduation presents to continue on for a while longer.

Phillip was getting ready to go on Phish tour. He invited Lucy out to dinner. Over the next week, they spent almost every day together. Lucy still slept at the hostel every night, but every morning she had Genesis juice with Phillip at Out of the Fog. He led her on adventures for the rest of the day from there. One day they hiked Spencer's Butte, and Lucy swore she could see the Pacific Ocean from the summit.

The next day he took her to the beach and showed her a cave where he sometimes came to spend the night. The day after, they drove up to Portland and he took her out to see Karl Denson at the Roseland Ballroom. It was an old ballroom, where people used to dance in the twenties and the hardwood dance floor was set on springs so that it bounced beneath you as you danced. Lucy loved it.

Later that night he got them a nice hotel room and he and Lucy made love for the first time. In the morning, as they lied in bed together, he invited her to come on Phish tour with him.

He explained how he'd be running drugs and would need her to follow behind in her car. She'd be a decoy if ever there was any trouble. "Just swerve around if you see a cop start tailing us. Tell him you were fixing your make-up or something, but I'll be rolling with a couple of felonies."

He' d pay for gas and everything if only she'd come.

As they sat in the Ferris Wheel together, both of them were glad with their decision.

"We need to find Melody," Lucy said.

"Yeah," Phillip laughed. "I'm sure she's all right. I hope those mushrooms didn't spin her too bad."

"She can handle herself. I saw her for a minute during the show. She was running around on Paige's side, dancing her ass off during that sick 'Sneaking

Sally Through the Alley.' I almost went up and told her something but she ran off. She's having a great time. I'm so glad she came along."

"Me, too. I hope she comes back to Oregon with us. You think she'll be down?"

"I don't know. Maybe. Probably. She's never really been involved with anything like this before. It might be too much for her."

"It would be so much better to have the both of you there. I'd be glad to know she was watching your back while you drive twenty pounds of weed down to San Francisco or up to Seattle. It's not that I'm worried about you being able to handle it, but it's always better to have someone around who's got your back."

The Ferris Wheel started spinning again. Lucy was quiet. She still held Phillip's hand.

"We should probably get to work pretty soon. Maybe Melody's back at the van," Phillip said. They got off the Ferris Wheel.

"I'm hungry," Lucy said.

They strolled through the lot and headed towards Shakedown. They weaved their way through the crowd and got into the now short line in front of the No Deals Café. Kale spotted Phillip through the crowd.

"What's up, bro?" He called.

Phillip nodded back at him, "Hey, man."

The crowd thinned out and Phillip and Lucy found themselves at the front of the line. Hugs were exchanged over the table. "Great show, huh?" Kale said.

"Fucking right," Phillip said. "How about that 'Funky Bitch' second set opener?"

"That was good, but what about the 'Wolfman's,' 'Sneaking Sally' sandwich. That shit was the heat."

To an outsider, this conversation makes no sense. But to the gentlemen engaged in it, they are talking about things that mean the world to them. There's an unspoken brotherhood between people on tour like this. It's prevalent in every exchange, and people on tour sometimes take it for granted what a pleasant interaction it is. When you see the same person in the lot, city after city, and know, without a doubt, this person is going through some kind of trial and adventure similar to your own, a very real and deep bond is created.

People respect each other.

In the real world, people just don't develop this bond with acquaintances. And really, Phillip and Kale are only slightly acquainted with each other. They see each other on lot, but know absolutely nothing about each other's families or lives beyond tour. The bond they share, however, is on a level completely removed from their families and whatever lives they have beyond tour. Here, in this situation, they trust and respect each other a great deal.

"Hi guys," a feeble voice injects into the conversation from behind the kitchen.

"Holy shit. It's Melody," Lucy exclaimed. "Where did you find her?" she asked Jessica.

"I picked her up out of the grass after the show. Is she with you guys?"

"Yeah," Lucy said. "She's my friend from high school."

"You know these guys?" Kale looked back at Melody and motioned towards Phillip and Lucy with his spatula.

"Yeah. They're my friends." Melody smiled sheepishly. "Is that all right?"

"It's better than alright. It means you're family," Kale said.

"I could tell there was something special about her," Jessica smiled. "You know me. I don't usually go picking up newbies and bring them into the kitchen."

"Well shit, let's smoke a bowl," Kale said.

He took off his apron and sat down. Just then a guy walked up to the table and ordered a quesadilla.

"Hey, sorry. I'm closed right now," Kale said.

"C'mon. Why?"

"Because I'm fucking tired and I want to smoke a

bowl with my friends. That's why."

"Alright, man. Fine. I'll just go get some French Bread Pizza."

"You do that, man. Vegas Mike needs your money, too." Kale waved the guy away and shook his head. "These people think I'm out here working just for them. If they knew me any better they'd know I can't stand having a boss," he laughed.

Phillip pulled a glass pipe out of his pocket and packed a bowl. He passed the fresh hit to Kale, who took a puff, touched the pipe to his forehead, and passed it to Phillip. The pipe went around the circle. When it got to Melody she took a hit and passed it to Jessica.

Jessica waved her hand at it. "I don't puff," she said. Melody was confused, looking at Jessica's long dreadlocks.

"Damn, did you see Schwilly Billy, tonight?" Kale asked Phillip.

"No, what was he doing?"

"He got his dog into the show."

"That fucking mean ass pit bull?"

"Yeah, that one. He got the dog and a handle of Jim Beam in. He was fucking plastered way back on Paige's side and his dog kept trying to bite every cute hippie momma he was trying to hit on. I was laughing my fucking ass off. He'd stagger up and try to share this bottle of Jim Beam with just about any lady he'd run into. They'd reach out to pet his dog and the bitch would try to bite them. Schwilly Billy would get all pissed off at his dog and smack it around like he does and this hippie momma would get all freaked out and run away. It happened like three times. It was fucking hilarious. Then we moved to Trey's side."

"That guy can't find a woman for shit."

"Who's gonna hang out with a fucking drunk all the time?"

"Yeah. I thought he'd found his match when he hooked up with Boozin' Susan."

"Yeah, you'd think Schwilly Billy and Boozin'

Susan
would've been a perfect match."

"I heard she's in AA now."

"No shit?"

"No shit."

"I guess they don't call her Boozin' Susan anymore."

They all bust out laughing.

Although they never see each other off lot, Phillip, Jessica, and Kale have spent years together and independently at the same shows. Anytime they get together the conversation and banter flows. They continued talking about friends they knew on tour, shows they'd been to, when the last time Phish played "Mound" was, and hotels they'd partied in throughout the country.

The girls quickly evaporated from the masculine scene.

"Hey Kale," Jessica said. "Do you mind if I take off and stroll around with these young ladies Phillip brought to the show?" She smiled at Phillip.

"Nah, it's fine. I might cook a little more tonight, but probably not much. We're gonna sit here and smoke some weed for a while."

"Love you, baby," Jessica said. "C'mon girls. Let's leave these guys to their guy talk."

Melody pulled herself out of the chair for the first time in hours. "Oh my God," she said. "I have to pee."

They took off towards the porta-potties.

13

It was late. The moon had set long ago and the sky was dark. The airport, however, was lit up with mobile light towers. The clatter of diesel engines could be heard through the night, powering spotlights high above the crowd. Beyond the diesel engines was the murmur of thousands of voices conversing, laughing, congratulating, crying, bargaining, singing and doing all the things human voices were meant to do. A few drum circles throbbed in the distance. Dogs barked. Somehow, amongst all this noise a sense of peace pervaded.

Everyone had slept or hidden as much as possible throughout the long, hot day. Now it seemed as if everyone was out patrolling the airport. Melody was finally coming off the mushrooms enough to successfully navigate her surroundings.

Together, the girls found their way to the porta-potties. There were about three dozen disgusting, overflowing, and awful smelling plastic closets to piss and shit in.

"Oh my God, am I really supposed to go pee in there?" Melody asked.

The girls laughed. Jessica offered up her experience. "I hardly ever go in the porta-potties, unless they're just cleaned of just delivered. I'd rather pee on the ground between some cars. Those things are gross. I don't even want to go inside of them, much less sit on the seat."

The girls weaved between the parked cars, found a spot that seemed secluded, and all three of them pulled their pants down and squatted to pee on the ground. They were laughing hysterically. "Stop making me laugh, I can't go pee," Lucy said.

Melody was laughing like crazy, "I have to pee so bad you're making me splash it all over myself."

"You girls are gross," Jessica laughed.

The giggles subsided and all three of them went about peeing in relative silence.

It was at that time a shady kid in a patchwork hoodie and a college kid in a ball cap ducked between the same cars. Neither one of them noticed the girls, they were too busy discussing what was in the little baggie the kid in the hoodie was selling to the college kid.

Jessica piped up, "Excuse me! We're peeing here."

The guys noticed them for the first time, "Oh shit," the kid in the hoodie said. "I'm fucking sorry. I didn't know this was the line for the bathroom."

The guys slipped out. The college kid shielded his eyes as he walked away, but the kid in the hoodie took another look. "Damn, those girls are all super hot," he said to the college kid.

The girls laughed and splashed some more pee on their legs. When they were done they pulled their pants up and slipped back out from between the cars. The kid in the hoodie had made the deal and was waiting for them. "Hey, I'm Nathan," he said. "But everyone calls me Natron, cause I'm like a machine built just for tour."

Jessica straight laughed in his face. "You're a fucking tool, Natron. What? Are you gonna offer us some molly now and try and get one of us to sleep with you? We'll eat your molly, but none of us are putting out."

Natron may have been a machine built for tour, but he wasn't programmed to handle someone like Jessica. Really, he was rather new to the scene but had fit right in and found his groove. He was only nineteen, but he thought of himself as a player. He'd been to 26 Phish shows now and planned on finishing out the tour.

He was, in fact, selling molly. Molly is slang for MDMA, or the active ingredient in ecstasy. It comes as a powder and the name, molly, is supposedly short for molecule. The reasoning is that molly is just the MDMA molecule, without all the mixers that make up the cocktail of drugs in an ecstasy tablet.

57

At 19, Natron was blessed with thick facial hair, but he kept his head trimmed short. His features were soft, his beard dark, and in some ways, he looked kind of like Phillip without the dreads and a little taller.

His smile was sincere and defeated as he pulled his head bag of molly from his pocket. "Well, can I at least hang out with you beautiful women if you're gonna eat my molly."

"C'mon Natron, it's like 1 in the morning. Put that shit away," Jessica shook her head. "There's a show tomorrow," she said.

The girls started heading back towards the "No Deals Café." Natron watched them longingly as they were walking away. Those girls were smoking hot and Natron really wanted to be hanging out with them.

Jessica really wanted to eat his free molly tomorrow night for the show, so she turned around waved at Natron.

"C'mon, silly," Jessica said to him.

The girls locked arms, Jessica in the middle, and skipped through the lot. They left Natron a good twenty yards behind so they could talk. He followed blindly behind them. The tour machine had been reprogrammed and was now a do-the-goddesses-bidding machine.

"We're going to get along beautifully, girls," Jessica was saying. "It's so hard to find strong young women to hang out with." Jessica was truly glad to have some girlfriends with her. Her locks, her kitchen, her boyfriend, and her attitude distanced almost everyone. Other women were generally intimidated by her.

Melody and Lucy were both genuinely glad to be around her. Jessica was special, and both the girls could see it. She was forever looking for women to spend time with who could match her strength. Part of her reasoning for going on tour had been the lack of strong women she met in the real world. Sure, some women held good jobs, but they were as much a slave to the system as they had been slaves to their husbands a hundred years ago. That was what passed for strong. She didn't want that for herself.

She saw more happiness in the eyes of the demure girlfriend whose sole purpose was to please her man. Even though sometimes she wished she could, Jessica knew she just couldn't be that person, either. She was an explorer. She explored the country and explored the strength within herself. She also explored other people's reactions to her.

She felt that if she approached any situation without passion then she had failed herself somehow. The result was that life had been very exciting for her for quite a few years now, but disturbing to some of the people around her.

Pleasant suburban wives at the grocery store saw her long dreadlocks, heard her mouth, and saw her cart full to the brim with tortillas, cheese, broccoli, and salsa. These women who saw her at random could become deeply confused and generally left the scene questioning themselves and their choices in life.

Jessica's mother was one of these women; dumbfounded, nervous, and oddly proud of her daughter all at the same time.

Jessica was determined to suck the marrow from the bones of her life. Melody and Lucy both recognized this quality instantly and knew it was one they wanted to emulate.

Once the girls got over their laughing fit, Lucy chimed in. "Phillip's gonna be pissed we've been gone so long. I'm supposed to help him work a tank tonight."

"Oh well. He'll get over it," Jessica said.

"So, what does molly do, anyway?" Melody asked.

"Oh shit, have you never eaten molly?" Lucy asked.

"No," Melody smiled again.

The girls both looked at her.

"What? I didn't get invited to your cool kid parties in high school."

"Fuck the cool kids!" Jessica screamed.

"Yeah, fuck those punk bitches," someone yelled from the distance.

"See, he knows what I mean," Jessica nudged Melody.

"What are we gonna do with Natron?" Lucy asked. He was still following them. He kept almost catching up, but would run into someone he knew. Natron seemed to know everyone. He would have a quick exchange with the people who stopped him, but was intent on following these girls.

"He's kind of sleazy," Lucy said.

"No doubt, but I want to eat his molly tomorrow night," Jessica said. "We'll bring him back to Kale and Phillip. If he's not cool, those guys will run him off quick."

Melody looked back to Natron. He smiled at her. She didn't think he was sleazy, she thought he was kind of cute. She hoped that Kale and Phillip wouldn't run him off.

When they returned to the "No Deals Café," the business was still closed. Instead of quesadillas, Kale and Phillip were serving up their favorite dish: drunk sarcastic remarks at people passing by. Kale had produced a bottle of whiskey from the van and he and Phillip were chasing it with beers they bought from some kid with a cooler.

As soon as the girls walked up, Kale hollered at Jessica. "Damn, that was a long piss break." He and Phillip laughed.

"Did you have to take a shit or something?" Phillip said.

"No, we had to clean the porta-pottie with our tongues before our diarrhea exploded. Kiss me baby," Jessica grabbed Kale, pulled him up from the chair and stuck her tounge in his mouth. They kissed deeply and as they pulled apart she looked him in the eye, raised her eyebrows, and flirtatiously grabbed his crotch.

"Good to see you too, baby," he said.

She let go and Kale beamed down at her. He was deeply in love with this woman. She had something no one else seemed to have: a joy for life that was unmatched. She brought him along for the ride, even though people thought he was in charge judging by his size and stature. They had it all wrong. He would do anything for her. He loved her as deeply as any man can love.

Natron walked up, eyed Jessica and Kale making out, met eyes with Phillip and said, "Hey. What's up?"

"Whose the fucking cool kid?" Phillip laughed sarcastically to his friends.

The girls all laughed as well.

"I seem to have a knack for picking up strays tonight," Jessica confessed.

"Man, if I'm too cool for you guys, I can stray right along. No sweat off my balls. There's like 70,000 other people I can go hang out with. But what's up? You guys wanna puff a bowl or something?"

"I like this guy," Phillip said

14

Natron was forever moving. It was partly due to the cocaine he'd done earlier, but he was also just naturally an energetic fellow. He sure couldn't sit still behind the kitchen for very long.

"Man, I'm kind of hungry. I don't think I ate today. Can I buy a quesadilla off you?"

"Sure. If you want to cook it," Kale said.

"Just tell me what's up."

Kale directed Natron through the mechanics of firing up the grill and told him where all the ingredients were. His explanation was as brief as possible. Somehow, Natron figured it out and fired up the stove. As soon as he started cooking, a skinny guy wrapped in a blanket and shaking from too many drugs walked up.

"Can I buy one of those?" He asked.

"Sure," Natron said. He fired another quesadilla, took the guys three bucks, and passed it back to Kale. Kale shrugged, "I like this guy, too" he said.

A small, late-night crowd gathered around the kitchen. Nobody else was cooking nearby anymore. Natron fired a few more burners and went to work. He was laughing and joking with the crowd, serving quesadillas, and passing money back to Kale.

"Damn Jess," Kale said. "This guy fits right in, too. Seriously, what's with the people collecting tonight?"

"I guess I'm on a role. Maybe I'll find my true love tonight," she flashed a wicked grin at Kale.

"Poor bastard. I feel sorry for him," he smiled right back at her.

They sat and watched Natron cook for a while, laughing with him and the customers. It was kind of weird to even think of the people on the other side of the table as customers. The exchange was more personal. There was far more to it than simply exchanging a product for some cash, saying 'have a nice day' and moving along to the next transaction.

There was actual gratitude involved, from both

sides. From the far side of the table, the person buying the quesadilla was so glad some other crazy person was up this late, camped out at an airport, and had the good sense to be making food. From the kitchen side, the person handing over three dollars was providing a way to stay on tour and purchase another gallon or two of gas in the tank.

This support economy was acknowledged by the management of the "No Deals Café" when the original blanket kid came back with his blanket girlfriend.

"She's really hungry now, but I ate all that quesadilla. We got like two dollars in change between us. Can we get like just a cheese quesadilla or something?"

"Keep your fucking change!" Kale bellowed at them. The blanket kids curled deeper into their shells of polyester hotel blankets. "Kick those blanket kids down a quesadilla, Natron."

"Word," Natron said.

The blanket kids smiled meekly, and bowed as they gratefully walked away with their quesadilla.

"C'mon Lucy," Phillip said. "We've got work to do, too."

"Oh, can't we just wait until tomorrow? I wanna hang out with these girls.

Phillip shook his head. He wanted to make some money tonight, but he didn't want to push Melody and Lucy into doing something they didn't want to do. He turned to Natron.

"You ever run a nitrous tank?" he said.

"All the time, man. I got you." Natron had once operated a tank to fill balloons, for about three minutes at a party one time. It wasn't fucking rocket science. He was confident he could handle it.

"The trick is that you don't hand balloons to anyone but me. Got it? Don't pass out balloons to randoms in the crowd that tell you they've already paid me. I take the money from them, take the balloon from you, and pass it to them. That's how it goes. You'll make some money."

"Cool man, cool."

"Kale, I'm stealing your cook."

Kale flipped his middle finger at Phillip. "Ah fuck you, man. I was making money sitting on my ass. You know how rare that is?"

"Well, get off your ass and flip some quesadillas," Phillip said.

"Fuck you. I'm gonna drink some more whiskey and go to bed. Hopefully Jessica gets horny later and wakes me up," Kale winked at her.

"Kale, you're such a fucking pig."

"And you love it right?"

"Sometimes." Sometimes their banter got to her and she did just want him to hold her close, tell her everything was okay, that she was beautiful and he really loved her. Kale would've loved to do that, really, but Jessica's strong exterior, in some ways, held even him at bay.

Like it is with most exceptional people, the trait that distinguishes them from everyone else, at times also alienates them.

How was Kale to know when she wanted him sarcastic, witty, and dirty, or when she wanted him sincere, simple, and clean? He wasn't a fucking mind reader. It was a fine line he walked, trying to maintain a relationship with such a strong-willed woman.

And all within the confines of a minivan.

15

Natron and Phillip marched off on a mission to blow at least 2 nitrous tanks and stack a few thousand dollars. Kale, in a way, was envious of them. Beyond the time he spent in the kitchen, the encores he missed rushing out to set up for blowout, and the hours at the grocery store, prepping, and cleaning up, he still had to find time to have fun and let go. It was sometimes bitter, unrewarding work. He would make as much on the whole two-day Oswego run as Phillip would make off one tank. Some nights Kale felt like giving up. Like he worked his ass off to make food for these people and it never really paid off.

"Fuck this," he said. "I'm going to bed."

He stumbled from his chair and swerved into his bed inside the van.

"What an asshole, "Jessica said. "He didn't even clean up this fucking kitchen."

"Don't worry. We'll help you," Melody said.

They closed bags of tortillas, put a lid on the salsa, wrapped the shredded cheese, organized the coolers, wiped down the tables, and closed up the stoves. The whole process took almost an hour in their dilapidated and tired state, giving the girls plenty of time to talk.

"So, what do you think of Phish?" Jessica asked Melody.

"I love it. I've never seen anything like this. The people are amazing, the music is amazing. I just feel so lucky to be here."

Lucy told Jessica the story of Melody walking out on her job. Jessica laughed, "I've lost so many jobs from going on tour it's funny. I walked out on a waitress job in Asheville, North Carolina just before this tour started. They just couldn't seem to understand why I needed four weeks off from work."

"This is our church," Lucy said. "Did you tell them it was a religious holiday?"

The girls laughed again. Melody's cheeks hurt

from smiling so much.

"I definitely felt something religious earlier tonight," Melody said.

"I could tell. I saw the way you were dancing," Jessica smiled.

Melody smiled back, "It was strange. I wasn't thinking about anything beyond the music. I've never felt like that before: so perfectly in place at just the right time."

"I know what you're talking about. It's such a great feeling," Lucy said.

For a moment everyone was quiet, remembering the feelings of the night before.

"Have you ever seen Widespread Panic?" Jessica broke the silence.

"No, we haven't," Lucy answered for both of them. "So far just Phish, and some Deep Banana Blackout shows when I was in high school."

"You never told me about that," Melody said .

"Cool kids," Lucy smiled sheepishly. "Sorry, but you're here now."

"You know, Widespread Panic almost does more for me than Phish. Keep that in mind and go see them sometime." Jessica grinned as she swam through the warm night air, busy with the tasks of closing her shop. "Tomorrow I want to hook you each up with a sexy momma dress."

"Do you sell clothes, too?" Lucy asked.

"Yeah, just never at night. There's no point. Everyone's too high and it's too dark. Something usually ends up getting ruined. What are you girls doing to get by?"

Melody and Lucy looked at each other and shrugged. "I guess we're just kind of rolling with Phillip," Melody laughed.

"That kid's a baller, for real," Jessica said. "Just make sure you don't get too dependant on him. If things go wrong you could find yourself stranded. You've got to figure out your own way to get by."

"Like what?" Melody asked.

"Whatever. T-shirts, stickers, food, crystals, water, beer, glass, clothes, posters, drugs, whatever it takes, you know? Don't expect to get rich doing any of those, though. It's not about coming to the shows to make money, it's about making money so you can keep coming to the shows."

By this point the kitchen was cleaned up and Jessica was tired. "Good night, girls. I'm going to bed. Come over tomorrow and let's go to the show together. I'd love to dance with both of you."

Jessica slipped into the van and pushed Kale over. He was sprawled over the whole bed. He grumbled as she shoved him, but didn't wake up. Jessica was asleep inside of five minutes. Off tour, she had insomnia problems, but here she never seemed to be able to stay awake once her head hit the pillow. She drifted into sleep to the sound of Kale snoring.

The girls went walking back towards the van but were stopped along the way. They spotted a shirtless guy out back of his 70s dodge van. The back of the van was open and two huge monitors blasted out some kind of trippy electronic beats. He even had a few lights, including a spinning disco ball that sent spots of light spinning around his area of the parking lot. The lights made Melody a little dizzy. It had been a long night.

"These fucking lights," Melody giggled. "They're messing me up."

"Watch this," the shirtless guy said. He took a drink from a bottle, grabbed a flaming stick, and spit burning fuel high into the air. Melody had seen people blow fire on TV before, but never in person. She was mesmerized.

As was Lucy. When he produced two oil lamps on the ends of ropes, lit them on fire, and started spinning them through the air, Lucy fell in love. Not with the man, though he was pretty cute, but with the flames spinning through the air around him as he danced. The way he whipped the lamps through the air turned the flame from orange to blue.

Lucy seated herself on the ground and watched the whirling fire for a few precious moments. Melody relaxed next to her, mesmerized more by the shirtless guy than the fire (but the fire was cool, too). When the fire-dancing guy's girlfriend came out of the van with her own poi (as the oil lamps on the end of chains are called), kissed her man, and went into dancing with him; that was when Melody got up and said, "C'mon, let's go."

Lucy hung on as long as she could. Stealing glances back over her shoulder as she followed Melody away. The woman was beautiful and her body was moving so gracefully in tune with the fire.

When Melody and Lucy got to the van, they were confronted by a sight that might have seemed weird to Melody three days ago. Tonight, it was business as usual.

A crowd of deranged looking people were gathered around the van, most with balloons in their hand. Phillip and Natron were busy pushing out balloons and bringing in dollars as quickly as they could. They both wore huge smiles on their faces, laughing and talking to each other above the crowd. They were the only two people with any kind of awareness in their eyes as far as Melody could tell.

The girls shoved their way through the crowd of simplified people and approached the tank.

"Hey, the next balloon is mine," some guy said.

"Yeah, whatever," Lucy said, and kissed Phillip. "Hey honey, how's it going?"

"Natron is a fucking machine. We've already blown two tanks and are into the third. I figure we might as well make the money while it's easy."

"Word," Natron said as he passed Phillip three more balloons.

Phillip was focused on passing out the balloons and taking in money. He didn't have time for Lucy. She frowned and waded back through the crowd of zombies towards Melody.

"Hey, you wanna sleep in the van with me tonight?"

"Sure, what's up with Phillip."

"He's busy," Lucy shrugged.

The girls pushed through the crowd again and made their way to the van. Lucy took out her keys and unlocked the door. The girls climbed back in and locked it behind them.

"Jesus, these nitrous people are crazy," Melody said. "How long do you think they'll be out there?"

"That stuff really is like crack. They'll be out there as long as Phillip and Natron keep blowing balloons."

"I'm not sure I want to do that stuff anymore. It's kind of gross seeing those people out there. I don't want to be like that."

"Yeah, it's nasty stuff. But it's good money."

It might be a lot of money, but that doesn't necessarily make it good, Melody thought. She just nodded at Lucy and laid down on the bed next to her.

Melody couldn't help but thinking maybe Jessica and Kale had a better way of getting around, feeding these people and giving them nourishment, than Phillip, taking without really giving back.

They went to sleep to the sound of the nitrous tank hissing. Every now and then the back door would unlock, open, and Phillip would take something out or put something in.

16

Again the van was sweltering in the morning, and again Melody got up before Lucy. She threw open the doors to a mess. There were people passed out in the sun amongst leftover debris from the night before. Beer bottles lay tossed haphazardly and everywhere empty balloons scattered the ground like confetti after a parade. She looked around and felt a little ashamed. Their campsite was fucking ghetto. By far the messiest around. Even the guys down the street, already drunk today, selling "Ragin' Cajun Quesadillas," even those guys had a cleaner kitchen than Melody's campsite.

Self-conscious, she started picking up balloons and trash and putting it all in a garbage beg that was smooshed into the ground. Four empty tanks were lying in the middle of it all. She drug these under the van. About that time Lucy stirred and rolled out of the van.

"Damn, it's fucking hot again."

"It's July, silly." Melody smiled at Lucy who was trying to rub the sleep out of her eyes, stretch, and wake up. It was hot, though not quite as hot as yesterday.

"Hey, where's Phillip?" Lucy asked.

Melody shrugged, "I haven't seen him since last night."

Lucy looked around at the rubbish still left on the ground. "It looks like there was a party here last night."

"Look under the van."

Lucy looked under the van and saw the four empty tanks.

"Damn, they really got to work last night. I wonder where the hell Phillip is? He never came to bed last night."

They hung out around the van for awhile, brushed their teeth, put on clean clothes, and still no Phillip.

"Well, I'm fucking hungry," Lucy said. "Let's go

see Jessica and Kale."

Shakedown during the day looked like a completely different place. The people who had been up so late last night were asleep or gone off somewhere. The day shift was on and a lot of them looked very sober. Melody even noticed a group of little kids playing together.

Two little boys were playing swords with sticks they'd found somewhere along the runways or in the woods nearby.

They were both seven or eight years old, one with long dark hair and another with tangled little blonde dreadlocks. Their joy was obvious as they darted in and out of the crowd of people, chasing each other around. Every now and then they would bump into someone who they instantly included into their game. Each person interacted with the children in an open and
accepting way.

In the course of their dashing swordplay, they ran around Melody for a few moments and used her for cover. She was like a shield between the two of them as they held onto her. The blonde one snuck his head around Melody's waist, and jabbed the dark haired boy playfully in the back while he was peering around Melody from the other side. A fit of gleeful laughter erupted amongst the boys that spread to Melody and Lucy.

The two boys both beamed up at Melody as their eyes twinkled with honest happiness. Lucy was laughing off to the side, and the boys noticed her.

"You girls are pretty," the dark-haired boy said.

"Why thank you," Lucy kneeled down to the young boy's eye level. "And you and your friend are both quite handsome. What's your name?"

The boy blushed as he answered, "I'm Travel, and this is Noble." He gestured towards the little blonde boy, who bared his teeth and snarled at Lucy.

"Well I'm Lucy and this is my friend Melody."

"Okay, bye." The little boys resumed their game,

chasing each other along through the crowd. The blonde-haired boy, Noble, stopped as they were running away. He turned back the Melody and Lucy. "I think you're both pretty, too."

Lucy and Melody exchanged a glance with each other. Now it was their turn to blush.

They continued down Shakedown and walked past a kitchen folded out from a brown Ford van. The man working the grill was in his fifties, as his grey hair and bald spot insinuated.

Melody smelled bacon cooking. She looked at his handwritten sign. It said, "Potbelly Grill: Bacon, Egg, & Cheese Sandwiches $3."

"I don't think I can eat another broccoli cheese quesadilla," Melody said. "How about a breakfast sandwich?" She pointed at the Potbelly Grill and the gray haired man smiling from behind his coke bottle glasses.

"Sure, that sounds good," Lucy said.

They ordered two sandwiches from the friendly man in the kitchen. "Can we get 2 for $5," Lucy asked.

"Well, that deal's only for friends. Bacon is expensive. My name is Paul." He held out his hand.

"I'm Lucy and this is Melody," Lucy shook Paul's hand and Melody nodded.

"There, now were friends. I'll give you the deal."

He cracked two eggs onto the flat grill. "How are you girls liking the show?"

"It's awesome," Melody said. Lucy was looking off into the crowd trying to spot Phillip while Melody talked to Paul.

"How long have you been on tour?" she asked.

Paul chuckled, "My first Dead show was in 1972. I was pretty much hooked right away. When Jerry died, I didn't know what else to do. Thank God for Phish."

"Do you like Phish's music?"

"Yeah, I do. Their shows are huge. But it's Widespread Panic that really does it for me these days."

"I've heard about them, but I haven't seen them

yet. People have been talking to me about them a lot lately."

"Really? Here on the Phish lot? That's weird."

"Why would that be weird?"

"These Phish kids don't seem to like Widespread Panic and Panic kids don't seem to like Phish. It's stupid if you ask me. I mean, I'll go see anyone if I can sell some food and the music comes from the soul. Here's your sandwiches."

Melody took the breakfast sandwiches from Paul and thanked him. She handed one to Lucy and they continued down Shakedown.

"You know. I think I'd like to try doing a kitchen," Melody said.

"What? Are you serious? That would suck. Those people work so hard for next to nothing. They get greasy and dirty and have to leave the show before the encore. They're the first ones on the lot and the last ones to leave. I've seen it. Don't get me wrong, I'm glad someone does it. But it's not for me. Selling nitrous is easy, and way more profitable."

"Yeah, I guess you're right," Melody said. But what she really wanted to say was that nitrous is evil and the karma from selling it is bound to come around sometime. It just didn't feel right. Would she be selling nitrous to Travel and Noble when she was Paul's age?

"Hey beautiful ladies!" It was Jessica calling from behind her table as the girls walked by. Kale was flipping quesadillas and smiled at them as well.

"Good morning!," Melody said.

Kale laughed, "Good morning? It's 2 in the afternoon."

"Have you seen Phillip?" Lucy asked.

Kale and Jessica looked at each and shrugged. "Not since last night," Jessica answered.

"Damn, I wonder where he went?" Lucy was obviously concerned.

"Who knows," Jessica said. "But I've got something here for both of you."

She went over to the rack of clothes set up beside the kitchen and pulled out a handmade green dress. It was sewn together in patches of different shades of green with a butterfly embroidered on the chest. Jessica had spent hours on the dress and had been hoping to sell it for $80-$100. Now all she really wanted was to see Melody wearing it.

"This one's for you, Melody," she said.

"Oh my God, really? I love it. Thank you, thank you, thank you."

Jessica also pulled out a deep purple patchwork dress of the same quality with a crescent moon embroidered on the front.

"This is yours Lucy Moon."

"How did you know?"

"I heard Phillip call you that the other night. Is that really your name?"

"It is now," Lucy smiled. She figured Moon was a better last name than the Italian tongue twister she inherited from her father.

"You girls should step behind the van and try those on. I want to make sure they fit."

The girls slipped behind the van, took off their shirts, slipped the dresses on, then took off their pants. They fit exactly right. When they stepped out in front of the van and twirled like models they were met with an instant response.

Someone whistled from the crowd. "Damn. I said it before, I'll say it again. You girls are super hot."

"Natron, where the fuck is Phillip?" Lucy said.

The tour machine danced over through the crowd. "Don't worry, he's fine. Let me see that twirl again and I'll tell you."

Lucy gave him the evil eye, but Melody spun around again and smiled at Natron. She really liked her new dress. It made her feel more at home on the lot already.

"I don't want to take mine off," Melody said. "Can I leave my other clothes here?"

"Sure, of course," Jessica answered and nodded

at Lucy before she even had a chance to ask.

"Seriously, where's Phillip?" Lucy asked again.

"He's asleep at my campsite. Let me get something to eat and I'll take you there."

"How late were you guys up last night?" Lucy asked.

"I'm playing through. It's still last night as far as I'm concerned."

"Jesus Natron, you haven't slept?" Melody eyed him but couldn't tell he'd been up all night. He seemed to be functioning fairly well. In reality, Natron was doing excellent and just barely holding it together at the same time.

He and Phillip had blown off those four nitrous tanks at the van while the girls were passed out. Then they drug another one over to Natron's campsite, blew it off over there. They were out so late people actually quit coming for nitrous. So they started doing it themselves. Just after sunrise Natron broke out some of his cocaine.

Phillip took a bump and then passed out in Natron's tent. Natron shook his head, did another rail, and figured he'd go get some breakfast. He had one of Paul's sandwiches early in the morning with a cup of coffee and a bottle of water. Then he took some more cocaine and had been selling molly all day.

Kale passed Natron a quesadilla across the table, "Here man, this one's on me."

"Bullshit," said Natron. "You're out here busting your ass to make this food. I'm making wicked easy money on drugs, man. Here's five bucks."

Kale took the money with another tinge of envy. If he hadn't seen so many of his friends get busted in the past, he'd likely turn to the same line of work. But for Kale, tour was about freedom, not money. There was no way he was going to risk his freedom for money. Prison would never be the punishment for illegally vending quesadillas. The worst he'd ever had was a small fine in Tallahassee, Florida; which he didn't pay anyway.

"Are you girls gonna go find Phillip?" Jessica asked.

"Yeah, wanna come?" Melody asked.

"Yeah, kind of I do. But I better stay here and work my clothes, you know?"

As if on a cue a pretty young girl was flipping through Jessica's clothes on the rack. Her eyes settled on a pretty blue sun dress. "How much for this one?" she asked.

"Take care girls. I'll see you in a little while, okay. We're gonna dance together tonight." Jessica hugged both the girls and Melody heard her say, "Oh, that would look so pretty on you," to the girl eyeing her blue dress as they walked away.

"Alright, we ready?" Natron said.

The group collectively nodded.

They set off down the runway towards the trees on the edge of the airport. It was a long, hot walk through the sun, and took them close to an hour. Natron made a few stops along the way for beer and for business.

When they got to the shade, the temperature cooled off considerably. Natron hiked them through the tall grass towards his campsite.

In a little blue and white one-man hiking tent, Phillip was sleeping soundly in the cool shade. Natron unzipped the door and Lucy crawled in. "Hey baby," Phillip mumbled, put his arm around her and breathed a sigh of relief.

Lucy snuggled up in the shade next to her man and decided it was a great time for a nap.

Natron looked over at Melody and shrugged. "Well, shit. I don't think they're gonna get up. What are you up to?"

"I don't know."

"Wanna go ride the Ferris Wheel?" Natron asked with a smile on his face.

"Sure," Melody said.

They left Phillip and Lucy to their snuggling and walked back across the airport. Along the way they found someone selling SnoCones. Natron bought one for Melody and one for himself. The fake blue coconut ice lowered Melody's temperature to a tolerable level and helped to refresh Natron enough that the grumbling in his engine subsided. The presence of the beautiful young hippie girl in her brand new dress helped him a little with keeping it together. When she smiled or laughed, it seemed to Natron that the whole world just lightened up a little.

"It's so cool you can get a SnoCone out here," Melody said.

"You can get just about anything you want out here," Natron replied. "I love it. I really do."

"I know. Me, too."

"So this is your first show, huh?"

"Yeah, how'd you know?"

"Phillip told me. Plus, I can kind of tell. You've just got this look and this glow that almost everyone gets at their first show. I've even seen security guards and cops getting down in the show."

"Really?"

"Yeah. Just the other day I got a miracle from a cop. I was outside of the show in Jersey looking for a ticket and this cop points at me from behind the barricade. 'Hey, kid. Come here,' he says. I was fucking worried. I almost ran away, but my pockets were clean so I walked over. 'Here,' he said, and handed me a ticket. Then he actually said, 'Have a good show.'"

"How cool."

"I know, right?"

"Everyone is just so happy here. It totally amazes me."

"What's not to be happy about? I mean, we're surrounded by the coolest people, we get to dance to some sick music, and we're in a pretty cool place. Although, I guess it is a fucking airport. I think it even used to be an Air Force Base," he laughed.

"Are you serious?"

"I don't know. It's seriously big enough to be

though. Look at that control tower. It's huge. It doesn't matter where we are, really. We're in Tourville, USA."

Melody and Natron were walking side by side and laughing together. He was in prime form. Something about approaching this level of drug use and sleep deprivation really excited Natron. In a strange way, he felt that it honed his senses.

Natron was walking in the spirit world. The beautiful woman next to him smiled and spoke, and he seemed to know exactly what to say to her. They laughed their way across the hot, black tarmac towards the Ferris Wheel.

At the Ferris Wheel, there was a line an hour long. Melody and Natron hardly noticed the time passing. They befriended the couple in line next to them, and took turns saving each other's space so they could run to the bathroom or get a beer.

Clouds were rolling in, but they were welcome. The afternoon cooled off nicely. Eventually Natron and Melody found themselves sitting high above the festival at the top of the Ferris Wheel. Melody was amazed at the expansiveness of the place.

There was a place called "The Green" in the middle with lush green grass where people were hanging out. A really good band was playing on the side stage, some old bluegrass guys.

Phish's gear was set up onstage and it looked like they might be playing soon.

"This is just so amazing," she said to Natron.

He reached over and held her hand.

17

Nathan was from Kentucky. He grew up in a little town outside of Louisville. When he was a kid his dad used to take him to watch the horses run in the Kentucky derby. Nathan liked watching the horses gallop as fast as they could. His dad liked to gamble and drink. At home, Nathan was known to crank the volume on his dad's stereo and run circles as fast as he could around the coffee table in the living room. For hours on end.

Sometimes in the middle of the night.

His mother caught him more than once and put him back
to bed.

He played the trombone in high school marching band during the football games, but wasn't much for football. Mostly he kept his eye on the cheerleaders, not on the ball. His freshman year, he convinced his mom to buy him a drum set. It was a good outlet for his energy.

He had a drum instructor, Todd, who introduced him to more than just rhythm. Nathan smoked his first joint with Todd while listening to a bootlegged Phish show on a cassette tape.

Todd also took him to his first show, when Nathan was 15, at the Louisville Gardens, an old brick armory turned into a multipurpose arena. It was 2 days before Halloween and only a 3,000 person show. They opened with "Buried Alive" and closed the second set with "Amazing Grace." The encore was "Funky Bitch."

Todd had tickets to the sold-out Halloween show in Chicago two days later at the Rosemont Horizon and convinced Nathan's mom and dad that it was in his best interest as an aspiring musician that Nathan attend as well. He got the name Natron at that show, since he used silver spray-painted boxes to dress as a robot.

If the show in his hometown had given him a taste

for Phish and the scene, being amongst everyone at such a blowout as Halloween hooked him permanently. The band went through three sets of music. The second set was a complete rendition of The Who's entire Quadrophenia album, including a horn section. The third set, Natron was perfectly high and the music was exactly right. The long, wailing guitar note from "You Enjoy Myself" burned it's way into his brain.

Phish closed the show with an acoustic cover of "My Generation." Fishman had a kid's drum set with "The Who" written on the front drumhead. At the end of the show they smashed the toy drum set with Trey's acoustic guitar. Then Trey detonated an explosion onstage. That show opened up an entirely new world for Natron and ended his old one with a bang.

Every summer thereafter he went on as much Phish tour as he could convince his parents to let him. When he graduated high school, at the same time as Melody and Lucy, in May of 1999, he saw himself as entering his career as a full-time tour kid. Maybe he'd go to college in a year or two, but for now there was a something out there waiting for him to come and find. As far as he could tell Phish tour was where he was going to find it

~18~

Phish took the stage in the afternoon. Melody and Natron were just getting off the Ferris Wheel. They held hands and ran towards the stage. As they got closer, Natron looked over and smiled at Melody. "Alright, 'Punch You in the Eye'. I love this tune."

He and Melody started dancing together about halfway back on Paige's side. They were throwing energy back and forth between each other. Suddenly Natron felt someone grab him from behind. His heart shot up into his throat. He turned around and saw it was Phillip. Lucy was with him.

"What's up, bro?" He yelled to Natron over the music. Natron just nodded and kept dancing, playing an imaginary guitar along with Trey.

Lucy gave Melody a hug and they started dancing together. The four of them were in a circle of bobbing heads, shaking hips, and flinging arms. There was an electricity conducted between the four of them.

Jessica spotted them from a distance, grabbed Kale and pointed. He nodded and smiled. Jessica ran over, clapping her hands and smiling, locks flailing through the air. She hugged Melody and Lucy and shouted over the music, "Yeah! I'm so glad we found you."

The girls engaged in a three-way hug, and got back to grooving with the music. After PYITE, the band slowed down into "Farmhouse." It was such a nice afternoon.

Natron reached into his pocket, pulled out a bag of molly, took a dip with his finger and passed it to Jessica, who was eyeing him already.

"This is a much better time to take molly than 1 in the morning," she said, and passed the bag to Kale. Natron took another gram bag out of his pocket, dipped into it, and passed it to Melody.

"How much should I take?" she asked.

"Take a little at first. See how it makes you feel. If you want some more you can have it."

She licked her finger, dipped it into the bag of white powder, then licked off what stuck. It tasted awful. Jessica instantly passed her a bottle of water to wash it down with. Melody welcomed it.

A wash of anxiousness at the oncoming trip flooded Melody's stomach. Would she be alright? From the stage she heard, "Each betrayal begins with trust." It made her nervous. The clapping after the song was awkward for her. She smiled at her friends and they smiled back knowingly.

They had all done molly to varying degrees themselves, and they all knew it was Melody's first time. She felt strange, looking at her new friends. Did she really belong here?

The next song started and she started shaking her hips. She heard the words, "Listen as she speaks to you. Hear the voices flutter through the barriers arranged by you."

The grin reached down into her soul. It was just her own insecurity questioning her friends. She truly loved these people: for who they were, for where they came from, and for where they were all trying to go; together. She looked each of her five friends deep in the eye and felt the connections. They truly loved her, too.

"I can hear you when you sigh."

It seemed impossible to feel so right and so right at home. Melody had never known such a feeling before. It was like a gift given to her by the sunshine, the cooling clouds, the grass, the people around her, the music, and the spirit that moved in all of it.

"Listen as she speaks to you."

The song ended and she smiled back to her friends. Melody's face wouldn't relax for the rest of the night. She was in such a state of enjoyment that she was experiencing a phenomenon known as perma-grin.

The next tune started and they all six formed a circle looking in at each other. Each one felt the precious and fragile nature of this connection. They held onto it.

"We're all in this together."

Natron was the first to enter the circle, shake a comical dance with a goofy expression on his face, and incite a fit of laughter. Phillip went in next, shook around violently for a minute, then fell clear to the ground. The second wave of laughter hit them.

Jessica snuck in next, her face curled in a mischievous expression. Once inside, she stood up all the way, forgot her friends were looking at her, and danced with the spirit for a moment. She was radiating the same gentle understanding she felt within herself.

This was real.

These people were experiencing a powerful combination of countless enhancing agents. Molly was one of them, sure, but MDMA alone will not make a person feel as these six people were feeling. It takes the combination of surrounding, situation, self, accompaniment, and magic to bring someone face to face with the gods that dwell within and around each of us.

As Lucy entered the circle, she felt the fire burning within herself. She twirled in the most sexual way, eyeing Phillip the whole time. She moved her hips in time, and approached him. They connected for a minute, she yelled, and then jumped back. She let go of Phillip and connected herself to the flaming soul she felt inside of herself and everything around.

The focus shifted over to Kale as Lucy returned to the outer ring. He bobbed his head, smiled, nodded, but stayed where he was. Jessica waggled her nose at him, but he just smiled, stayed where he was, and went on bouncing in his own way. Jess figured that was all she was gonna get out of him, so she turned to Melody.

Melody, at that exact moment, was the incarnation of youth, freedom, love, and acceptance. In her new green dress, her new green eyes were lit up in the same vibrant fashion. Jessica was so happy to see her dancing in the afternoon sun. It made her proud to know that a new young person was joining this feeling of pure love, excitement, and joy that Jessica had already known so many times herself.

She felt that everyone deserved to feel this way at least some of the time.

Melody felt it. She entered the circle and again met eyes with each of her new friends in turn. She concentrated on the positive energy flowing within herself and focused it out and into each of them. She used her dancing, in her own mind, as a way to instill a personal message into each of them. The message was this: "Thank you. I Love you."

They all felt it.

Abruptly, it seemed to Melody, the song came to an end.

By the end of Bathtub Gin she felt great. The tingling in her face, the dryness in her mouth, the sweat, and the sensual amplification to her sense of touch were all quite pleasant. Everything felt wonderful. She ran her hands over her stomach and felt waves flowing through her body.

Clapping, her legs wobbled beneath her. She stumbled into Jessica.

"Hi," Melody said.

"Yes I am, and it looks like you are, too."

Melody laughed and hugged her. Onstage, the band was bringing out more musicians. Offstage, halfway back on the left side, six people were stumbling into each other and laughing. Jessica, Kale, Phillip, and Natron knew that this stumbling around between songs served a purpose. They were keeping their dancing space clear.

It was also fun to bump into your friends, hug them, and laugh together.

The band was playing again. The kids were dancing. The Del McCoury Band, a bluegrass legend, had joined Phish onstage. Instead of something traditional, they were playing Phish's song.

"I left it all behind me and I've traveled far."

So much of what she was hearing was exactly right for Melody. It felt to her like the band had chosen their music to coincide with her life, her feelings, and her experiences. It was eerily odd to her. Phillip and Kale were now talking over to the side as the bluegrass music went through a few songs.

They were debating the nuances of the tour: the quality of the shows that had been played; what songs had been played, and which ones hadn't. Melody and Lucy never stopped dancing. Jessica and Natron joked with each other about the people they saw, the things happening, and the musicians on the stage.

In their own way, each of these six individuals were exactly in place and exactly in time. That extrapolated throughout the crowd to a factor of ten-thousand, as there was hardly a person in that show who had thoughts of being anywhere else or doing anything else. There was no other place to be but here and no other time to be but now.

They were going to be breaking the Guinness Book of World records during this concert, Trey was saying from up on stage.

"For those of you who don't know the world record for the most number of people ever doing one dance at a time is the Macarena which was done by 50,000 people." Melody was trying to listen, but couldn't quite understand.

"My sources have told me that there's more than 50,000 people here tonight. So at some point during the night, we're not gonna do it now. We're gonna save it and wait 'til later and get a little more, you know, ready," Trey smiled the same goofy grin half his audience was smiling.

Jessica, Natron, and Lucy laughed with each other. Kale and Phillip grinned and shook their heads. Melody just wanted the guy to stop talking so she could start dancing again.

"We will be doing The Meatstick and you can take part in that."

Melody turned to Natron, "Did he say Meatstick?"

"Yeah," Natron was very pleased to say. "He did."

Out of nowhere the music kicked in again. Melody could relax, close her eyes, feel the bass move through her, and move along with it. For a long time it was just the music, with no words. Melody felt that it more than made up for all the talking moments ago.

"The moment ends."

As if on cue the mother of all things made her appearance at the show. Melody, literally and metaphorically, felt winds blowing different than ever before.

After that is was time to lighten up, float around, and lighten up again.

"Bag it, tag it."

The days were the longest of the whole year. The solstice was only three days away. The sun was still high in the sky, hiding behind just the right amount of cooling clouds when that song finally ended. There was more stumbling and clapping.

With the next song Melody got to shake her ass as much as she could for almost fifteen minutes. She wished it would never end.

"Can't I live while I'm young." And the set ended.

~19~

They sat in a circle, passing two water bottles. One had almost two grams of molly dissolved into it. The other was a chaser. Natron was happy to share the ecstasy with his new friends. There was a bond cementing between all six of them that would last forever.

Together, they were witnessing the gods peek in and out of existence within themselves, in the people around them, and through the musicians channeling it onstage.

Those four guys snuck back onto the stage right before sunset. They picked up their instruments and started playing. Melody jumped off the ground and yelled. They were playing her song!

"Run away, runaway, runaway."

They played her song for nearly half an hour. The sun was slinking closer to the horizon as they flowed nonstop into the next song. Ecstasy was flowing through Melody in every way possible. She floated up, left the crowd, left her friends, left parts of herself, and everything that couldn't transcend with her far below.

"I feel the feeling I forgot."

When she would think back to this show later, Melody would recall "Free" as the moment when everything was the most perfectly lined up. It was the pinnacle for her, spiritually, but it didn't diminish the rest of the show in any way. From there on out, everything became hilarious or comforting in some way. The epiphany period of the evening was over, or so she thought.

Anyway, it was time for some good fun.

Natron eyed her, "Here comes the Meatstick."

Did he just say what I thought he said to me? she thought.

"Whoa, shocks my brain."

Trey was talking again. Melody was trying to listen. He was teaching everyone how to do the Meatstick, a silly dance to go with a silly song.

"Once you've learned how to do the Meatstick, life is never the same again. It's just....you know...it's all better after you know how to do the Meatstick."

A lot of the kids were dancing along to the goofy dance. Melody was one of them. She twirled her finger in the air, spun a circle, and patted herself on the head with everyone laughing around her. Phillip and Kale stood to the side, not dancing and shaking their heads. Sometimes, Phish can be so stupid, Phillip thought. Shit like this makes me miss Jerry more and more.

There was still enough light in the sky for the picture, but someone thought not enough people were doing the silly dance to make the Guinness Book of World Records that night. No one felt disappointed.

Finally that nonsense ended, and some more nonsense began. Melody had to ask Natron to make sure, and he confirmed, that yes, they were actually singing about a pig. Melody laughed and laughed and almost fell apart.

"I hope this happens once again."

When that was over, there was some kind of funky bounce that made Melody feel dirty and love it. She hardly caught any of the lyrics (acts of love?), and there were a lot of them. The lyrics didn't necessarily matter as much as the jumping up and down with the rock and roll.

The next song started instantly and picked up speed to an insane frenzy. Melody moved as fast as she could and couldn't even begin to think of slowing down.

"It was the loudest thing I ever heard, and I knew my time had come."

It seemed that everyone else but Lucy and Melody had to stop and sit down for a minute. The two young women bounced and twirled and the crowd around them backed away. They had plenty of room to frolic and used every bit of it. Eventually, even the band couldn't keep up with the frenzied pace anymore. The song broke down into crashing notes and dissonant noise.

Trey spoke out over it, "Everybody have a good time, because we're coming back for another set."

The audience welcomed the break. Someone lit a bottle rocket.

Melody just melted into the grass. Fresh bottles of water circulated amongst the group. Melody's eyes were twitching. Natron was grinding his jaw. None of them were feeling any pain.

The third set began and the onslaught continued. The first song was funky and Melody liked it. She smiled wholeheartedly at Natron, locked her eyes with his, and moved her hips closer and closer to him. Jessica pointed it out to Lucy, who screamed, "Owww!"

"It's my soul."

Natron knew he was dancing not just with Melody's gorgeous and shapely body rubbing up against his, but also that part inside of her she usually reserved just for herself.

"Why do I sit and cry without a reason?"

It was a very fulfilling experience for both of them. Melody hadn't ever really allowed herself to feel this way about anyone. Natron had plenty of skill at getting girls into bed with him, but they were generally stupid, couldn't keep up with him, or didn't want to. He couldn't believe his luck that this gorgeous woman was actually dancing with him and enjoying it.

That dance ended and the next one began. It was quiet in the beginning, but there was a gradual crescendo. The increase was more in substance and feeling than in volume. The crowd felt it and a barrage of glow sticks were flung into the air. Tens of thousands of red, yellow, blue, purple, green, and orange iridescent lights were bouncing all over the crowd.

This time Melody couldn't decipher a single word in the only refrain of the whole song. It didn't matter, it was the notes of the excellent music that were carrying her across this ocean of understanding and acceptance. She held Natron close to her and tried to talk to him. A flurry of words erupted from her mouth and he knew it was something important so he tried to listen, but he couldn't really hear her over the music.

Instead he shrugged, smiled, and danced with his eyes looking lovingly into hers, nodding towards the stage. Melody laughed, it didn't matter anyway.

"Her words were words I sailed upon."

For half an hour there was nothing to say as "Piper" just kept playing. Natron and Melody were dancing just with each other now. Kale and Jessica had wandered off to get a couple of beers. Phillip and Lucy slipped away to the bathroom. The soaring instrumental morphed uninterrupted into the next song.

During the transition Melody and Natron laughed with each other and hugged each other close.

"You're so warm," she said to him, his arms wrapped tightly around her.

"You, too," he said.

"I feel good," she said.

Natron gave her a mischievous look as he squeezed her just a little closer. "You're right. You do feel good."

Their eyes locked. They kissed. The next song began. Natron felt something profound in his chest like anticipation; and also something just a little like fear and pain. Melody felt something new. Her regular apprehensions were overwhelmed by the pure ecstasy of warmth and security. They were kissing and she wanted to feel exactly like this forever. She'd never let herself be kissed like this before. She'd only ever been kissed like she was a little girl playing games or as a reluctant teenager full of mistrust.

Nathan kissed her like she was a woman who wanted to be kissed.

They had this song to themselves.

"Afloat upon the waves."

The song ended, but for Natron and Melody the feeling would remain. Lucy and Phillip met Kale and

Jessica in the beer line. Lucy hid off to the side while Phillip bought her a beer. She was underage, after all. Then the crowd started chanting "Wilson" as they came running back, trying not to spill their $6 beers.

This wasn't a song for lovers and Melody and Natron split apart but kept their eyes on each other. The others noticed it, especially when Natron sang parts of the song directly to Melody.

"I'll make it all true for you."

The interaction between the crowd and the band was almost telepathic. The crowd loved their part in this song, even if was just one word. Melody shouted it at the top of her lungs. "WILSON!" When that song was over, the drummer was singing. For the first time Melody noticed he was wearing some kind of maternity dress or something.

This song was just nonsense. Trey was talking over it. Melody's head was spinning. She fell into Natron's arms. He held her close. This wasn't a song, it was just noise.

Melody wanted another song. The music had held her and made her feel safe all night, but this wasn't music. For now, at least, Natron was taking care of that. This soft woman in his arms seemed so fragile and so vulnerable. All he wanted was for her to be safe and never to have to experience any darkness at all in her life.

They ignored Trey babbling onstage and kissed instead. Jessica nudged Lucy, pointed to them and they both laughed.

Kale and Phillip were listening to what Trey was saying, "You know, you should never really overlook the knowledge that you can take from certain books. I think people are too hung up on fucking T.V. Stop watching so much damn T.V. and read a book once in a while. You know what I'm talking about?"

The crowd cheered, Kale and Phillip laughed, and someone had an idea that would manifest ten years later.

"I just think it's important in this day and age with

the computer and the TV and everything that you should stop watching so much damn TV and read a fucking book. You know? Not just any book. There's some books with something to really say."

"I think there's one book in particular that we all talk about. And we know what book I'm talking about."

The crowd cheered again. They knew what book Trey was talking about.

"I think you should all read it. You should stop watching TV, and you should stop listening to that evil heavy metal music, except Deep Purple, cause they're the best heavy metal band ever."

"Read the book, okay."

"Read it. Read it!"

"READ THE BOOK!!"

Now they were playing "Smoke on the Water," by Deep Purple.

Lucy had tears running down her cheeks she was laughing so hard. Melody might have, too, but she was engulfed in kissing Natron. It felt so good, her lips were like direct nerve lines to her entire self and she completely tuned out the guy babbling onstage.

Trey was going on about the book. He was explaining how to find an imaginary book at Barnes and Noble. Not just any book. "The Helping, Friendly Book," written by an imaginary man from Gamehenge named Icculus.

"The children are old enough to read Icculus."

Trey tried to become a stand-up comedian, riffing on about Icculus. He introduced the band: on bass, Michael Jordan, on guitar, the Bad Lieutenant, and Vajohna on drums. He neglected to mention the Chairman on keyboards.

Afterwards, in Trey's own words, the band was now, "Gonna mill about aimlessly and decide what we're gonna play next."

They really didn't take themselves, their music, or the scene too seriously and it was part of what made it great.

While the band milled about aimlessly for a few

minutes, Jessica reached out and lightly punched Melody in the shoulder as she was relaxing into Natron's arms. Melody looked over. Jessica shook her head and laughed. Melody shrugged and smiled back.

Mike finally decided the next song Phish would play. It was a Bob Dylan cover, "The Mighty Quinn" or "Quinn the Eskimo."

"Come all without. Come all within."

~20~

After Quinn the Eskimo was Fluffhead, which Melody readily identified with this evening. After Fluffhead the band left the stage for the encore break. Kale darted away instantly. Jessica hung around for about 35 seconds telling everyone to meet them at the kitchen after the blowout. Jessica hated leaving early. She hated it so much that sometimes Kale told her to hang out and he would fire up the grills. Not tonight. Shakedown would be crazy busy tonight and they had to take full advantage of it.

Melody didn't want for it to end. She cheered and cheered during the encore break for the band to come back out. Everyone knew they would. Melody slipped out of Natron's arms, looked back at him seductively, and sidled up next to Lucy.

"This has been the best time of my life," Melody said to her friend. "I'm definitely going on tour with you guys."

"Of course you are," Lucy replied.

Behind them, Natron and Phillip were making quiet plans for blowing off that last nitrous tank and other things. It wasn't like any big decisions were made, they were just going with the flow.

"I can't believe how tired I am, but I just want to keep dancing," Melody laughed.

"Does the molly feel good?" Lucy asked.

"Oh, so good."

For a minute they just swayed next to each other. Then Lucy looked at Melody as seriously as she could. "So, you're hooking up with Natron?"

"I don't know. He's cool. We're just having fun."

Lucy giggled, "He is cool. Have fun, girl!"

Then the band came back onstage. They slunk through a quiet part at the beginning of the song, then dropped some loud notes that required full crowd participation. "HOOD!" There were some silly lyrics that didn't mean anything to Melody, then everyone shut up and played their instruments beautifully in the warm night air of summertime.

Another glow stick barrage erupted during the song. The music just kept flowing. Out in the parking lot, Shakedown was reopening for business. Some of the vendors had stayed in the lot during the show, for whatever reason. Some were too tired, some were too messed up, and some didn't like the music and were here strictly for the purpose of making money.

The vendors who were making money just to be here and dance to the music (which is most of the vendors) were running out of the show, cursing they wouldn't see the encore again, and setting up their kitchens, booths, and displays as fast as they could. The encore might last only fifteen or twenty minutes then everyone would flood out of the show hungry, thirsty, and happy.

For Jessica and Kale, time was once again a factor in their lives. For those still in the show time was standing still. Natron and Melody danced close. He tried to wrap his arms around her again, but she just wanted to dance. This was the last song of the evening, the last song of the festival, and the last chance to get it all out.

So many epiphanies had already flown into her that night and so much frustration had exited that she couldn't believe there was anything more she could take from this show.

She was wrong. Dancing to the uplifting jam, which seemed almost freeform but was actually very practiced and orchestrated, she had no idea that the biggest understanding was yet to hit her. It would come in the final minutes of the show. She let herself float above the crowd again, as she had earlier in the day during "Free."

The music intensified and she floated higher and higher, until they started singing again. She only heard four words and they made everything different.

"You can feel good."

It was alright to feel like this.

Melody knew that she was supposed to feel

ashamed with herself for being so high on drugs. She knew she was supposed to feel irresponsible for walking out on her job to be here. She was supposed to be sad for her mother, depressed for herself, and angry at the world. Everyone expected these feelings out of her, including herself.

What she never knew was that she could feel good, and it was okay to feel good. It didn't matter she didn't have a job, or she was profoundly high, or she was making out with a drug dealer she'd only just met. She could feel genuinely good and satisfied and it was alright. There wasn't any need for the weight of guilt.

It was a foreign experience for her.

When the band left the stage a fireworks display began. Melody relaxed into Natron's arms and like the explosion at Natron's second show on Halloween a few years ago, the fireworks signaled the end and the beginning of something for Melody. The brightly colored explosions in the sky went on for awhile. Melody thought it was all so beautiful. She was content, fulfilled, extremely tired, and hungry for more.

"Oh my God, is it really over?" Melody asked.

"Only until the next show," Natron whispered into her ear.

The breathe of his voice tickled and excited her at the same time.

"What are we going to do now?" Melody directed her question at Phillip. She knew who was making the decisions.

"I tell you what we're not going to do. We're not going to drive up to Toronto tonight."

"Jesus, why would we?" Melody asked.

"That's where the next show is. Tomorrow's a day off, then there's the show in Toronto which we're skipping. A lot of people are leaving tonight. We're gonna hang out here tonight, rage it, and start heading towards Pennsylvania tomorrow. We'll get a hotel room, and relax until the show on the 21st. You're in, right Natron?"

He nodded, "Sure," and Melody felt her stomach jump, and just like that Natron was riding with them. He'd hitchhiked up to this show anyway, unable to convince anyone in Louisville to go on tour with him. Bunch of losers, he thought.

Natron was powering down. He wouldn't last until the sun came up again. He helped Phillip blow that last tank, then he and Melody went off to his tent in the trees.

Melody thought at first that she was going to get laid. She was wrong. Natron was too tired for sex. Anyway, Nathan really did like Melody and didn't want their first time making love to be with her also tripping ecstasy for the first time. It seemed cheap, and he told her so. He said he didn't want for their relationship to be cheap.

Melody felt any reservations melting away with the warmth in his voice. Instead of sex, she lay in his arms and simply told him everything about herself. She let it all out, her mother, her father, her naivety, her wonderment at where she was, and her strange new feelings for life and for Natron. He listened until he fell asleep and dreamed about her all night.

Everyone who had been involved in the dancing circle that night slept peacefully in someone else's arms. Phillip and Lucy counted an obscene amount of money, split it into Natron's and Melody's separate cuts, and locked the rest in Phillip's box for which he had the only key. Then they drifted to sleep next to each other.

Jessica and Kale served food until all they had left was half a bottle of salsa and a 12-pack of tortillas. They cleaned up their kitchen, locked themselves in the van, and counted their relatively modest pile of greasy bills. It was almost $4,000, the best they'd done in a while. Jessica felt sticky and wished for a shower to wash the smell of broccoli and cheese quesadillas off. Kale didn't mind, and the two of them snuggled into bed together.

The festival was over. Melody had survived her first show.

21

Phillip kept his promise and set the four of them up in a swanky hotel in Pittsburgh for the night before the show in PA. Melody was glad Natron was riding with them. They rolled in a two-car caravan, consisting of Phillip's brand new van, loaded with drugs, and Lucy's battered Oldsmobile, the clean decoy car.

If Natron hadn't been around, Melody would have been driving the decoy car all alone. Instead, they laughed and talked down the highway together. She was quickly falling for Natron. He had a certain quality she couldn't quite put her finger on. Now matter how dirty they got, or how crazy the nights were, Nathan always seemed to hold himself together.

Before Phillip could re-up on nitrous, Natron told him even though the money was amazing, he didn't want to sell nitrous anymore. It just wasn't right, Natron had said.

Melody fawned over him for this, and she thought it might have been something she said to him that inspired this moral standing. He really liked her and said it often, "I really like you." She smiled and being with him made her feel excited about everyday to come.

Especially the day they spent sleeping with the curtains drawn in the swanky hotel outside of Pittsburgh. Phish was in Canada, so they had the day off again. All anyone wanted to do was sleep. That evening, Phillip and Lucy went out to score some work from Phillip's family connections in Pittsburgh. Natron and Melody stayed in.

The softness of the bed and the expensive hotel pillows were in perfect contrast to the hard and determined way in which Natron made love to her for the first time.

The next week was a blur to Melody. The nitrous was gone, but Phillip had picked up an excessive amount of molly. It was the only work he could find that Natron didn't mind selling. In Pennsylvania they ran into Jess and Kale again. They had gone up to Toronto and said it was the best show they'd seen the whole tour.

"That's the way it always is," Jess said. "The show nobody comes to is always the best. That's why we said 'fuck it' and drove up to Canada. We didn't make any money, in fact we lost some, but it was totally worth it."

Pittsburgh was a fun show, but the work was slow again. Phillip and Natron were frustrated they didn't sell very much molly. Really, it was pointless for Phillip to keep working the shows, as he had plenty of money to finish out tour in style from the nitrous in Oswego. But he felt like he had to work every show. He couldn't relax unless he was hustling more money.

After Pennsylvania they had a day off to make the long drive to Columbus, Ohio. The day between the shows was almost as fun for Melody as being on lot. The lot was stretched out everywhere in between the two shows. Every rest area they stopped at was invaded with tour kids. The average traveler on a business trip or a family vacation, was utterly baffled by the scene.

Tour kids were everywhere. Dreadlocks, baggy patchwork clothes, a few tie-dyes, and an attitude of knowing something other people don't know permeated every stop.

At the rest areas and gas stations kids were making trades or trying to sell their wares for gas money. Some were begging for gas money. Some were sleeping on the picnic tables and drinking beer in the parking lots. It was hilarious for Melody to see all these normal people intermingled in such a mundane setting as a rest area with these outrageous kids. Every stop was a new adventure.

The gas stations were a riot. Phish was blaring through seven different car stereos while barefoot young girls in sundresses with hairy legs caught the eye and imagination of every truck driver. Melody felt like she was part of the circus. Somehow, she knew it was a good thing that these normal people were witness to the unencumbered insanity of the Phish tour.

Little kids pointed, laughed, and made faces, while the tour kids pointed and laughed back, making faces to the mortification of the young suburban parents just trying to make the trip to visit Aunt Flo in Indianapolis. What the hell were all these crazy people doing on the Interstate and where did they come from, anyway?

Throughout the day, Melody counted a total of twelve VW bussed putting along in the slow lane with enraged truckers growling behind them. It was a wonderful city to be a part of.

On lot, the same people were at every show. Melody started recognizing faces. She was friendly and waved and they waved back. Hello again from the same place in a different city. They came into town, established the village, worked their economy, went to their church, and moved on to the next one.

Alpine Valley was epic. Melody and Natron had the happiest night of the tour, ditching everyone else and going off on their own. Natron didn't want to work Alpine, and Phillip agreed. The police presence there is easy to feel and has affected everyone who's ever been there in some way.

Still, Phillip felt like he had to do something. He emptied his pockets and scouted out the under-covers and the uniformed cops. When he spotted one, he'd stroll through the crowd ahead of them. "Six-up," he said to anyone and everyone, pointing out the under-cover cops especially. They were generally easy to spot. They were older, wore crisp, clean Grateful Dead tie-dyes and ball caps. Also they were the only people on lot wearing nice running shoes (for chasing down hippies in sandals).

"Six-up," and Phillip pointed them out. Even Phillip didn't really know why "Six-up," meant police, but everyone on lot who needed to know knew exactly what he was talking about. Business deals were stopped. Groups split apart and scattered. Phillip left gratitude in his wake and probably saved at least a dozen kids from winding up in jail.

While Phillip was engaged in this noble occupation, Lucy had wandered off and found the couple in their disco van. She was getting her first lesson in spinning fire. She bought practice poi (soft balls on the end of the leash), as well as purchasing the flaming option for when she got better. The fire dancing had enchanted her and it was something she knew she absolutely had to learn how to do.

Natron and Melody washed through the crowd, madly in love with each other, everything, and everyone around them. Their enchanted reverie was disrupted by a gruff and angry voice in an accent that might have been Middle Eastern, Pakistani, or Indian. Melody couldn't be sure. Natron recognized the voice instantly.

"Natron, you filthy motherfucker," the voice was yelling, except it sounded more like, "Nay-tradn, yew fildy muthafocka."

"Oh shit," Natron said and walked briskly over to the kitchen set up behind a dirty brown Ford Econoline van. The man working the kitchen, and responsible for cursing Natron in his strange dialect, was a short, swarthy man. He was older than most anyone except Paul in The Potbelly Grill. He had a crazy look in his eyes that kind of disturbed and excited Melody at the same time.

"Russo, it's good to see you," Natron said.

The short man snarled at Natron, set aside the French bread Pizza he was cooking and picked up his ten-inch long gleaming chef knife. He held it menacingly towards Natron. "Is good to see me? Is bullshit! You owe me money motherfucker."

Melody could hardly tell what the man was saying, his accent was so thick.

Natron shook his head, "Russo, I know I owe you three-hundred bucks, but you fucking disappeared after Oswego, man. I've got your money, I just haven't seen you anywhere to pay you."

"Is bullshit, Natron. I'm everywhere. You find me when you owe me money. No more cuffing work to you."

"Fine, here's your money. Hey, sell us some pizza, too."

Natron pulled the wad of bills from his pocket he'd grown accustomed to carrying since he started working with Phillip. He peeled off 15 twenty dollar bills and a single five-dollar bill for the pizza. Russo smiled, but still held the gleaming chef knife. He took the money and put his arm around Natron in an aggressively friendly way.

Russo pulled Natron in close, and smiling from ear to ear told him, "Is good you pay me, my friend. Otherwise I was going to find you and cut out your liver." At this Russo gestured with his chef knife towards Natron's abdomen. Natron flinched, but Russo just laughed.

The pizza wasn't anything special. It was the cook who was exceptional. Russo was blatantly hitting on Melody and Natron was powerless to stop it. He kept thinking of that menacing chef knife. Melody felt okay about it. There wasn't a chance in hell she'd go anywhere with Russo, but something about his impish grin and huge laugh made her like him nonetheless.

Still, she was thankful when she heard her name being called. She turned and there was Jessica and Kale set up across the way. She waved goodbye to Russo and skipped over to her friend's kitchen. Natron shook Russo's hand again.

"No hard feelings," he said to the deranged little man.

"Never," Russo smiled. Then he picked up that sharp knife again and pointed it at Natron, "As long as you pay me motherfucker." He laughed like a crazed hyena as Natron slinked away.

Jessica and Melody were already deep in giggling conversation beside Kale's van as Natron approached the "No Deal's Café." Kale was flipping quesadillas and saw that Natron was visibly shaken from his encounter with Russo.

"Shit, you got a bowl, Kale?" Natron asked.

Kale produced a packed pipe from his pocket, made a clicking sound with his tongue and passed it to Natron. Natron took a deep puff of weed smoke and went to pass the pipe back to Kale.

"Take it to your head," Kale waved off the pipe.

Natron lifted the glass pipe to his forehead and bowed slightly at Kale. He smoked the rest of the bowl to himself as Kale was dealing with people buying quesadillas.

After every toke he touched the pipe to his forehead. The murmur of Shakedown began to blur into a steady hum. Nathan scanned the crowd, taking in the smiling faces, the laughing people, the happy children, and the occasional burnout who'd taken things too far. Nathan was still hot from his discussion about drug money with a knife-wielding man of indeterminate nationality.

He took a deep breath and then another toke off Kale's pipe.

All in all it was a beautiful day. Sure, it was ridiculously hot, like it had been for most of summer tour, but somewhere through the sweat and the blistering sun a refreshing breeze was blowing. Natron felt the air stir and his internal temperature dropped twenty degrees. Russo wouldn't harm him. Nothing could touch him out here.

It is truly a beautiful life, Nathan thought. Concerns like rent or making it to work on time never entered his thought process. He couldn't even remember what day of the week it was. All he knew was that Alpine Valley was tonight, tomorrow was a day off, then it was two nights of camping out again; this time at Deer Creek.

The simplicity of his existence did not escape Nathan. He hit the pipe again, touched it to his forehead and let his gaze drift over to Melody. God, she's beautiful, Nathan thought. He shook his head trying to fathom how he'd come to be so lucky with such a remarkable young woman. He watched her telling Jessica a story. Her face was lit up and expressing the emotions of surprise, fear, relief, and finally hilarity as she articulated whatever story she was telling.

Watching her, Nathan couldn't help but to think of her crying to him about her home and her mother and the mistakes she felt she'd already made in her young life.

Seeing her now, laughing and being so casually intimate with Jessica, there was no indication whatsoever she had ever concerned herself with anything too deeply in her entire life. Nathan stood in the middle of Shakedown and no one bothered him as he continued to smoke his pipe and gaze at Melody.

That now familiar sensation of apprehension and pain deep in his chest overwhelmed him as he focused on this weightless young woman. He would do anything just to keep her laughing and smiling like she was now. He knew she was his destiny. Whenever he had thought of falling in love, this is what he had always thought it would feel like. She was perfect and he was overwhelmed by her. He hadn't had a thought that didn't include her since they'd met.

Melody felt similar. She was giddy with love or infatuation, she couldn't be sure. Either way, it was amazing and she was, for the first time in her life, forever with a smile on her face. She felt like she had fallen in love twice. Once with the new life she had discovered and again with Nathan.

Everything she learned about him fascinated her. This kind of life was unimaginable to Nathan even just a few years ago. He was certain he would just do what he was supposed to do. His parents were friendly, understanding people, and encouraged Nathan on everything he tried. They bought him the drum set he learned to play on and let his friends come over and jam late into the night.

Still, they were successful southern suburbanites. There were expectations and unspoken understandings. Even though he drug his feet through the applications, he figured he's just go to college, get some stupid degree, then some stupid job, maybe a stupid wife, some stupid kids, and a stupid house with a stupid mortgage.

The notion that there was anything else available was slow to set in. Once he convinced his parents it would be good to let him go on tour for the summer everything changed. After a few shows the expectations he'd had for his life simply faded away. There was a freedom and a joy in this life on tour that he couldn't overlook. He felt he had to grab as much fun and enjoyment or else he would be wasting his life.

Nathan was reprogrammed. Natron was born. He knew there was no way he was going to go to college in the fall. He'd had enough of school. He wished he could tell his parents that, and he knew he would have to. He fretted at the thought of this and hoped he would have the courage to stand by his convictions when the time came.

He just didn't know how or when to break the news to his loving mother that her baby boy was a complete fuckup and wasn't going to be living any kind of life she would find respectable. How could he tell his father he couldn't imagine doing anything that would make him a success and instead wanted to spend his life chasing something unspeakable around the country?

In his vision of the future he saw himself and Melody on tour years from now, living in a van. Maybe they'd be working a kitchen like she kept saying she wanted to, something legitimate. They could even have a few kids and a dog or two. They could make a family on the foundation of this love.

The thought of this made the painful feeling in his heart subside and as he looked at Melody a wave of warm comfort washed over him. She saw him looking at her. She smiled and waved him over.

"Hey beautiful girl," he said as he approached.

"Hey sexy man," she said in reply.

"I love you," he said. It just came out. He hadn't said it to her before and hadn't really meant to just then. A surge of fear climbed from his stomach to his heart.

"I love you, too," she said instantly. It just came out. She hadn't even thought about it before saying it. She shook her head in disbelief.

Nathan grabbed her and kissed her with everything he had. Jessica stood to the side, feeling the warmth radiating from the young lovers. It brought moisture to her eyes.

Nathan never imagined he would be lucky enough to know this perfect feeling. It was a mix of love, accomplishment, freedom, security, and acceptance and it wrapped Nathan and Melody snugly together.

22

The cornfield is an interesting place. Row after row of genetically modified and identical plants stretch in endless lines from Iowa to Ohio and beyond. Once upon a time, corn was a smaller plant. The natives called it "maize." It was the primary food staple of most agricultural societies on this continent six-hundred years ago. However, the natives never had a notion to grow maize the way we grow corn.

Goddamned civilized people got over here and saw real estate and some easy slaves. In the blink of a planetary eye the whole place was transformed. Life that had found it's place over eons of evolution was plowed under in favor of the obscenely straight line of toxic corn.

In the middle of the modern cornfields north of Indianapolis some of the corn has been plowed under so that 25,000 people can get together at a venue known as Deer Creek to dance to whatever kind of music makes them feel better.

Natron looked out the window of the Oldsmobile as the cornfields were rolling by. He and Melody hadn't said anything to each other in a while. It wasn't an uncomfortable silence, it was just silence. For the last week their lives had been filled with so much musical sound that they actually cherished the silence of being next to each other. The tape player in the Oldsmobile wasn't even spinning out a tune.

Nathan turned his gaze from the hypnotizing regularity of the endless rows of corn passing by to the young woman who piloted them down the highway. The curve of her profile enchanted him far more than the scenery. She was relaxed and easy behind the wheel. Their destination was the last show of Phish's summer tour, 1999. The thought of this caused a familiar apprehension to rise in Nathan again. What would happen when tour was over? Would Melody still want to be with him? He wanted to stay with her, wherever she was going.

She looked over and noticed him noticing her.

"What?" she smiled questioningly.

"I just couldn't help thinking how beautiful you are."

She blushed, "Stop it."

"I'm serious," he said emphatically. "I've never felt like this about anyone before."

"Thanks," she shrugged. "Me neither."

She took her eyes from the road and turned to gaze at him.

What is it that makes people fall in love? Are we so empty that we need someone else to validate our existence? Is it our destiny? Psychologically it either greatly empowers a person or destroys them. On a brain scan it resembles mental illness. Chemically, it affects us in much the same manner as amphetamines.

Poets have spent millions of words trying to decipher love and every person alive has been overwhelmed by it at some point in their life. Still, it remains a mystery. Circumstance and chance place another person in our path and something overwhelming occurs. Logic and reason disappear and strange, reckless feelings become the only guide.

"I want to stay with you after tour. I can't stand for this to be our last show together. I want to be with you." Nathan made himself completely vulnerable to this woman he'd known little more than a week. She had the power to instantly destroy him if she wanted to. This power surged through her and she was swept away herself.

"I'd go anywhere with you," she said.

Then she smiled and looked right into him. "I want to go everywhere with you."

In the middle of nowhere the corn stretches from horizon to horizon. Cars whiz by, full of people unaware of the environment they're traveling through. There are no destinations out here.

However, wedged between two cornfields on a rarely traveled dirt road, two young people were finding a kind of destination in this transient landscape. The Oldsmobile was hidden amongst the corn. Inside Melody and Nathan were taking their emotional love for each other and transferring it into physical action. Everything was perfect, except the seat belt was digging into Melody's back.

~23~

Phish's summer tour of 1999 came to what seemed to Melody as an abrupt end. One day, there just wasn't another show to drive to. She felt kind of depressed and confused about what to do next. She couldn't go back to her old life, she knew that, but what to do now?

Nathan was just as unsure. He was supposed to go back to Louisville. He was supposed to go to college. He didn't want to do what he was supposed to do. All he knew was that he wanted to stay with Melody. He wanted to be with her wherever she was going. He wanted to hear more music.

Lucy wasn't thinking about the future too much. She never did. She lived her life completely at the whim of the moment. Whatever impulse came next, she would follow. She'd go with Phillip, for now.

Phillip, on the other hand, had plans. He had to get back to Eugene, Oregon, where his plants were growing. He wanted to bring Melody and Nathan along and it didn't take too much convincing.

They drove straight through from Deer Creek to Oregon. It took the better part of two days. They slept in their cars and took turns driving. "I have to get back," Phillip urged them on. "It's time to harvest my next round and I haven't talked to my partner in a week. I'm wondering what's going on." By the time they pulled into the driveway of Phillip's house just outside of town they were all delirious from lack of sleep and sheer distance.

Phillip's delirium quickly turned to outrage. His rooms were empty. The plants were cut off at the stem and most of his equipment was gone.

"What the fuck?" He screamed as soon as he walked into the house and saw the devastation. "Every plant is gone! Every single one! That motherfucker. I knew I couldn't trust him. I'm gonna kill John next time I see him. I've got to start all over!"

Phillip was raging around the house, breaking

dishes and kicking holes in the walls. Lucy cowered in the corner. Her attempts to calm him down had been met with more rage.

"Who's John?" Nathan asked Lucy quietly.

"Phillip's partner. He was supposed to just stay here and watch the grow while we were on tour. I never really trusted him, but Phillip did. I told Phillip he was a liar."

Phillip overheard, shook his head at himself, and calmed down a little. "John's a piece of shit who's gonna fucking die if I ever see him again," The house was in tatters. Thousand watt lights had been torn from their hangers and one of the flood tables had been cracked in the process, leaving a bedroom saturated in the hydroponic solution used to feed the plants. The place smelled of mildew.

"Okay," Phillip said, regaining his composure in the tatters of his livelihood.

He nodded his head a few times, coming to terms with the situation.

"This is a blessing," he finally said. "That motherfucker just kept getting greedier and greedier. I should've known something was up when he didn't want to go to any of the shows this summer."

Phillip placed aside the gruesome thoughts of what he wanted to do to John, saving them for another time. "Now we've got a chance to start over, together." He looked between Lucy, Nathan, and Melody, telling them what he wanted them to hear and believe. "I trust you three more than pretty much anyone I've ever met. I know Lucy's in with me all the way, and I know neither of you would do anything to fuck up a good situation and a friendship. Nathan, Melody, you want a job?"

"Yeah, man. Of course," Nathan said.

Melody looked at Nathan, then Phillip, and nodded.

"Okay, here's what we're gonna do. You girls go to town, rent a U-haul and get a newspaper. We need to move. Nathan and I are gonna stay here and clean up this mess. We gotta patch drywall, paint, change that fucking mildew carpet and get the hell out of this house. We'll find something better."

"Can't we sleep first," Melody asked.

"Not now. This is too sketchy. We need to get the rest of the equipment out of here as soon as we can. Who knows, that motherfucker might try to come back and get the rest of my shit. I can't believe I've got to start all over."

Once Phillip had a plan in place, things moved forward swiftly. He dug up the lock box buried in the backyard. Everyone helped for the two weeks it took to get the house cleaned out, and whatever was left was moved into a new rental near Hendrix Park, at the top of Capitol Drive. The place was huge and the landlord lived in California. He came up to meet them and Lucy and Melody were the front. They were just a couple of rich college girls renting the house for themselves. Sometimes their boyfriends came over. The landlord never batted an eye when they paid first and last months rent, as well as the security deposit, in money orders.

Meanwhile, Nathan and Phillip returned the other rental to a pristine state so that the owner could never tell it had been an indoor farm. There was still a faint scent of mildew, but even though Phillip broke the lease he still got his security deposit back.

Within two weeks they had three of the four bedrooms in their new house turned to grow rooms. Phillip and Lucy took the empty bedroom, while Melody and Nathan set up camp in the living room. Phillip dug deeper into his pockets to replace some of the lost equipment.

However, he couldn't replace his lost genetics. The girls drove ninety little cloned plants up from California in Phillip's van. He was kind of back in business, running really short on money, and now he had Nathan as an understudy and two extra people to support.

He was irritable and snapped when Melody

mentioned fall tour. "Someone has to be here all the time," he told Melody and Nathan. "I don't know who's gonna get to go, if anyone. Ya'll got any money?" he asked.

Everyone shook their heads. Phillip shook his head back at them, "Not until the crop comes in."

Even though he had been cleaned out, Phillip was still able to get things back on track.

It was work. Lots of work. They had to run ducting all over the house to bring in fresh, cool air and expel the heat created from the thousand watt lights. They had to hang the lights, and adjust air flow to keep a constant temperature, preferably in the eighties. It would take the whole harvest to work out all the kinks and Phillip already knew the crop would suffer because of it.

Nathan and Melody suddenly understood why weed cost so much. Day in and day out they were constantly working on the system. In addition to getting the fans and the lights to work like they ought to, it entailed filling reservoirs, spraying for bugs, trimming plants to grow certain ways, raising lights, and in the end everything still had to be cut down, trimmed, dried, and cured.

Then it had to be sold.

Phillip refused to bring in any outside help. "I don't trust anyone, anymore," he said.

They hunkered down, trying to come up. The grass slowly got taller. Money quickly got shorter. The crop still wouldn't be in when Phish's fall tour started on a Thursday night in September up in Vancouver, Canada. After that the band was coming down on Friday and Saturday to The Gorge in Washington. The Gorge is only about a six hour drive from Eugene. Then on Sunday there was a show in Portland, just two hours from Eugene.

"I kinda wish they were starting back East and coming this way," Phillip said. "We don't have any money to get started and I really wanna go to the Gorge."

"We all wanna go the Gorge," Lucy said.

"You got any money?" Phillip asked again. It was becoming one of his favorite lines. Lucy glared at him. He rubbed it in on her. "Of course not. You haven't had any money since I met you."

"Fuck you, Phillip." Lucy turned and walked out of the house. Melody followed her.

"Lucy, wait up."

"What?" Lucy was visibly agitated. "I'm sick of him being such an asshole know-it-all. He's arrogant and thinks he's better than everyone else. I think I'm gonna leave."

Melody tasted fear in the back of her throat. If Lucy left, what would she do?

"Lucy, you can't leave. I wouldn't know what to do here without you."

Lucy was shaking with frayed nerves. This wasn't about Melody. This was about being treated like an unwanted accessory for too long. She'd put in her time with Phillip and had done work to help them along, still he made her feel inferior. If he didn't need her, maybe she should just leave and let him fend for himself.

Melody was waiting for Lucy to speak again. Lucy couldn't look at Melody and not feel some sense of responsibility for her being out here. Lucy had convinced Melody to come along for the ride, and she knew she couldn't leave her stranded. She didn't want to.

"Do you wanna get out of town for a few days?" Lucy asked.

"Sure, where do you want to go?"

"Let's go soak in some hot springs before it gets too cold. I'll go in and talk to Phillip. You talk to Nathan and get packed. We'll go spend a couple of nights up at Cougar Hot Springs. Then I won't feel so bad about missing the Phish shows."

Lucy smiled and forced the feelings of anger and resentment deeper inside, hidden by her radiant smile. It was something she'd become very good at doing.

After a long talk that ended with Phillip apologizing, everyone agreed it was a good idea for the group to split along gender lines for a few days. The boys would stay behind and work the garden, while the girls went off to the mountains to relax and clear their heads.

There are places on earth that are just too wonderful to be created by chance. Divinity is all around us, all the time, but in certain places it becomes completely impossible to ignore. The voice of this magical world sings with clarity and volume in those places. Melody and Lucy were in such a place, listening.

Cougar Hot Springs bubbles up from the primordial forests of the Cascade Mountains in Oregon into a large pool of 112 degree water. That pool flows downhill into larger, & cooler soaking ponds. All this is surrounded by the lush, dense, old-growth rainforest of Oregon.

The hot spring water fell as rain thousands of years ago. Slowly, it seeped through the earth until it came close enough to the magma that it heated and rose back through the layers. Rich with dissolved minerals this water retains some of the core heat as it graces the surface on its way back to the ocean.

Lucy and Melody sat completely naked in this pleasantly hot water. The city, their boyfriends, Phish tour, the bills, the weed, everything seemed so far away. They were in the womb of the world, relaxed and perfectly at ease and at home in their own bodies.

They ignored the other scattered bathers and conversation flowed between them through the afternoon.

"This world is amazing," Melody said. "I used to think everything was working against me, and now it feels more like I'm flowing with everything. Life is this wonderful gift, and I've been ignoring it for too long."

Lucy smiled and pulled her head beneath the water for a minute, where all she could hear was the beating of the earth. When she came back up Melody continued talking.

"I mean, I've traveled across the country, dancing at concerts. I've got a great boyfriend, who I love very much, and look at us. We're chilling in a hot spring in the forest in Oregon and there's no job to go back to Monday morning. We're living the dream."

Lucy laughed, "Yup. And you'll never have to check groceries again."

Melody smiled, that life seemed so far away and so unreal now. She splashed some water on her face. The girls had brought a tent and enough food for three days or more. Phillip and Natron waved forlornly from the porch as they drove away.

The women waved back, but were laughing as soon as they were around the corner. They were out of town after stopping for a few bottles of red wine.

In those days, you could camp at Cougar Hot Springs for free and there were always people taking advantage of the situation. Still, there were times, when the day trippers would clear out of the pools, and a few people could sit there alone all night.

After the girls soaked for a while, they hiked in their camp, set up the tent, and heated up dinner on the camp stove; refried beans, tortillas, spinach, tomatoes, and avocados. They ate like royalty, and then hiked back to the springs with their towels, some flashlights, and a few bottles of wine.

They were happy to find the pools deserted.

"Thank God there's no creepy boys here trying to check us out like earlier," Lucy said as she took off her clothes.

Melody giggled and joined her in the water.

"This is exactly what I needed," Lucy sighed. "Hand me that bottle of wine, will you?"

"I know. I had no idea places like this existed. Did you remember the corkscrew?"

"It's in the backpack with the wine. It's amazing, isn't it? There's nothing like this in Massachusetts. No matter what happens, I'm so glad not to be there any more. I don't think I could ever live there again. Do you?"

Melody thought wistfully back to her old home, but couldn't see herself occupying that space. She'd moved past it and there was no going back.

"Never in a million years," Melody said flatly as she popped the cork free. She took a healthy drink from the bottle and passed it to Lucy.

At first they were laughing and telling stories from their childhood, but as the bottle got lighter, the conversation got heavier. Melody finally cornered Lucy on what was going down between her and Phillip and Lucy was happy to talk about it.

"I really do love Phillip," Lucy said. "I just don't know if I can deal with everything that goes with him. I mean, he's crazy, right?"

"Sure, but so is Natron."

"Yeah, but he's fun crazy. Phillip can get scary crazy. I wonder if he's gonna flip out and kill someone or something."

Melody shook her head, "Phillip would never do anything like that. He's got his control issues, but he's definitely family. He's got your back no matter what. Hell, he's got us all out here working. It's gonna be fine."

"I hope we make as much money as he says we're going to," Lucy shook her head as she spoke. "Sometimes, I don't know if it's worth it. I get all paranoid thinking about what would happen if anything happened."

"Nathan says you just can't think about that. Put it out of your mind, like it doesn't even exist. It's not about the money, it's about getting to live the kind of life we want to live. And if we keep our focus on the good side of things, then things stay good."

"You're lucky. He's so positive. Phillip has told me before he'll probably end up in prison or dead before he turns thirty. It's hard to live with someone and love them when they don't really think they deserve to live or be loved."

Melody nodded her head in understanding, "I get it," she said.

"But when he's being positive and on a roll," Lucy continued, "There's not another person I'd rather be with. I just don't know what to do. I don't know which person he'd rather be."

"Luckily," Melody chimed in, "Things like that usually get decided without much input from us. If it's gonna work out, then it'll work out because you and Phillip both make it work out for each other." Melody smiled at her friend who smiled back.

"No matter what, I'm glad you and I have got each other."

Lucy felt more than just the warmth of the water.

Phillip was going crazy. He'd never been so broke in his entire life. He knew he could call his family for money, but the idea of it didn't appeal to him. He'd done his best to stay away.

They had moved into the new place and got everything running by mid-August. He let the little clones veg for just about two weeks. Then, it was a game of waiting sixty days or so until the plants were finished blooming and the herb was ready to harvest. Then there'd be a day or two of trimming and about a week of curing. He wasn't gonna get paid again until mid-October at the earliest.

There was enough money for rent and bills, if Phillip was careful with his money. Phillip hated being careful with his money.

There was always another option. He could take the rent money, invest it in something profitable and easy to sell and go about living his life without the stress of being broke.

Cocaine.

Phillip knew these Mexicans down in Tucson who could get the stuff across the border real cheap. If there was a ready supply of white people to consume it he could make plenty of money in no time at all.

While Lucy and Melody were away, Phillip began formulating his devious plan.

"So, were just gonna go camping for a few days, maybe a week, like you girls did. We've been stuck in the house for too long." Phillip was listening as Natron unwittingly convinced the girls of going along with his plan.

"Where are you guys gonna go?" Lucy asked Natron, while eyeing Phillip, trying to bring him into the conversation.

Natron shrugged, "We're thinking of hitting the beach. We just need to get out, you know? We're super bummed we missed the Portland show the other day, but we've finally got everything running smoothly: the timer's are working, the pumps are working fine, and the reservoirs are full and clean. All you gotta do is keep the water full and watch the temperature. Maybe turn off one of the exhaust fans if it gets too cold."

"I'm sorry we missed the Phish shows," Lucy said and smiled sheepishly at Phillip. Since they'd come back from the hot springs Phillip had been sweet and attentive and she couldn't help thinking that things were going to be just fine.

"It's okay," Phillip smiled back and walked over to hug Lucy. "I've seen that band before. I just need a break from this house. I wanna go somewhere with you, but Natron has got to get out of here as bad as me."

"The hot springs were really refreshing," Lucy said. Since she came back she'd made a conscious decision to make this work with Phillip. She loved him, after all.

"It's just gonna be a few days, maybe a week." Nathan was playing his part perfectly and the girls relented without a fight. How could they say no?

Once again the group split apart. When they got back together again, everything would be different even though it still seemed the same.

"You gotta be fucking kidding me. You're not serious are you?"

Phillip laughed at the absurdity of Nathan even asking. Of course he was serious. He was always serious.

"Tucson? For fuck's sake, man, that's like a 20 hour drive." Nathan kept whining while Phillip laughed.

"So we've got plenty of time to get down there, take care of business, hit the Phish show, take care of more business, and get back to Eugene before the girls even start missing us. Four days, and everything lines up perfectly. We come home rolling in cash again."

Nathan was skeptical. He couldn't believe that Phillip was actually making this move. They'd settled into a safe routine with the plants in Oregon, and here Phillip was just coming out of nowhere with this crazy idea.

"I've gotta call Melody and tell her."

Phillip glared at him as they rolled south down Interstate 5.

"You're not gonna tell Melody shit. You're not gonna call her now, and you're not gonna bring this up later, either, or we're fucking done, man. You hear me? Done. And when we get back from this you're gonna notice an increase in your walking-around money 'til the plants finally come in and we split that 50/50. But this trip never happened. Deal?"

Nathan shut up and watched the miles roll by while Phillip maniacally piloted the vehicle. They were both lost in thought. Nathan didn't want to do this. Phillip was pissed he didn't work it out to get a few tanks before the Portland show and had to make it up. Neither of them could really believe they were driving all the way down to Tucson, Arizona to score a bunch of coke and take it to the Phish show.

"Don't worry," Phillip said. "We're not gonna break it into little bags, we're gonna sell the whole kilo to four or five different friends that I've got on tour; a half-pound for eighty-five-hundred, a quarter pound for five-thousand. I'll get the kilo for twenty G's, so we'll make almost twenty G's for less than a days work. They'll take it on to Austin and make even more on those college kids. It's a fucking cake walk. We're gonna have a kilo of coke on us for about three hours."

"I still don't like it." Nathan finally emerged from his thoughts.

"Tough shit. Learn to like it. Quit being a little bitch about this work or find something else to do. This is how you make money. See what happens when you tell that pretty little girlfriend of yours that she's gotta go back to checking groceries while you get a job flipping burgers because you're too scared to put your balls on the line."

"Fuck you, Phillip. You goddamn well know I'm not some fucking custie. I work my shit all day long, every show. I'm just saying that coke ain't really what we ought to be feeding those kids. Our kids."

"Fuck those kids. Coke is what they want and I know where to get it and I'm gonna take their fucking money. You watch me. Just like blowing balloons."

A tension mounted between them that had never existed before. Nathan looked over at Phillip and knew they were different people to the core. The only time that Phillip actually cared about anyone besides Phillip, thought Nathan, was when their well-being directly affected his own.

Nathan told himself that he actually cared about the random people at the shows. He had gone to the shows seeking something deeper in himself and life and he hoped that other people were finding that same feeling.

He wanted to help them find that feeling. He wanted to be part of the solution and not the problem. Coke was a problem, just like nitrous. Couldn't Phillip see that? All he saw was false security in the form of flowing cash.

He relented to this devil in the driver's seat because he had to. He was this far in and he had to get to the end. By the time they crossed into California and saw Mt. Shasta on the horizon, Nathan began making plans to separate himself and Melody from Phillip.

It was another delirium inducing drive that brought them down to the Sonoran Desert. They checked into a ratty motel next to the busiest Wal-Mart ever seen and promptly fell asleep.

But not before Phillip phoned his connections and confirmed their meeting for tomorrow.

The next day Phillip left Nathan in the hotel room, explaining, "These guys are pretty serious and seriously paranoid. They don't want to meet you and you don't want to meet them. I'll be back in a few hours."

Natron paced around the hotel room, trying to get the TV to take his attention but it was the telephone that he kept gravitating towards. He wanted to call Melody. He wanted to tell her what was going on.

He chewed his nails and paced the floor and watched daytime TV.

Finally Phillip came back. He was grinning from ear to ear as he set the backpack down on the empty bed. "Went off without a hitch," he said.

"Can I see it?" Nathan asked, finally relieved and completely frightened at the same time. "I've never seen that much cocaine in my life."

Phillip smiled, happy to show off, and pulled the white brick of powder carefully wrapped in cellophane from out of the backpack and displayed it for Nathan to see.

"Beautiful, isn't it?"

All of his ethics aside, Nathan had to admit it was a beautiful sight. His mouth watered in anticipation of breaking into it. Coke was always so easy, none of the mental calisthenics of psycadelics. Coke would keep him going when the shows were stacking up.

"This is what twenty-thousand dollars looks like. We're gonna split it up and it will look like forty-thousand dollars."

"So we gotta break it down now?" Nathan asked.

"Yeah, but I bought a scale and some masks and gloves and a vacuum sealer while I was out."

"Man, that sounds like work. I guess if we're breaking into it then we might as well do a few lines, right?"

"Now you're thinking, Natron," Phillip laughed. "But we can't do very much until later. We've got work to do. You don't wanna get all coked up before you go sell coke. It's bad for business."

Natron smiled and locked the deadbolt and the chain while Phillip pulled the full length mirror off the wall of the hotel room. Carefully he slit into the sealed plastic brick of severely intoxicating powder that was once a plant.

"Damn, that's a lot of blow," Natron said, shaking his head. Phillip started shaving chunks off the brick and setting them on the digital scale. Natron busied himself with breaking down some of the lump into snort-able powder.

"This breaks up funny, coming off such a big chunk I guess," Nathan laughed.

Within minutes Phillip was sealing up the first half-pound and Natron had cut two big fat rails out on the mirror.

"Jesus, man," Phillip said. "That's way too much for what we gotta do. Cut that shit in half, at least. Natron swiped the blade and pulled half of the rails back into the pile. There were still two fat lines about three inches long.

Phillip laughed, "Man, that's still too much for me. I'll just pull a little bump for myself, but you can hit that line if you want."

Natron bent over the mirror with a straw stuck up his nose. He inhaled half of the rail with his left nostril then came up rubbing his face. It tingled and burned in a way he wasn't familiar with. There was no numbie.

"Man, this is some shitty coke."

"What?!?" Phillip was obviously confused and pissed off at the same time. He licked his finger and stuck it into the line Natron had cut out for him. He tasted the powder and his eyes opened wide.

"Holy shit, man! This is fucking awesome! This isn't coke. This is the best fucking heroin there is. China white. I didn't think those Mexicans could get anything but black tar. This is the shit Jerry used to do. Do you know what this means?"

Nathan felt his heart pound frantically in his chest. He'd just done Heroin for the first time. Heroin. With a capital H. What did this mean?

"This means we're gonna make way more money than I first thought. I wonder if those Mexicans knew what they were doing? This is fucking crazy. Oh shit, are you alright Nathan? You just did a bunch of fucking Heroin. Ha-ha!"

The color drained from Nathan's face. He wanted to kill Phillip. Literally kill him.

"Man, let's get this shit bagged up and hit the road. Don't do any more, though. Fuck, you're gonna be wasted."

Finally Nathan broke his silence. "Man, I've never done Heroin before."

Phillip nodded and hummed while he examined Nathan. "You're gonna be in for a ride. Just relax and go with it. Seriously, you just did a bunch, so make sure you don't let yourself nod out completely. Stay awake as long as you can and keep moving."

Nathan scratched his chest and did his best to beat back his rising fear.

"You're gonna be fine, man," Phillip assured him. "I've seen people do more than you, no problem. It's just another drug and you just gotta take the ride. You know how to do that. I'll handle the work. You're probably gonna get a little sick. You'll be alright. Just go with it. It's never as good again as it is the first time." Phillip smiled at him and patted his shoulder. "I'll be here for you, man."

Somehow, this wasn't very comforting for Nathan.

28

It was a crazy place for a show. They pulled into a dirt parking lot at the fairgrounds outside of Tucson and Nathan could barely keep his eyes open. He was constantly falling into himself then bolting back into his current situation.

His mouth was dry and his whole body itched. They parked and Phillip looked at Nathan. He scratched his chin and exhaled slowly, shaking his head while Natron slumped over in the passenger seat.

Nathan exhaled, squirmed around, then looked over at Phillip. "Fuck man, this is some serious shit. I didn't see this coming. I just wanted a little gacker to get me through the show and now I'm totally fucked. I think I can maybe walk."

Phillip laughed, "No man, you better stay here. I'm gonna leave the shit stashed in the car for now and go scope the scene. I gotta run into these guys, but I know they're here and expecting me. You just chill. Get out of the car, sit on the trunk, and watch the pretty girls walk by."

Natron squirmed in his skin again. His skin didn't feel like it belonged on him. He was like a cicada trying to get out. "I'll try man. I'll chill here. You go do whatever."

"Cool, I'll be back in fifteen minutes."

Natron saw Phillip leaving as eight snapshots that flashed through blinking eyes, starting with Phillip smiling at him and ending with the car door slamming.

Within minutes the strange, floating euphoria was replaced with the distinct sense that he was about to vomit. He crashed out of the car and started retching. Nothing would come out. He would jump just to the point of throwing up and stay right there. It was even worse than actually barfing.

Nathan had no idea how long this went on. Eventually he was panting and rubbing the sweat off his brow, hoping he'd gone through the worst of it. It was going to be a long ride. A few more breaths, and he crawled back into the passenger seat.

This was nice to relax here and drift through this. It was an ocean. He lolled around in it until Phillip came back. It seemed like he had been gone hardly any time at all.

"Holy shit, man." Phillip said smiling.

Nathan grinned out of from behind the fluff of his existence. "You're feeling it now, aren't you," Phillip laughed. He rubbed his hands together in hateful glee.

This was the kind of situation where Phillip excelled. Everything seemed to be falling apart around him, but actually it was all working out and he was adapting and changing instantly not only to suit his surroundings, but to work them more for his benefit.

It was perfect that Nathan was out of the picture for the evening. Phillip had seen John strolling the lot and John hadn't seen him. The same piece of shit John who ripped off his house in Oregon and put him in this shitty situation to begin with. The same piece of shit John that Phillip was going to destroy later tonight. Phillip was giddy with the revenge he was going to have. First he had to get through the work.

The best part was that the lot seemed to be completely unguarded. There was absolutely no security anywhere in sight. This actually made Phillip a little nervous, because it meant that security might be just out of sight, watching.

Still, he wanted to get this deal done before the show, before everyone was high and before everything got crazy. He could deal with John later. First he had to deal with Dirty and a few big bags of heroin.

Dirty was a big guy from the East Coast that Phillip had known for years. He would do anything, and heroin definitely wasn't off his radar. Phillip knew he was gonna be here from simple phone conversations they'd had before tour. They were usually into something together. Dirty had helped Phillip move molly before and Phillip had helped Dirty move L in the past.

He was easy to spot and Phillip kept an eye out for him while he was walking the lot, but he saw John first and hightailed it back to the car. Dirty would probably just walk by, anyway. Sure enough, within a few minutes he was strolling down the aisle towards Phillip and Natron.

"Hey Dirty," Phillip yelled.

The greasy, bearded man, who completely lived up to his nickname, turned in surprise. "Holy shit, Phillip! Is that you?" Dirty smiled through his ragged beard, an incomplete row of stained teeth making an appearance in the daylight. He came over to hug Phillip, who embraced his friend while wincing at the prevailing body odor.

"You got any work for me," Dirty asked. "This tour has been hobbled. I made a pretty good haul on nitrous to begin with, but I'm burning through it. No one has any work until we get back east."

"Man, I got you covered. Think you can move any H?"

"Is it any good? It's not that black tar shit, is it?"

"It's the real deal. China white. Did you meet my friend, Natron? Hey Natron, come here man. Meet my friend, Dirty."

Nathan staggered over from the passenger seat. "What's up man?" he said through half blinking eyes, while swaying back and forth on wobbly legs. He held out his hand. Dirty shook his hand laughing, "Alright. I see what you mean. It's the real deal. How much you got?"

"A kilo."

"A fucking kilo? Are you serious, man?"

"Yeah, I broke it down into half-pounds for $10,000 each
or quarter-pounds for six G's."

"Man, a few years ago I woulda said no way, but all kinds of kids are doing H these days. I can move that shit. I'll take two half- pounds at 10 G's to my head, but can you drop the price to $8,000 on the others so I can make a little on moving the weight."

"How about $8,500."

"Done."

"But it's till 6 for the quarter-pound."

"No worries, man. That shit's gonna be gone in a few hours. Lemme get to work. You gonna be here?"

"Yeah, I'll be chilling at the car. Hey, is that piece of shit John on tour?"

"Yeah. He's here. Fucking guy. He talks a big game, about how cool and connected he is, but that motherfucker is always asking everyone else for work."

"Fuck that guy. I hope nobody gives him any work. He shouldn't be on lot anyway."

"That's fucking right. Little bitch got desperate today. He bought about a dozen vials of Visine and he's out here selling it as liquid LSD."

"What? That motherfucker! I'm gonna get him later, you watch me."

"Fuck yeah, man. I got your back on that shit. Wrecking crew!"

"Whatever you do don't tell him I'm here and don't work any of this out to him."

"You got it man."

Dirty kept coming and going, bringing tons of cash to Phillip and taking away big bags of heroin. Natron continued squirming and swaying while Phillip counted his money. Pretty soon all the drugs were sold and the sun was setting. It was time to go to the show.

Phillip lead the way and Nathan staggered along behind. It was his first time away from the car all day long.

The security was so lax they weren't even really checking tickets. Phillip breezed through the gate while Natron staggered along behind.

The show started and Natron did his best to wade through it. Something was off, not just with Natron, but with the band as well. Maybe it was just his perspective, but the music seemed awful. He couldn't dance at all. He didn't even want to be here, so when Phillip asked him if he wanted to head out just after the second set started, Natron said, "Sure."

He was still walking through a nightmare daydream in the parking lot when Phillip bolted away from him. For a minute, Natron thought he was hallucinating as he watched Phillip run over and cold cock some guy Natron had never seen.

When the guy fell to the ground, Phillip started kicking him in the ribs. This was right in the middle of Shakedown. Some people went to pull Phillip off of John and some others stopped them. Natron heard snippets of conversation while the beating continued.

"That guy sold me some bunk acid, fuck him."

"Yeah, he ripped off Phillip. You don't fucking do that. You don't steal from other kids."

Soon, Phillip wasn't the only one beating on the kid. A few others jumped in and pounded him with skateboards. John was a bloody mess lying on the ground and Natron was watching in shock while Phillip went over to a vendor's booth and ripped the lid off of one of the drink coolers. The vendor shouted at Phillip, but Dirty stepped in and told him, "Be quiet and mind your own fucking business. Here's fifty bucks for the cooler."

At that moment the vendor made eye contact with Nathan. It was Paul. The same gentle soul who'd been there all along.

Phillip walked over to John who was crying on the ground, blood soaking everything.

"Fuck you, John. Nobody rips me off."

Phillip bludgeoned him over and over with the cooler lid. Eventually he was satisfied. Then someone walked over and spat on the bloody pulp that used to be a kid. "Sell me bunk acid, huh? Well this is real acid, motherfucker. Have a good trip to the hospital." Laughing, the young kid poured a vial into John's open wounds.

Flashing lights appeared in the distance and everyone scattered. Nathan staggered back to the car, soaked in tears over what he'd seen and what he'd been a part of. He found Phillip smiling in the driver's seat, soaked in blood, and twitching with adrenaline.

"That's how the wrecking crew works right there. I told you I was gonna get that motherfucker," he shouted. "Nobody fucking steals from me. I hope I fucking killed him. I hope he's fucking dead."

29

John died five days later in the hospital. No one will ever know the hell he went through between the pain and the acid and coming in and out of consciousness before he died.

Nathan was going through his own hell the next day. He didn't remember actually falling asleep, but when he woke up his stomach turned inside out. Phillip had to pull over while Nathan wretched on the side of the highway. He puked until nothing came out, then they started driving again. In less than a half-hour they were on the side of the road again.

There were times last night, when Nathan really enjoyed the sensation. He'd wished he were just sitting on the couch at home and melting into nothing instead of trying to keep it together at a Phish show. Part of him hoped Phillip had saved a little of the drug. He could see the appeal.

Heroin is an evil mistress who can completely own the user's heart. She's the most beautiful woman ever, who willingly gets in bed and fucks harder, faster, and better than any other woman in the world. At the same time, she is full of hate. If she is your mistress, she hates everything about you; your job, your friends, your dreams, everything. However, she will always be there in the end, ready to take you into her bed and touch you in a way you've never been touched before.

Natron went back and forth between guilty reminiscing and adamant denials of the evil he'd witnessed and been a part of. How many other kids would die from overdosing on that pure heroin they'd brought to the Phish lot?

Not to mention the piece of dying meat that Phillip had created out of one young man's future.

John hadn't even gurgled his last helpless breath through the respirator by the time Phillip and Nathan were safe and sound back in Eugene. Phillip was all smiles and laughter when he told the girls about hiking down to a cave on the beach and spending a few nights there.

"Then we went and soaked in Bagby Hot Springs," he told them with a sincere smile on his face. "It was great. You girls gotta try it sometime. Tell them about the pools, Natron."

Then Phillip would look at Nathan and smile in such a way that it made Nathan's skin crawl. He knew Phillip would attack him instantly, and he was scared. So he choked back the bile and went along with the contrived journey they'd had that Phillip had dictated on the way home, even filling in details.

"The thing about lying," Phillip had said, "Is that you have to know every little thing about the lie so that it starts to seem true even to yourself. We were never at that show. I never beat the shit out of that stealing motherfucker. We were camping on the beach and soaking at the hot springs. You ever been to Bagby? You know what it looks like?"

Phillip had even thrown some desert sand into the car to give evidence of the beach.

Nathan had never been to Bagby Hot Springs, but when Phillip prompted him to tell about the pools, Nathan forced a smile and supplied the information he'd been given. "It's great, they've got these hollowed out, old-growth trees turned into tubs. It's like the log ride. The water comes in through the old style plumbing of little wooden creeks all over the place. It's amazing."

"It sounds like it," Melody smiled at him and her smile tore through him. Surely she could read his mind and tell he was lying. Surely she could see how tortured he was.

All she saw was the same young man she'd fallen in love with. He looked a little tired, but surely he hadn't been sleeping as good all alone on the ground. She would make love to him later and he would get a good night's sleep afterwards.

She couldn't see that he would never be the same again. Always he would feel that heroin in the back of his mind tempting to let go of trying and sink into her vicious embrace.

The entire event remained a secret that was never mentioned again except in the occasional look exchanged by Phillip and Natron.

Furtive glances aside, Natron found himself with more walking around money, just as promised. He would take Melody out for dinner or to buy some new clothes, and she would smile at him and he felt so trapped. He wanted out. He wanted away from Phillip.

When the first harvest finally came in, it wasn't as big as they had hoped. Too many of Phillip's lights were gone to keep up with the production he was used to. They hadn't been in veg cycle long enough to get much mass. Most of that crop went to keeping the rent and the electricity paid. Whatever was left over, Phillip invested in lights, still surfing on the stash he'd made in Tucson and convincing Natron this was the way to invest the harvest and that he and Melody would still be taken care of.

There were never any visitors to the house and there were no concerts. Melody and Lucy desperately wanted to go on Fall Tour, but it didn't happen. Then the girls wanted to go to Florida for Phish's Millennium concert at Big Cypress, but Phillip wouldn't hear of it. Nathan didn't object because, after Tucson, he really didn't care to see Phish ever again. He'd lost interest and now there were these evil memories of heroin and death tied into it all for him.

Y2K came and went and the world continued to function as it always had.

They spent what seemed to Nathan like endless months hunkered down in the house, just watching the grass grow. It was too much. He needed to get away from here. To get away from Phillip. He just had to make a little more money, first.

So he spent his time watching Simpson's reruns and drinking excessively. He cultivated a fine depression that quickly took the gleam out of his eyes. Instead, it was replaced with the gleam of sodium lights. Melody couldn't stand to see him like this. She was happy just about anywhere, as long as he was happy. He wasn't.

The months spent locked together in the mansion on Capitol Drive had served to bring them closer together as a couple. Except for that one thing, Nathan broke down to her often about his relationship with his father, his disconnection from the world, and his confusing and conflicting dreams for his life, but never told her about the murder.

Melody likewise divulged her confusing love for her parents and her guilt for leaving home. They wore down their individual personalities and exposed raw wounds, especially on nights when they got blackout drunk together. In the morning they would wake up sheepishly grinning at one another, scared of all the secrets they'd divulged and hoping to find themselves still in love with each other.

If there was one thing certain in this time, it was the feelings between Nathan and Melody.

However that one hidden thorn festered in Nathan. He would work himself up to the edge of coming clean with her, but always backed down. After all, he had been involved in smuggling heroin into the country, distributing it to people Melody cared about, then been an accomplice in a murder, and lied to her about the whole thing. Worst, after all of that, he had continued to associate with the murderer.

And he couldn't help but to like Phillip. He was irreverent, confident, and determined. All the things that Nathan wasn't anymore.

It was because of Phillip's encouragement that even when Nathan was in the blackest pits of his depression he still managed to keep up with the work Phillip and the indoor marijuana farm required of him. He actually excelled at it and together they made money, good money.

Whenever Lucy and Melody drove a trunk full of weed down to California or up to Portland or Seattle they came back with thousands and thousands of dollars in cash. The rent was always paid and the fridge and the liquor cabinet were always well stocked. It was a hard situation to imagine leaving behind, even with the constant stress of making a living through an illegal enterprise.

The summer of 2000 came and went. It was a beautiful summer in Eugene, but the added heat forced them to entirely rework the exhaust system. It was constant work, most of it done during the twelve hour period from 7 pm to 7 am when the lights were on.

Phillip knew what he was doing and the weed he produced was top quality. Phillip cut Nathan in 50/50 on everything, just like he said he would.

They pulled in a steady $4,000 for every pound they produced. They staggered the harvest to be trimming one of the three rooms devoted to marijuana production every month. Each room yielded nearly ten pounds. Once, with a particularly vigorous strain of OG Kush they got 12 pounds out of a room.

Somehow, it wasn't enough for Nathan or Phillip. Phillip kept expanding the operation and Nathan just wanted out. But he had no idea what else to do with his life. He certainly didn't want to get a job and blend into the inbred corporate landscape of modern America. He wanted to be free, but now he was rooted down with these plants. He buried cash under his mattress and waited for something to change. Melody was growing restless, too. Their love life suffered. For the first time, they were fighting.

One day, Nathan came home with a nice, used Chevy van he'd gotten for a few thousand dollars. He was getting ready to leave soon, no matter what. He explained his anxious feelings to Phillip and Phillip did his best to keep him around.

"You're the best partner I've ever had," Phillip assured him. "No one else has ever been able to take care of the plants as well as me. You've got talent and should stick with this. I was thinking we both outta move out soon and just have this as a work house.

We can get three more rooms up and running and even sell clones. We're just about to really break through, man."

"I just need a break. I need to go to a show and dance."

"You know Phish is going on hiatus soon," Phillip said. "They're playing their last show down in San Francisco at Shoreline next week. You wanna go?"

"Honestly, (and don't tell Melody this) no. I'm not really into them anymore. I wish I could see The Grateful Dead. I wonder how that Other Ones tour with Bruce Hornsby was? Anyway, we're taking down the big room next week and I need to be here for that."

"I knew you would say that," Phillip smiled at him. "So I got you a present." He handed Nathan two concert tickets.

"I'm not the biggest fan, but I hope you'll like it."

Nathan studied the tickets. Widespread Panic at the Hult Center in Eugene on November 8, 2000. Maybe this would do.

"We'll have everything trimmed up, cured, and sold by then and get the next round underway. If you like the show they're also playing a few shows in Montana afterwards and you and Melody should go to those, too."

Phillip looked deep into Nathan's eyes "But then come back and get to work. I need you, man. I can't do this by myself."

Part 2:

The Spirit Moves In All Things

~30~

The Widespread Panic scene has always been a very different animal than Phish. To the casual observer, the two seem almost identical. Dreadlocks are still everywhere, likewise patchwork dresses and sandals. It looks like the same people in the same vans are there as at the Phish show.

The differences lie beneath the surface and are as subtle as they are defining.

Phish's music is very technical. The band members were braving long winters in Burlington, Vermont, taking psychedelics, and going to school to study music. Their first show was in 1982 or '83, depending on who you ask. Their mix of intricate musical refrains, nonsensical lyrics, and freeform jamming was met largely with disappointment and confusion by their early crowds. The four of them crafted a compelling musical comedy that, for a long time, no one else got. Once people started getting the joke, the band steadily amassed a horde of loyal listeners that would grow exponentially after Jerry Garcia's death and the disbanding of The Grateful Dead.

Coming from New England, they carry with them something of that abrasively honest vibe most people from the Northeast carry as well, most accurately exemplified by the apparently rude New Yorker who is really just being themselves.

Widespread Panic formed in Athens, Georgia in the mid-eighties; around the same time as the guys in Phish. Eventually there would be six in the band. All of them were southerners; hailing from places like Mississippi, Tennessee, and Georgia. There is a decidedly different vibe down south. People are initially friendly, even if it's just a false front for the same brutal honesty.

The guys in Panic weren't at school studying to become musicians like the guys in Phish. Panic was formed kind of on the side, around two friends, John Bell and Michael Houser, and their intense desire to become musicians because it was the song singing in their heart. The other members were recruited along the way and heard the same song. Like Phish, they developed a following that also increased exponentially in the wake of the flood that ensued after the death of Jerry Garcia.

The difference in their musical aspects is also visible in the difference between Phish and Panic fans.

Phish fans tend to be more cerebral. If they are into drugs, they tend to prefer chemically mind-altering drugs like ecstasy, LSD, or DMT. Panic fans who use drugs are more physical. They tend to prefer whiskey, cocaine, and mushrooms.

Phish is the cities and Panic is the small-towns and countryside. Phish causes intense thought while Panic causes intense feeling. The paradox is that Widespread Panic's lyrics and storytelling are generally much more involved and easily decipherable than Phish's.

With Panic, you don't have to think about what the song means, so you just feel it.

With Phish, you feel what the song is about, but have to think of how the story matches that feeling.

For Nathan and Melody it was surreal walking into the familiar downtown setting of Eugene and seeing a lot in the parking garage outside of the Hult Center. For the first time in over a year the excitement bubbled to the surface in Nathan and he became Natron again. He didn't have to go to the show, the show had come to him.

He had a spring to his step that Melody hadn't seen in too long. She watched him with a smile creeping across her face as they strolled through the parking garage. Her own legs tingled in anticipation. There was a muted Shakedown with a few kitchens in operation.

"Hey, Melody, is that you?"

The female voice sounded familiar and Melody whirled around to see who it was. A joyous scream erupted from Melody as she ran to hug Jessica. Her locks had grown longer and reached further down her back. Kale was standing behind the table grinning with a spatula in his hand. They both looked wonderful to Melody.

That same once-familiar sense of placement filled her. "Natron!" Melody called, distracting her lover from the animated conversation he was having with two tour kids regarding Phish's hiatus. Nathan turned and spotted their old friends.

"Holy shit," he said. "Imagine seeing you guys here."

"Well, what else are we gonna do, now that Phish is gone?" Kale answered.

"Get a job, hippie," Nathan joked.

Warm embraces were exchanged and it was as if no time had passed since that wonderful summer tour of 1999. They picked up their conversation right where it had been left off. The quesadilla business was slow so there was plenty of time to converse.

"Did you guys do that last Phish run?" Natron asked.

"Of course," Jessica responded with a roll of her eyes.

"So how was it?" Melody pressed.

"Actually, it was pretty sad. The music wasn't that good and the last show was just like any other. They just walked off the stage without a word while 'Let it Be' was playing over the sound system."

"Fuck Phish. I can't believe they quit." Nathan said.

"No shit," Kale agreed.

"So, what now?" Nathan asked.

"Panic tour, finally." Jessica smiled.

Kale explained, "Jess has wanted to go on Panic tour for years, but there's just so much more money on Phish."

"Now, there's no excuse," Jessica smiled. "Have you seen these guys before?" She asked her friends.

"Not yet," Melody said. "I remember you talking about them at Oswego, but we've been stuck here in Eugene since '99."

"I wondered about you guys. We didn't see you down in Big Cypress, but that place was huge. Anyone could've been there and we missed them."

"Oh my God, how was that?" Melody asked.

"Fucking amazing," Jess smiled. "They played from sunset to sunrise. It was hands down the best Phish show I've ever seen. Why weren't you guys there?"

"Check this out," Nathan pulled a sack of nuggets out of his pocket and handed it to Kale. He opened the bag, took a whiff and nodded his approval. "Nice," he said. "Is this you?"

"Yeah. We moved out here with Phillip and Lucy and have been growing weed ever since. It's alright, but I'm getting ready to move on," Natron said.

Melody saw the excitement in his eyes and was so happy to see Natron back in his element. It warmed her heart against the cold November sun.

"You should come on Panic tour with us," Kale said.

Natron nodded, "Maybe we will. Let's see if they're any good, first."

There is a point, in some people, when the fairy tales of modern life become completely intolerable. Once past that point, panic becomes the only appropriate response. People will destroy their own lives and those around them just to interject some chaos into the regulated existence they feel they've been forced into. We see this every day in varying forms.

In extreme cases, schoolchildren pack weapons to math class. Husbands murder their wife and kids. People join religious cults and spike the Kool-Aid with cyanide. Anything to shatter the status quo of everyday the same mundane and pointless toiling.

Melody had passed that point long ago. It happened months before Lucy walked into the grocery store. Melody, however, wasn't willing to externalize any chaos into her life. She was too afraid of becoming her mother. Her panic was on the inside, creating an internal turmoil without damaging her bland existence.

She had no visions of taking out her co-workers with an automatic rifle, but she occasionally thought about buying a gun to shoot herself. Walking out the door of the grocery store and opening her life ended those thoughts. She valued her life more than she ever had. It was precious and fleeting and moments of wonder and excitement make the whole thing worth it.

Nathan was finally reaching that point in himself. Phish tour had been kind of like a game. Now, he was feeling like he had to do something different, but didn't know what. For more than a year his life had been a regiment of growing plants and cutting them down. Sure, the money had been good, even great at times, but he'd never looked at money as the purpose for his existence. Freedom was his purpose and he had constructed a prison of his own in that mansion on top of the hill. Albeit, it was a comfortable prison, but he felt trapped nonetheless.

"Hey Mel," he said to his girl as they were strolling towards the front entrance to the Hult Center.

"Yeah," she smiled back into his eyes, enjoying the comfortable feeling of his arm around her as they walked together. They'd left Jessica and Kale to dismantle their kitchen, planning on meeting them inside the venue.

"I've been saving these for a special occasion," he pulled a small bag of mushrooms out of his pocket and dangled them in front of her. "Wanna eat some mushrooms?" he asked.

She smiled mischievously, "Yeah."

They split the bag and slipped in the front door. Security was searching pretty heavily, but they avoided Melody's bra where she had a few joints rolled up for the show.

"Hey there Eugene," John Bell grumbled into the microphone as the band took the stage. The concert hall was plush, and used to housing performances by the Eugene Ballet Company, the local opera, and a symphony orchestra. Panic dropped the first notes of "Disco" and the building rumbled with a sound it hadn't heard before.

Instantly Nathan's grin grew exponentially. Watching him, Melody felt the same infectious joy. They began to dance, their bodies moving like they hadn't in far too long. The shit-eating grin spread across their faces moved into their legs as the band delved into a sexy cover of J.J. Cale's "Ride Me High." Melody was pressing her body against the man she loved and he felt her softly melting into him. This was how it should be. The keyboard player was singing now and someone next to them shouted, "Go Jojo!"

Together Melody and Natron were already going higher together they ever had a Phish show. Maybe it was because they knew each other so well now. Maybe it was because they weren't thinking anymore.

"The less you want, the more you got. So don't

you cry for more," Jojo screamed into the mic.

The message tore through Melody.

Jojo insisted "Go down on me baby. Get down on the floor. Yeah! Yeah! Yeah! More! More! More!"

Her body shook almost violently. She looked to Nathan who was pumping his fists in time with the music. He had a look in his eyes that almost scared her: the look of an animal. She had to touch him, and brushed her body against his. He looked at her with his animal eyes and a shiver ran up her spine. There was still more to him than she would ever know, but she was positive she would spend a lifetime getting to know everything about him.

"How high can you go?"

The peak dropped back and gave everyone a chance to breathe. "I love you so much," Nathan had to shout for Melody to be able to hear him above the roar of the band. She smiled, kissed him, and suddenly they were in another song.

It sounded familiar as J.B. resumed the role of lead singer. It was "No Sugar Tonight/New Mother Nature," made popular by The Guess Who in the seventies. There was a new twist to it here tonight. Even though neither of the last two songs had been written by Widespread Panic, there was a pervasive sense that the songs belonged together under the same roof.

There is this feeling that can only be described as Widespread Panic, an idea that everything has kind of gone wrong and we're all messed up because of it. So let's dance and embrace it and see where that takes us.

Everything the band was doing seemed to contain this dark understanding that the world is fucked up beyond belief. Eventually the oceans, the air, and the Earth itself will be clogged with the byproducts of the most wasteful and destructive way of life ever witnessed on this planet. Something has to change.

Even though the songs are filled with anger and a little hate there's no animosity among the people in the crowd. It's like they're all on the same team against the rest of the crazy world.

Then there was a space. The band finally took a break between songs and Melody and Nathan looked into each other's now dilated pupils. The mushrooms were kicking in. Melody rubbed her stomach as she swayed back and forth in the empty space. She was about to travel out of her body and she could feel it coming.

There were no worries about the marijuana crop, no indecision about herself, and no questioning where she was supposed to be. The anxiousness she usually felt with mushrooms just wasn't there. Or maybe it was there, but she was embracing it. She was supposed to be here and now, dancing alongside the greatest love of her life, and questioning everything. During "Greta," Jojo asked the question, "How's it gonna be?" and Melody was beginning to think she might be forming an answer.

Mother nature was in a fighting mood, and Melody didn't feel like being a happy flower child anymore. Neither did Nathan. He'd seen too much darkness to have that outlook anymore. They were coming to the same conclusions at the same time and the glances they exchanged were like telepathic agreements between their subconscious.

One thing Melody knew for sure, and she thought about it as she danced, all this was going to come to an end sometime. One way or another, the landlord was going to call, and the Earth was going to be rid of the destructive machine of civilization. The music told her so. For now, she could dance.

The sonic assault grinded on, dirty and honest. Melody forgot about everyone around her and threw her fists in the air. She felt like she was trying to knock down the walls that separated her from becoming who she needed to be. She was dancing for her life.

Alongside her, Nathan was doing the same. Phish had never touched either of them so directly, brutally, and without restraint. A strange dissonance developed in the music and it was something that scared and excited them at the same time. They were only just coming to the end of the fourth song of the night, and already they felt as if a locomotive were chasing them down.

Melody tried to look around at the crowd, but the strong mushrooms were taking over and all she could see were fractals reverberating from the music.

Fungus is different from every other organism on this planet. It's not quite a plant and not quite an animal. There is even some speculation amongst people who think about such things that the introduction of hallucinogenic mushrooms into the diet of upright monkeys instigated the ability to think and reason.

Melody's mind was certainly turning a million miles a minute while her body followed suit. And yet, there were absolutely no thoughts in her head either. Everything she was thinking seemed to be more of a feeling than a thought. She slipped in and out of time, feeling like she was in a dozen different places and a dozen different times all happening congruent to one another. The only constant was Nathan dancing at her side.

Whenever they touched, electricity raced through them. It wasn't merely sexual energy. It bound them together in something transcendental. New life was forming between them.

They had known each other before, in another life or something. They would be joined together for the rest of their lives, she was certain. It was here, in this time out of time and this place out of place, that they both experienced it fully. A few songs slipped by, the words and the music penetrating and consuming them.

The band didn't let up: "Thought Sausage," "Impossible," "Radio Child." It was an onslaught and Melody felt her legs were in danger of giving out. Sweat was pouring off her body as she struggled to keep up with the energy bouncing around the room. Could the band really keep up this level of excitement all night long?

Thankfully they took a set break after "Radio Child."

"I need to go pee," Melody smiled at Nathan, finally feeling the physical needs of her body once again.

They staggered happily into the lobby and went in search of the bathrooms. Melody had to go it alone into the ladies room, dancing a different kind of dance while she waited in line. The men's room wasn't nearly as backed up and Nathan beat her back into the lobby.

While he was waiting for her to appear from the exit of the women's restroom, an extremely attractive young blonde girl, obviously rolling on ecstasy approached him. She reached up and ran her hands through his hair. "Oh my God, you're so cute," she cooed at him. "I love your hair."

He pulled away from her and instinctively said, "Why don't you just leave me alone?" He couldn't imagine another woman's touch beside Melody.

The girl was taken aback. It was obvious she wasn't used to this kind of rejection. She stumbled away, back to her friends.

Nathan was curious about the power he felt inside of himself because of this encounter. As she walked away, he laughed at not having flirted back with this extremely attractive woman. But he was in love, deeply and truly, and even the most stunning woman in the world couldn't compare to the feelings he felt for Melody.

"I saw that."

Natron turned to see Jessica smiling at him.

"Saw what?" he smiled back,

"I saw you dis that gorgeous little girl."

"Yeah, well. She's not Melody. I love Melody."

"Aw," Jessica melted. "You're so cute."

"Thanks," he smiled back.

Melody found them standing in the hallway and crumpled into Jessica's hug.

"This is great," Melody said. "I love this band. I love you. I love Kale. I really love Nathan." Then she paused, laughed, and continued. "I'm pretty messed up. These mushrooms are strong and this music is so good."

Jessica led them back to the spot on School's side where she and Kale had been dancing the whole first set. Melody dug out a crumpled joint from her sweaty breasts and the four friends laughed together and sparked it up while they waited for the second set.

"I wanted to go to the show," Lucy was pouting to Phillip as they lounged in the mansion on Capitol Drive.

"It's just fucking Widespread Panic."

"Yeah, but you made me miss the biggest Phish show ever and their farewell tour for your stupid weed."

"My stupid weed pays the bills around here. You need to check yourself Lucy."

"No, you need to check yourself Phillip. When is it going to be enough? How much money do we need before we can have fun again?"

"Fuck you, Lucy. If you don't like it, you can leave."

"Maybe I will."

"No you won't," Phillip was really getting angry now. "You won't because you love the money and the lifestyle just as much as me. Maybe even more."

"You really think that?" Tears instantly formed in her eyes. "You're so wrong, Phillip. I never loved the life, I loved you! Don't you get it? I can't stand it anymore. String Cheese is playing for New Years up in Portland and I'm going, with or without you."

"String Cheese," Phillip laughed. "They're worse than White-bred Picnic. You go. Put on some fairy wings, glitter yourself up, and don't forget your hula-hoop."

"Sometimes, you're such an ass."

She slammed the door behind her, leaving Phillip alone with his precious weed crop. She was crying as she drove towards the Hult Center. If she wasn't going to get to go to the show, at least she was going to find an after party.

The second set started sweetly. Melody leaned back into Nathan as J.B. crooned "Nobody's Loss." There wasn't much time left to take things slow, and Nathan held her close. This was his lady love, and it was the only thing he was interested in anymore. Phillip could keep his weed business and his fucking money, but Nathan and Melody needed to get to somewhere nobody could find them.

Melody couldn't decide if the place she was in was make believe or reality. While a storm was raging between Phillip and Lucy, Melody and Nathan had turned their eyes into a new sunrise. They could both feel this energy flowing through the music, the crowd, the universe, and into them together. Holding hands, Nathan couldn't tell where he began and Melody ended.

Jessica nudged Kale and pointed to the two of them. "See that?" she asked.

"See what?" Kale said.

"They're so in love. Remember when we used to be like that?"

"What are you talking about? We're still like that."

"Yeah," Jessica nodded apprehensively. They had been like that, but years together on the road had worn them down. They were frayed around the edges and Jess didn't know how much more she could take. Kale kept promising they would come up, and they just kept struggling.

"They say it takes hardship to let you know the joy."

Jess and Kale had certainly known hardship. It had become a way of life. The food vending scene was always hard work for minimal pay. Whenever she talked to him about settling down, getting off tour, maybe having some kids, Kale dismissed the idea. Maybe later. She loved him and could wait. She held his hand as the band went through "Pleas," one of her favorite songs. She was determined not to let things get too sad. Kale knew this was her song and he held her close.

The music was flowing, and Natron was soaking it up. He'd never heard any of these songs before, but it was as if he knew every word and it was directly applicable to him and his life. He felt as if the band were playing directly to him. He looked at Jessica and Kale holding each other and nudged Melody.

"Check out Jess and Kale."

Melody did and saw what looked like a dream.

"Maybe we could be like them one day," Nathan suggested. "They're so in love."

Melody nodded, pretty much unable to speak through the mushrooms.

The band carried on, painting a musical landscape of acceptance and gratitude simply for being alive and getting to experience the full range of emotions we're all blessed with.

A few more songs wound through this maze of emotions. Then the band delved into a cover of War's classic hit, "Lowrider." Everyone was dancing. The crowd moved, swaying together more like a field of grass than individual people.

It was a religious experience. Melody felt like she was in church. If she believed in any gods, then there was at least one in the room with them right now.

She tried to look to the faces dancing along next to her and wondered how many of them felt the same presence. The jam carried on, lifted up, turned around, and then slowly slipped away. There was space in the music for the first time during the evening. The keyboard player and the two guitarists slipped offstage, one at a time. Each fading out in their own way.

Then it was just the drums.

All music is born from the drum. Long before civilization, long before agriculture, and probably even before fire was utilized, some distant primate ancestor beat on a log to a certain rhythm and was able to convey something no words could express.

Dance began around the same time. The crowd clapped along with the beat. With language came song, and the voices of humans filled the world with joy and wonder. With the advent of civilization came the enslaving of humanity. Still, there were songs in our hearts and they reminded us of a time when we were free. Like the tiger pacing his cage in the zoo, music is a scent of freedom born of instinct and the wilderness.

As civilization overran the Americas, it carried with it a slave caste seen as little more than human machinery. They were shipped over from Africa, stripped from the music of their tribes and the song that was their way of life. Still, they continued to sing. In the fields their tribal rhythms evolved.

As their religion altered to accommodate the wills of their masters, so to did their song. In the slave houses and cotton fields of this new world carved from the death of indigenous tribes and species, a new kind of music was born that would be the basis for blues, jazz, and eventually all the various forms of rock and roll.

At the heart of all of it was the drum. As simple and complex as the heart that beats within all living things.

Melody wasn't exactly dancing, but she was on her feet, with eyes closed, melting into Nathan and swaying to the rhythm. She was thinking these long lines, inspired by all she saw and felt.

What Melody didn't know, and what most slave owners didn't know, is that the spirituals the slaves sang in the fields often contained hidden meanings. Sure, they sang about Christ and heaven and it pleased the master, but in some cases these songs were codes. Christ was code for a conductor on the underground railroad, and he would lead them to heaven, or Canada.

So there might be a spiritual in the field one day when all the slaves sang, "Tonight we meet Jesus by the old oak tree where we'll be forgiven and welcomed into Heaven." The next day, all the human machinery would be gone.

The band came back onstage and the rock and roll continued. Melody was aware that the music she was dancing to was born from the voices of slaves. However, she didn't know that if she listened closely enough she might be able to find her way out.

Nathan could taste the freedom he'd once known so well and knew where to find it. He and Melody would pack that Chevy van and go back on tour. This time, it wasn't going to be Phish tour, it was going to be Panic tour.

34

"I swear, this is my favorite lot. I'm so glad they decided to play two nights this year," Natron said.

The southern sun was shining bright as Natron and Melody were setting up their kitchen. It was a hot afternoon in April of 2002 at Walnut Creek Amphitheater outside of Raleigh, North Carolina.

It had taken some time to figure out the whole kitchen thing. The learning curve is unforgiving when working with food out of coolers from the back of a van in a fold-out kitchen. One mistake and that 5 lb. bag of shredded cheese from Sam's Club would turn into a mushy orange glob in the melted cooler.

Miscalculating a show or your ability to vend it could result in piles of wasted and rotting food, or completely missing out on what could have been a blue moon bonanza.

Nathan and Melody had witnessed lots of kids try their hands at concert vending. Generally, it ended badly. Amongst scattered shreds of cheese and ripped tortillas in the dirt, there would be some blanket kid curled up in a ball. Empty beer cans littered the area; and the stove, even though it was set on a table, couldn't be cooked on even if someone had offered to buy whatever culinary concoction this broke and desperate traveler thought he could provide.

In the morning, the coolers would be left behind, the cheese, salsa, and tortillas given away to whoever would take them or left to rot, and the kid would be walking the parking lot with a pocketful of overpriced ecstasy or xanex trying to make an easier dollar.

There were many times when Natron almost went back to slinging ecstasy or whatever, but this was about freedom not money. There was never any real risk to their freedom vending food. No matter what, they weren't going to prison for quesadillas. The worst they could expect might be a night in jail or a ticket for vending without a license.

At Walnut Creek, they had no worry about any of

this. The concert promoters here seemed to understand that these vendors couldn't touch the money to be made inside the venue.

The only people with anything to worry about were the T-shirt guys using Panic's name, image, or likeness. The copyright guys frown on this. So much so that Panic had hired a real asshole, going by the name of "Gentleman Dave," to police the lot.

Melody and Nathan witnessed more than one poor T-shirt vendor get shook down and have his merchandise confiscated. Natron was pissed off when he saw this.

"Where are they when some idiot starts blowing a tank?"

They had discovered over their time as food vendors that nitrous was the bane of their existence. Whenever a nitrous tank was being blown off, hardly anyone was interested in buying food. People who might buy food instead of nitrous just wanted off the lot. Then, at the end of the night, completely broke and starving the used up nitrous junkie would be begging for free food. When this happened Nathan and Melody understood why Jessica and Kale were known as the "No Deals Café."

Speaking of Jessica and Kale, they were set up right next to Melody and Nathan. Often they purposefully placed their kitchens next to each other. With the prevalence of cell phones these days it wasn't too hard to co-ordinate. They worked together, picking up forgotten items from Sam's Club for each other, saving spots, and splitting hotel rooms.

The lot was also teeming with other vendors Nathan and Melody had come to recognize from seeing them across the country at dozens of different shows. Some of them, like Russo and Paul, they knew from Phish tour. Others only went to Panic shows. Each of them led a story as unique as Melody and Nathan's.

"Have you heard the rumors?" Kale was saying to Nathan.

"What rumors?"

They hadn't seen each other since the New Year's Eve shows in Atlanta. This was the start of Spring Tour and it was like a reunion amongst a large family.

"I heard Mikey was sick," Kale said, shaking his head.

"What do you mean sick?" Melody asked.

"They say he's got cancer," Jessica said with a tinge of sadness in her voice.

"Seriously?" Nathan said. "I don't know. There's always so many rumors flying around. For a while I heard they were gonna kick Todd out of the band, but that was bullshit."

"Yeah, but I got this from a pretty reliable source," Kale offered.

"No shit. Man, I can't even think about that right now. I've got all this steak to prep for later."

Nathan and Melody were beneath their EZ-Up tent with twenty pounds of top sirloin he was carving into fajita strips. Melody was slicing peppers and onions and the lot was still pretty empty. It was four in the afternoon and the show didn't
start until eight o'clock.

The day wore on and the prep got finished as the lot started to fill up. When all the meat was stripped up and marinating in tequila, lime juice, and cilantro, Melody, Jessica, Natron, and Kale all sat down to smoke a bowl together before they started serving the growing crowd.

"Man, it's crazy how big things have gotten on this tour since Phish quit," Kale was saying.

"No doubt. There's lost Phish kids at every show trying to sell molly and pills and nitrous," Nathan agreed.

"It's a wonder Phillip hasn't shown up here," Melody said.

Jessica laughed, "Have you guys heard from him lately?"

"Not since we left Eugene," Nathan said. "I

imagine he's still sitting in that mansion growing weed."

"What about Lucy?" Jessica asked Melody.

"I heard she was on String Cheese tour for awhile, but I have no idea how to get a hold of her."

Kale chimed in with one of his favorite jokes, "Hey, do you know what one Panic kid said to the other Panic kid on the way out of the String Cheese show?"

Everyone quietly waited for the punch line, and Kale delivered it with gusto. "Worst Phish show ever!"

This got everyone laughing. They sat in silent reverie for a minute, wondering where their friends were until the first customer approached.

"Hey man, you cooking fajitas?" a friendly southerner in a ball-cap asked.

"Tag, you're it." Kale said.

"Yeah, I'll get 'em started," Nathan said.

He fired up a burner under one of the griddles on the three camp stoves set on the folding camp table.

"Hey, didn't I see you guys at Red Rocks over the summer?" The random southerner asked in a heavy accent.

"Oh shit, man. We were there. What a clusterfuck that place has turned into. I almost got arrested just for selling fajitas."

"No shit? Why?"

"Vending without a license. They used to be pretty cool back in the day, but something changed."

"I heard that they changed management or something. Either Jefferson County used to own it and sold it to the City of Denver or the other way around. I can't remember. But yeah, this year there wasn't even really a Shakedown."

"Yup."

The griddle was hot. Nathan spread some oil, dropped some peppers and onions and then added the meat. The marinade steamed into the air and the lot was filled with a very pleasing smell. Nathan fired another burner to heat the tortilla. When it was done he wrapped some meat, peppers, and onions in with some cheese and salsa in a tortilla and rolled the whole thing into a foil wrapper.

"Five bucks," Nathan said as he handed the fajita over.

"Thanks, man," the guy said as he handed over a twenty. "Got any water?"

"Yeah, there's a whole cooler full by your feet. Open it up a grab a bottle."

"I'll take two."

"A buck each."

Nathan fished out a ten and handed it over then started to fumble for some ones.

"Keep the rest, man."

"Thanks."

The lot started filling up and Nathan was selling more fajitas. Kale fired up his kitchen. During the day business was steady but not outrageous. Nathan and Kale manned their individual kitchens while Jessica and Melody went for a walk.

They strolled the parking lot, eyeing T-shirts they might want to buy later, laughing with old friends they hadn't seen since last tour, and generally just glad to be back on lot.

"I'm so glad we got on Panic tour," Melody was telling Jessica.

"How long has it been now?" Jessica asked.

"Well, we set up our first kitchen in Atlanta for New Years into 2001. Then we hit nearly every show in 2001."

"That's right. Gosh, so it's been over a year now."

"Yup. Over a year and the only home we've known has been our van and the parking lot. It's crazy, but I love it."

"Me, too. But I'm starting to get tired. I don't know. Sometimes I just wish Kale would ask me to marry him and we could settle down and have some kids."

"Seriously?"

"I don't know. I've been on tour now, between Panic and Phish, for almost ten years. I guess I need to grow up some time."

"Look at Paul. He's still on tour. I mean, remember how much fun we had in Larkspur at the Field of Dreams."

"Yeah, but I also remember the dust there, too. It just seems to be getting harder every year. There's more vendors now. We don't make as much money. Sometimes it's like there's nothing new happening."

"Aww, Jess. Don't get down on me now. It's the first show of spring tour. We've got all of summer ahead of us. It's gonna be a great year. I heard Phish might even come back soon."

"Yeah, everyone hears that. I'm sorry. I don't mean to be down. Forget it. Let's find tickets and get back to the guys."

Tickets weren't hard to come by for the two pretty girls. They sold some food until about 7:30, then they shut down their kitchens, turned away whatever straggling customers came up and went into the show. It was like it always was. The music transported them. It was the same, but different for each individual willing to have the intention to be moved. After "Climb to Safety" at the end of the second set they hightailed it out of there and ran to rebuild their kitchens as quickly as they could.

The downside of vending food was that they never got to see the encore. The upside was that they got to see nearly every show.

The blowout was amazing. When the band left the stage hungry and thirsty people poured out of the venue and flooded Shakedown. Nathan and Melody moved as fast as they could to swing as much food as they could before the cops came to run them off the lot an hour after the show was over.

They nearly sold out, then crawled into their van and drove to a nearby hotel parking lot where they fell asleep. In the morning they made a quick trip to Sam's Club to re-up and were set up and ready when the crowds returned the next day.

By now, there was talk all over the lot about Mikey

being sick. Michael Houser was the lead guitarist for Widespread Panic and the band's namesake. He had severe panic attacks when he was younger that earned him the nickname, "Panic." As the story goes, one day he was heard to say, "I don't wanna be just Panic. One day I wanna be Widespread Panic."

He got his wish and helped to create music, and a lifestyle, that would live on long after he was gone.

John Keane, the band's producer and longtime friend sat in with them on guitar and pedal steel for every show of that spring tour. After the very successful two night run at Walnut Creek, the band, along with their traveling city, made their way into downtown Asheville, NC.

After that everyone found themselves on the Georgia coast for an amazing show in Savannah. By then, the rumor that Mikey was sick wasn't a rumor anymore. Although there had been no official release, everyone on tour somehow knew the details. He had pancreatic cancer, one of the worst cancers a person can get. It kills very quickly

Mikey was visibly ill on stage. He was skinnier than he'd ever been, and although his playing had the same energy it always had, there was almost a sense of desperation that drove it to a higher level. Mikey was on stage for all of every show, but John Keane was there to pick up the slack when he got tired.

Melody and Nathan were as in love as they had ever been, but Kale and Jessica were faltering under the long, hard years of tour. The work, the miles, the constant partying, and the sadness prevalent on that spring tour were really wearing on Jessica, especially.

"This might be my last tour," Jessica said to Melody in confidence when they finally got down to Oak Mountain Amphitheater in Pelham, Alabama.

Oak Mountain had been a staple for Widespread Panic, having played there at least once a year since 1990. It began like any other lot, with sunshine, friendly banter, and the setting up of kitchens.

There's always a moment of apprehension when

setting up on a new lot. The vendors never know what to expect from the locals. Most times they were greeted with incomprehension at what they were doing. Police would laugh at them, or sometimes buy food off of them. Every now and then they'd be shut down, but usually without any animosity: "I'm sorry, but you can't do this here."

In Oak Mountain, the police had something up their sleeves.

On Friday, as Melody and Nathan were setting up their kitchen a collection of swaggering southern cops walked up to the table.

"What're you doin', son?" the cop asked Nathan in a tone dripping with contempt.

"Just setting up my kitchen, sir. We like to feed people here, you know? Keep everyone healthy." Nathan smiled at the cop, trying to build some kind of connection, "Can't have all these people drinking on an empty stomach."

"You got a vending license?"

No sir. We don't actually sell anything. We give it away and accept donations."

At this the cop slammed his fist on the table, "I don't care what you call it. If I see any money exchange hands over this table, I'm not going to arrest you. I'm going to arrest your girlfriend." He pointed directly at Melody who felt her knees quake beneath her.

The cop laughed, "Have a good night." He walked off with his other cop friends. Everyone on Shakedown was accosted in a similar way. There was a scramble. It was the last three shows of tour. Money had to be made here to last until summer tour started.

"I've got a plan," Natron said.

They packed up the kitchen and moved. They found a spot hidden off to the side of the lot. Nathan set up his stoves inside the van.

"We're gonna do this like nitrous dealers," Nathan smiled at her.

They paid one of their tour friends in steak fajitas

163

and beer to stand on top of the van. He danced up there and held his finger in the air, under the pretense of trying to find a miracle. Jared already had a ticket. He was just being the lookout.

Melody stood outside of the van, whispering her wares as if she were selling drugs. "Pssst...hey. Hey? Wanna buy a fajita."

It was weird, but word spread and people began flocking to the van, one of the only places on lot to get food. Nathan was shut up in the van, sweltering near 150 degrees inside the metal oven with Coleman stoves burning away.

He rolled fajitas and passed them out the door furtively to Melody a dozen at a time. Whenever one of the many gangs of police would wander by, Jared would stomp on the roof.

Nathan would slam the doors closed and be trapped in the heat with his kitchen until the coast was clear again.

In this manner they managed to turn three days of vending hell into a decent, but sweaty paycheck. Jessica and Kale didn't have such luck. They both got tickets for illegal vending.

"I sold a pair of shorts to an undercover," Jessica would later say, shaking her head. "Seriously. There was an undercover trying to buy patchwork shorts from me and then three cops came out, searched me, and when they didn't find any drugs, they wrote me a ticket. I can't sell any of my clothes, I don't know what I'm going to do."

It wasn't Jessica's first time to get harassed by the police, and she doubted it would be her last if she kept this up. Jessica was seriously planning on doing something else with her life after these shows. She wasn't a kid anymore. Melody was 21, Jessica was 29.

Almost thirty years old. Maybe it was time.

The last night at Oak Mountain, the tour family passed out candles everyone would light at the same time after drums. It was a simple gesture of love for the guitar player who had filled so many nights with joy. However, the wind was blowing pretty hard that night, and the desired effect of thousands of candles lit at once was blown out.

Spring tour ended and Melody and Nathan spent the next month a half camping all along the gulf coast. They especially fell in love with a place called Dauphin Island, and stayed there for two weeks.

It was on that beach that Melody finally decided to let her hair lock up. For a long time it had been getting close and she would painfully brush the tangles out every few days. That night she told Nathan and they made love together in the van listening to a solo acoustic performance of Jerry Garcia at the Oregon State Penitentiary.

"I love you Melody," Nathan said. "I love you more than I ever thought I could love another person. It scares me. I want to let my hair lock up, too. I want people to know we're different just by looking at us."

Melody looked into his eyes and saw an honest devotion she had never seen from anyone before. It scared her, but it also felt perfectly right.

Everyone wondered during the break whether or not Mickey would be there when tour started and what would happen if he wasn't. Nathan was pretty sure the spring tour had included John Keane because he was the obvious choice to fill Mickey's place. He had been with the band since he produced their first album in 1986.

Widespread Panic has never been a band to do much speaking for themselves beyond their music. None of the members speak more than a few words at a time when on stage. There are no speeches. Occasionally JB grumbles something into the mic, or Schools makes a joke. Mostly, the music speaks for itself.

Before summer tour, Mikey released a statement on the internet confirming his illness. He thanked everyone for such a wonderful life and their continued support. He made it clear that Panic should continue regardless of his being a part of it, but that he would play as long as he could. It was what he most wanted to be doing and he felt lucky to have been given a life that allowed him to live his dream; even if it had to be a truncated life.

The music was more important than the individuals involved in creating it and Mikey understood this.

To everyone's surprise, even though he was visibly stricken, he kicked off summer tour with Panic and played the initial Bonnaroo festival in Tennessee the summer of 2002.

35

It was always meant to be. Like Isaac Newton deciphering the laws of gravity and discovering something that had always been there. Superfly Productions didn't create Bonarroo, they deciphered something that had always existed in the dreams of everyone on tour and made it a reality.

They picked 700 acres in Tennessee and brought in an impressive lineup of bands to include Widespread Panic, The String Cheese Incident, Les Claypool, Ben Harper, Blackalicious, Jurassic 5, The Disco Biscuits, Umphrey's McGee, Ween, Trey Anastasio (from Phish), Bela Fleck, and a whole slew of other acts.

Nathan and Melody would only get to see Widespread Panic perform. As they pulled into the festival grounds, Melody wasn't feeling very well. It had been a long, hot drive from Alabama, and Tennessee wasn't any cooler on the summer solstice of 2002.

They parked the van, while Nathan tried to cheer Melody up. "Come on. Let's go for a walk and see what's happening. Here, drink some water."

They were headed into the festival and Melody felt weak. The sun and the heat were really getting to her and she started feeling lightheaded. She almost fell over and Nathan caught her.

"Are you alright?" He asked.

She shook her head, "No."

Nathan stopped a passing parking attendant, "Hey man, where's the medical tent? She's not feeling very well."

The parking attendant eyed Nathan first and then Melody. She chose that instant to throw up her lunch from earlier.

"Woah, shit." The guy said. He stepped away from the two of them and called someone on his radio.

Nathan was brushing her young locks out of her

face and holding her up. She let her weight go and leaned on his shoulder. She felt like shit.

A golf cart arrived and Melody sat in the passenger seat. Nathan climbed on the back and held on. He was worried and felt powerless. In all his years on the road, he had never had more than a runny nose. Sickness was something he didn't handle very well.

They got to the medical tent, which was air-conditioned, and Melody felt a little better. However, she continued to throw up. No matter how much water she drank, it came back up as a clear and viscous liquid.

"I'm concerned she can't keep any water down. I don't want her to get dehydrated." the doctor said to Nathan. "I'm going to put her on an IV drip."

They sat in the medical tent for two hours while the first day of the inaugural Bonnaroo festival was going on outside. Melody drifted into a light sleep while Nathan sat on a stool watching her.

Was this really what he wanted? She didn't look so beautiful pale, passed out, and with an IV stuck into her arm. Nathan felt something slipping away.

Melody eventually awoke from her nap and the doctor inspected her again.

"I'm not sure what's wrong," he confided in Nathan. "She may have some sort of stomach bug. I can't tell. She has a coughing fit every time she throws up, so I'm going to write you a prescription for some Codeine cough syrup. You can get it filled at Wal-Mart. Also, here's a note so you can go in and out
the back entrance."

"Thanks doc," Nathan said.

"I hope she gets to feeling better."

"Yeah, me too."

They left the medical tent and went back to the van. Melody laid down in the shade of their EZ-Up. "I don't think I'm gonna be able to cook or anything," she said.

"I know," Nathan replied. "Are you gonna go see Panic?"

"I don't know. Not if I feel like this. You can go, though."

"Don't worry about it. We'll figure something out. I just hope you get to feeling better."

"You don't have to stay here with me. Really, I do feel a little better after the IV. Why don't you go for a walk? I know you want to. Then we'll go get my medicine."

They had been at the Bonnaroo festival for a total of 4 hours so far and she was right. All Nathan really wanted to do was take a look around.

"You sure you're gonna be alright?" He asked again.

"I'll be fine. I'm gonna take a nap, just don't be gone too long. I love you."

"Thanks, I love you, too. I'll be back and we'll go get your prescription filled."

He gave her a gentle kiss on the forehead and went walking down the aisle. It was the first year of Bonnaroo and as soon as Nathan walked away from Melody he felt an amazing tingle in the air. In some ways the promoters weren't ready for what was happening. It was said there were 70,000 tickets sold to Bonnaroo in 2002, but it felt twice that size. Nathan was pretty sure there were more than a few thousand people who had managed to get in without a ticket.

Nathan was walking, trying to really get into what was happening around him, but he couldn't get Melody out of his mind. He better get back to her. On the way back he passed the water tank where people were supposed to be filling up drinking water.

There was a problem. The water wasn't drinkable.

"Look at this shit," Nathan heard a passerby say to his friend.

"I know. The water is green. I'm not drinking it."

"What are we gonna do? I don't think I brought enough water and it's four bucks for a little bottle in there."

A light bulb went off in Nathan's head.

He went back to the van and found Melody still awake and groaning.

"I feel like shit again," she said. "And I threw up again."

"Come on, let's go get your medicine."

Nathan folded up the EZ-Up while Melody lay down in the van. They headed for the back entrance, showed their doctor's note to the security guard and came out right by Wal-Mart in five minutes. The line of cars coming into the front door of Bonnaroo stretched for hours.

At Wal-Mart, Nathan took Melody to the prescription desk and sat her down with the pharmacist. They looked over her prescription and began to fill it.

"I'll be right back," Nathan said. "There's something I want to get."

"Okay," Melody said and slumped back down in the chair.

Nathan headed over to the bottled water aisle. "Excuse me," he tapped a Wal-Mart worker on the shoulder. The guy turned around and eyed Nathan. What did this dirty hippie want?

"I'd like to buy a bunch of water."

"What do you mean?"

"Well, there's not enough drinking water at the festival so we were gonna bring some in."

"How much do you need?"

"How much you got?"

In about an hour they walked out of Wal-Mart. Melody was clinging to her bottle of Codeine cough syrup while behind them came a forklift and a full pallet of bottled water in cases of individual bottles and gallon jugs. They loaded the van until the leaf springs sagged under the weight. They spent $500 on $4 cases of water, 30 cent gallon jugs, and bags of ice.

Inside the festival Melody drank cough syrup and dozed in a camp chair beneath the EZ-Up. They used their doctor's note to get to the very front row of camping. Nathan set up a sign that read, "Water. $1 a bottle or $2 ice cold. Gallons $3 or $5 ice cold."

People were flocking to their setup, happy to pay $3 for a gallon when inside the little bottles were $4.

"Thank you, thank you," they said to Natron who was making 1000% profit.

"No, thank you," Natron said.

That night they went in for Panic. Melody, sick and now high on Codeine spent the evening sitting or lying in the grass. Nathan danced next to her.

The next day they had to go back to Wal-Mart and buy more water. Melody was still miserable. They used the doctor's note again to get in and out the back door. It worked like a charm. Melody was just along for the ride, miserable to the core.

What was wrong? She drank more cough syrup, hoping to feel better. At least she was keeping her water down now. That night, it seemed as if Panic opened the show just for Melody and Nathan with an amazing musical sandwich of Chilly Water>Makes Sense to Me>Chilly Water. The next day, after another run to Wal-Mart, Nathan changed the sign to read, "Chilly Water Makes Sense to Me," and then listed the pricing.

Melody never felt any better throughout the whole festival. In retrospect, everything became a blur to her. The last night, they didn't go in for Trey's solo set, but Melody heard him playing "Wilson" and a few other Phish songs over the fence and it made her think of that long ago summer when she first left with Lucy and met Nathan, Phillip, Jessica and Kale. Of all of them, only they were here. Jessica and Kale were visibly absent and neither of them knew where Lucy or Phillip were.

Her health deteriorated and Nathan continued to take her in and out to re-up on water. He never broke out the camp stoves to sell any food, but stuck with the water all weekend. He was torn between the easy money he could be making if he really hustled and needing to be available to see if he could help his woman feel any better.

Finally, the festival was over and they got a hotel room with blessed air conditioning. Melody was worse than she had been. She started to throw up again while Nathan counted money. They made $7,500 on water sales, their most lucrative show to date. Natron couldn't help thinking of all the money they'd missed because of Melody being sick.

Finally, Melody begged Nathan to take her to the hospital. He did and they immediately put her on another IV drip while they ran tests.

In about an hour the doctor came back in. "Well, I got good news. There's nothing seriously wrong with you Melody, but you should probably be getting more rest now that you're pregnant."

36

For a few more months their life would remain pretty much the same, except Melody instantly quit drinking, taking any drugs, or smoking anything other than the occasional bowl. After Bonnaroo they went to Red Rocks and somehow Mikey made it, too. He was skeletal on his side of the stage, knocking on death's door but still playing his guitar. His very last show with Widespread Panic was on July, 2, 2002 in Iowa just after Red Rocks, and then, without fanfare or announcement, he was gone. Panic staggered on in his absence, finishing the tour with George McConnell on guitar and Randell Bramblett on saxophone. The shows were not great.

Nathan and Melody stuck with the band. It was a hard tour. This awful sadness permeated the scene and everyone kept hoping Mikey would make it to one more show. It never happened.

Michael "Panic" Houser died of pancreatic cancer on August 10, 2002; just over a month after his last show. A week later Widespread Panic played two scheduled nights at Fiddler's Green Amphitheater in Denver. Fiddler's Green is on the south side of Denver, out in the suburbs. Everything is new and clean down there and the manicured nature of the setting made Melody and Nathan both feel a little weird.

They successfully set up their kitchen and sold some food next to Kale who had some disturbing news for them.

"Jessica left me. She cut off her dreadlocks and moved to Chicago. She said she was going to pursue a career in the fashion business and that she was done with tour. She said she's never going to work lot again."

At this news Melody instantly tried to call her friend, but the cell number she called was disconnected. Kale shook his head and turned down his eyes. No one had ever seen him so devastated. It was like he was just going through the motions.

Everything felt wrong. Whenever Melody looked over to the "No Deals Café," she felt like crying. She'd gotten over the sickness of being pregnant, but the emotional roller coaster wouldn't let up. She bounced between feeling ecstatic to be starting a family with Nathan, to being sad because she felt her youth was over. Something was growing inside of her. She wasn't really showing that she was pregnant yet, and they decided to keep it a secret between themselves.

They were both scared about what this meant for their life. Were they too young? Should they have an abortion? What if Melody miscarried? Nathan did his best to give her the notion that everything would be just fine, but deep inside he was a nervous wreck. The baby would come next spring, right before tour usually started. Would they have to stop touring? What would he do for work? He'd never had a normal job. He chewed his nails and lost sleep.

The show at Fiddler's Green had a festival atmosphere, with numerous other bands appearing, including Karl Denson's Tiny Universe, DJ Logic, Particle, Keller Williams, and Steel Pulse. The second night had Michael Franti, Ben Harper, and Angelique Kidjo, Since there was so much music during the day, the lot scene was very muted. Nathan was scraping by to make a dollar while Melody relaxed in the shade.

The first night the band was on for really the first time since Mikey left. Melody closed her eyes and felt that once familiar connection that reminded her the world is a safe and beautiful place and that she absolutely belongs here. When the music was right it seemed there could be nothing wrong.

The first set, the band said nothing about Mikey being gone, though everyone could feel his physical absence and spiritual presence. The setlist reflected this feeling. From the "Imitation Leather Shoes" opener ("I don't wanna fake it anymore), through trying to shake of the "Weight of the World," "Walk

On," and "Stop-Go" (we used to ride the highway, we used to know where we were going). Melody could feel a transition happening in herself. It felt like the end of an era. Nothing would ever be as simple as it had been before.

George McConnell, Mikey's replacement, was finally starting to get the feel of the band. The songs were flowing back into each other again. To help fill the empty space Panic also recruited Randell Bramblett on the saxophone. Somewhere between George's guitar and the mournful wail of the saxophone Melody could almost hear Mikey's guitar.

During "Stop-Go," J.B. started singing Bob Marley's classic, "Three Little Birds." When he said, "Don't worry about a thing. Everything is gonna be alright," the crowd exploded. Somehow, in spite of all the trials behind and yet to come the music would continue to play.

Melody closed her eyes and swayed with a feeling of joy and acceptance to whatever life would give her. She touched her belly and could already feel the small life growing in there. It was part of the cycle. As one life ended, another was beginning.

She did her best to avoid the danger of too much thinking, feeling the love all around her instead. Nathan was in the same space. She looked over at him, her companion of so many adventures, and she was glad he would be there for this one as well.

She turned and saw Kale, dancing all alone, tears streaming down his face, and a wave of sadness engulfed her. Jessica should be here, too. Lucy should be here, and so should Phillip. Along the way, so many friends had disappeared. It's hard to maintain connections when you live a life on the road. Friends get on tour and fall off tour without a warning. One day, they just aren't there anymore and nobody knows where to find them.

Supposedly, they all had homes outside of the lot. Supposedly, this was just a vacation. For a select few, this wasn't the case. This was their life. This was the only place they really felt at home. The first set ended with "Space Wrangler," and Nathan curled into Melody, rubbing her belly, thinking of the little one growing inside of her. It was going to be hard, but they would manage. Love would be their unshakeable foundation.

During the set break Nathan and Melody talked about their unborn baby.

For some reason, they were certain they would have a girl. Mikey and Widespread Panic deserved to be honored in their child's name. They chose a line from Mikey's song, "This Part of Town."

"Where there is love, there is hope."

"Her middle name could be Hope," Nathan said.

"I like it," Melody grinned. "How about Maia for her first name?"

"Perfect," Nathan agreed. "Maia Hope."

They smiled with each other and relaxed into the grass, watching the sky change from blue, to a vibrant purple and orange glow with the setting of the sun.

When the band returned for the second set the candles from Oak Mountain were finally lit. There was no wind and the flicker of thousands of tiny lights touched everyone. A familiar spirit was gliding though the crowd and smiling down on them all. There was hardly a dry eye in the place as each individual reflected on the joy this one man had brought them all.

J.B. acknowledged the presence of his dear friend's spirit and the amazing care the audience exhibited towards all of them. "That's heavy," he said in response to the flickering candles. "Bless your hearts."

"Thank you very much Michael."

Instead of observing a moment of silence, which would have been incongruous with what Widespread Panic is all about, J.B. called for "a moment of a big ole joyous sound." As the band went into "Papa Legba," strangers turned to each other, shook hands, hugged, and shared their tears. It was something to witness, all these people from various walks of life embracing each other in the warmth of their glowing hearts.

After "Papa Legba," the band went into a song of Mikey's that suddenly carried new meaning. "It was six o'clock on Saturday, when Henry Parson's died." It had been around six o'clock on a Saturday when Mikey left this world for the next. Could he have known, or was this just one of those amazing synchronistic experiences a person can have when they're in tune with themselves and the spirit that moves in all things?

When the encore break came, Melody saw Kale dart out to set up his kitchen. Nathan made no move to leave. Melody looked at him quizzically. "I can't go," he said. "This means too much tonight."

The first song of the encore was "Old Joe." Nathan lost it. Tears streamed down his face and Melody wrapped him in her arms. She'd never seen him cry like this. No matter what, Nathan had always been a rock. He managed to force a smile through his tears and held her close. "I'm sorry," he stammered.

"Don't be. I understand." Tears were streaming from her as well. Their life was on its way to changing forever.

"Someday, somewhere, some things get hit by lightning," J.B. sang. "Some things just don't. Hope we live long and lucky," the crowd erupted again. Never had Melody or Nathan been to a show where the crowd and the band were on such a common wavelength. Always there was a sharing of experiences, but tonight it felt like they were all on the same side of the music, playing into the heavens.

Melody and Nathan swayed in each other's arms, drenched in tears. They weren't tears of joy or of sadness. They were simply tears of acceptance.

"No matter where we are, its this life that we're living."

This sparked something in Nathan. He thought of Kale, and how sad he was with Jessica gone. Nathan couldn't let that happen to him and Melody. He held her close and whispered to her through the tears, "I love you. I love you so much. I want to be with you for the rest of my life. I want to marry you. Will you be my wife?"

"Somehow, somewhere, some things get struck by
lightning."

Melody felt the electricity race through her. This was exactly what she wanted. "Yes, of course," she managed to say through the emotions.

When the band went into "Porch Song" they separated enough to dance and shake. It felt good. Tears were still streaming down Nathan's face, but they were certainly tears of joy this time. They were having a good time here today. The familiar guitar line carried them to a different level, and it was smiles all around. Time stood still and they danced together for what seemed like an eternity.

As always, the show had to end. "Thank you ladies and gentleman," J.B. said. "For everything. Good night."

They slowly filed into the parking lot with the rest of the crowd. It was a strange feeling, not rushing out to set up their kitchen. Kale was working his kitchen all alone, desperately trying to keep up with demand and failing. The line stretched forever. He didn't look up as Melody and Nathan got in their van and drove to a hotel. They would make love that night like they never had before. It was soft and sweet and involved their entire souls.

Neither of them could believe the intensity and the scope of the emotions they felt for each other.

37

So many things changed that year. After spending the interim in Asheville, North Carolina at an RV park in their van, not finding any jobs, and not knowing what else to do, Melody and Nathan went on Fall tour. There were highlights, to be sure. Nolaween, their regular three-night run in New Orleans for Halloween was epic as usual. Also, Widespread Panic was the first band to play a two night run at the Von Braun Center in Huntsville, Alabama since Elvis had been there.

The thought of being in Alabama again, after Oak Mountain, unnerved everyone on tour. However, it was exactly the opposite. There was a massive police presence, to be sure, but they weren't out to get everyone. They bought food from the vendors, put Panic stickers over their badges and walked around with smiles on their faces.

As always, Nathan offered the cops free food when they walked by. "Free food for police officers," he said to them.

"What'cha making?" One of them asked.

"Tequila, lime, and cilantro steak fajitas."

"Hey, that sounds good. How much?"

"For you, nothing."

"Awww, c'mon man. I'm getting regular pay, plus overtime, plus detail pay. I'm making like sixty dollars an hour to be here. I'll buy a fajita."

"Okay, five bucks."

"You guys want one?" the cop asked the rest of his crew. They all nodded. "We'll take six." He handed Nathan a fifty dollar bill and told him to keep the change. Once they all got their fajitas, Melody asked if they'd mind taking a picture. So Melody, Nathan, and a few tour kids lined up in front of their van and took a picture with all the cops. They walked away and left Natron shaking his head in disbelief.

After a few more shows they reached the end of tour in mid-November: a two night run in Memphis at the Mid-South Coliseum. Cops were out in force again, unfriendly, but focused on taking down kids with pockets full of drugs for sale. They heckled the kitchens, saying, "If they want to eat this crap, then let them." The lot raged for hours after each show and Melody and Nathan were able to completely empty their coolers. Then tour was over again.

They returned to Asheville and the R.V. Park, not sure of what to do. Melody was obviously pregnant. They got food stamps to help their money last and Nathan went looking for work. Asheville is kind of a hippie enclave in North Carolina. There's a joke circulating around there that Nathan heard far too often on his job hunting excursions: You know why there's so many hippies in Asheville? Cause there's no jobs.

Time slipped by. Phish was coming back for New Year's with shows scheduled in New York City at Madison Square Garden. Afterwards they were coming down to Virginia to play at Hampton Coliseum.

Melody and Nathan returned to Atlanta for Panic's New Years shows at the Phillips arena. By this time, Nathan had developed a severe distaste for Phish. His reasoning went like this: "With Panic, one of the founding members dies and they keep going, without missing a single show. Phish went on indefinite hiatus just because of some personal issues. They don't understand, like Panic does. This is more important than just them. Plus, those kids on Phish tour are just ghetto. There's all this heroin and shit on tour now."

Tickets were pretty easy on the 30th, but New Year's Eve were hard to come by in Atlanta that year. For a while Melody and Nathan were afraid they weren't going to make it in. Then a middle-aged guy in a ball-cap came up to them. "Have you found tickets, yet?" He asked, noticing their sign that said, "Got an extra?"

"Not yet. Got any extras?"

"Yeah, lemme talk to you a minute. My name's

Dick and I work for the band. I've seen you on tour for awhile. Thanks for supporting us through these tough times." He pulled a stack of tickets out of his pocket and handed Melody and Nathan two floor tickets, which scalpers were peddling for hundreds of dollars.

"Are you serious?" Melody asked. She was almost eight months pregnant now, feeling great, but having a hard time getting around. She'd always been a petite girl and couldn't believe how big she was. She looked at her stomach and giggled. "I don't know if we belong on the floor this year."

"Don't worry about it. If you look it says 'V.I.P. floor.' We also got you guys a booth on club level. Have a good show and thanks for supporting the band." He walked away, presumably to dole out the rest of tickets.

Nathan couldn't believe it. When they got into the show, they were even more astounded. Panic had reserved a V.I.P. booth on the club level and it was stocked with a full bar and all the familiar faces they had seen at every show along the way. The tour kids all had wristbands and full access to the floor as well as the private booth. The band never said anything about this gift, but it was something the most dedicated of the fan base would never forget.

The shows were great, and soon after stickers starting appearing on lot extolling the new guitar player: "By George, I think we've got it." The fans were willing to give him a chance, even though sometimes his guitar playing just wasn't right.

After New Year's, Nathan got a call on his cell phone from a health food store in Asheville; a place called Earth Fare. They wanted to interview him and possibly offer him a job. "When can you get here?" They asked.

"When do you need me?" he replied.

"As soon as possible."

"I'm out of town for the holidays. Can we schedule it for
the 5th?"

"That works. We'll see you January 5th at 9:00 am."

They ran up to Virginia for the Phish shows and set up their kitchen. The demand for tickets far exceeded the supply. Some people were carrying around signs offering hundreds of dollars, and even their first born child for a ticket. Melody and Nathan didn't stand a chance of getting into the show. Nathan didn't want to, still sour on Phish, but Melody would have liked to see at least one show. She kept this to herself and they spent 3 days in the parking lot selling more food than they ever had before. In three days they made $5,000 just on quesadillas.

After the last show they drove through the night back to Asheville. Miraculously, even being sleep deprived, Nathan landed a job in the produce department of Earth Fare. They didn't even ask him to cut his hair. They used their money from tour to rent a nice little house in West Asheville and Nathan went to work as an apple-stacker.

Maia Hope was born on Valentine's Day 2003 in Asheville, North Carolina. She was born at home with a midwife. It was an indescribable night for both parents. The labor wasn't easy, but it wasn't hellish, either. Melody gritted her way through it without any painkillers other than the love with which Nathan showed her throughout the event. He was there with her for every minute of it.

Afterwards, when the midwife had finally assured them and herself everything was fine and gone home, the newborn Maia lay in bed with her parents. Nathan and Melody weren't just two people anymore, they were a real family. Nathan lie in the dark exhaustion, too worked up to get to sleep, but unable to move. It was such a wonderful feeling of peace just to doze in this soft bed with his young family. He was drifting off to sleep.

"She wet herself," Melody said. "Can you get up and get a diaper?"

Nathan was slowly pulled from his reverie. He just

wanted to lie in bed. He felt it was all he could do.

However, he made a decision then and there. No matter how tired he was, how badly he didn't want to, or whatever came up in his own life, he would do anything to protect and comfort this little child who depended on her parents for everything. He would also do anything for Melody, the woman who had given him this wonderful gift of being a parent.

He felt higher than he ever had from any drug at any show. He set his willpower as firm as he could and rose from the bed to get a cloth diaper and a rag to clean up his newborn daughter.

~38~

Meanwhile, in Northern California, Lucy was pursuing her own dreams and taking fire dancing classes. She was getting pretty good. Taking what she learned from her time with Phillip, she rented a nice house, and started her own growing operation. Her weed crop was coming in regularly and supplying her with enough money to live comfortably. Thoughts of starting a dance troupe were manifesting into real action as there were three other girls from class equally as interested. No one called her Lucy anymore. She went by here stage name, Gypsy Moon Angel. Most people called her Moon or Gypsy. She hadn't seen Phillip in years and didn't care to.

He was still in Oregon, still living his life pretty much as he always had. His locks grew longer and his marijuana crop kept getting bigger. He changed women as often as a tour kid changes socks. Which isn't terribly often, but it happens more frequently than a shower. He was unhappy, but didn't have the time to address his own unhappiness or where it stemmed from except through a constant supply of pharmaceuticals.

He was in bad shape. He walked up to Kale's kitchen at Bonnaroo in 2003 bleary-eyed, starving, and completely unaware of his surroundings. He didn't recognize Kale and he didn't have enough money on him for a quesadilla. Kale, of course, gave him some food and Phillip stumbled on into the night.

Aside from being wasted, Phillip had other reasons not to recognize Kale. Kale was still on tour, but had gone legitimate. He got a tax ID number and started legally vending shows on the inside.

He missed Jessica profusely and cut his own locks off.

She was in Chicago, working for a lingerie firm under the title "Boobologist." She was in charge of bra's and designing how they formed to women's breasts. It was somewhat mundane, but she felt like she was on the path towards becoming something in the fashion world. She still made clothes in her spare time, though she no longer made hippie clothes. What she was making was somewhere between those old patchwork dresses and more mainstream fashion. When she showed her co-workers pictures of herself on tour they were astounded by who they saw. They couldn't understand why she had spent so many years of her life traveling the country to see these bands.

She couldn't explain it to them either, but whenever Panic or Phish came through Chicago, Jessica was there. Kale made it a point not to be there.

Melody and Nathan domesticated themselves after the birth of their daughter. They were married in the Spring of 2003 beneath a waterfall in Chimney Rock Park outside of Asheville. It was a small ceremony. Nathan continued to work at the Earth Fare and eventually made his way up through the ranks to become head of the produce department. In some ways, it was the happiest and simplest time of their lives. While Nathan and Melody were both very happy, Natron was suffering quietly on the inside.

They deeply loved Maia and spent days just looking into her deep green eyes that mirrored her mother's. She was bright and aware and utterly receptive to the attention her parents paid to her.

In 2003 Panic released a new album, "Ball." The first track has the lines, "Maia, she dances." When Melody and Nathan first heard this song it gave them the chills. They had meant to name their daughter after a Widespread Panic song, but were completely blown away when Panic had, in turn, had written a song about her. 2003 slipped into the past and Melody and Nathan didn't attend a single show. From their friends, they heard things were going well, but most everyone really missed Mikey and was still having a hard time adjusting to George on the guitar.

Nathan was snobbish, and suggested the reason

they weren't going to any shows was because of George's playing. They downloaded some shows and Nathan really didn't like what he was hearing. Melody thought most of it sounded okay, but they stayed at home as a family.

Widespread Panic finally took a break and didn't play a single show in 2004.

At the end of their summer tour in 2004, Phish called it quits for good. For a minute there was nothing. Neither Phish or Panic played a New Year's show leading into 2004. Melody and Nathan felt justified sitting at home. There weren't any shows to be going to anyway.

Bonnaroo was still happening every summer and other similar festivals were spawning around the country.

Panic came back in 2005, ready to fill the void.

In 2005, Melody also found out she was pregnant again. Melody's second pregnancy was more sickening to her physically than the first, so there was no going on tour. For such a torturous pregnancy, her birth was miraculously smooth. Smoother than Maia's. Clarity was also born at home with a midwife, but this time in a birthing tub. Melody believed it made all the difference in the relative ease with which Clarity was born.

With the birth of their second daughter, Nathan finally gave up completely on being Natron ever again. He told Melody. "All I want to be is a good father and a good husband."

"You're a great father," Melody said.

The years passed and the children got older. Sometimes, Melody and Nathan missed their previous existence, especially Melody. During the day, when Nathan was at work, she would turn up Panic on the stereo really loud and dance along while the girls giggled.

She was even listening to Phish again. For the most part they were content with their life together. They were seemingly surrounded on all sides by beauty and love.

Children brought something to Nathan he had never felt before. There were now two legitimate reasons for settling down and focusing his energy, for being a part of the world instead of just a rootless vagabond.

Melody, on the other hand, felt a growing impatience inside of herself with everything. When Nathan went to work, she found herself resenting him. She'd walked in to the store on multiple occasions to see Nathan flirting with some pretty hippie girl asking how to cook some exotic root or mushroom while she was stuck at home with no company except for two young children. To his credit, Nathan was still as fiercely loyal to Melody as he'd always been. Sure, he'd chat it up with customers from time to time, but it would never go any further than it did with the pretty young blonde girl at their first Panic show together.

Together, they were lonely. Of the real friends they had in Asheville, none of them had children and were still taking off to shows all the time. The few friends they made who did have children were generally wary of Melody and Nathan because of their dreadlocks.

Panic had been going through some changes themselves. In 2006 they replaced George McConnell on lead guitar with Jimmy Herring. Melody and Nathan hadn't seen the band since the New Year's shows of 2002/03.

When they came through Asheville for Halloween, Nathan stayed home with the kids while Melody went to the show. Jessica was there and she had arranged for all of her collected friends from tour to dress as Girl Scout Troop 1013.

Dancing among these super sexy, free-wheeling women, something stirred in Melody. Her panic was coming back and she was going to have to do something about it soon.

Nathan relaxed into complacency. He went to work, brought home a paycheck, and drank beer on the weekends. He and Melody smoked a lot of weed together at night and watched movies.

Melody felt an anxiousness growing inside of her and mentioned it to Nathan. Panic. He shrugged it off, "Soon enough the girls will be old enough that we can have my mom watch them and go see a few shows or something."

Soon enough couldn't come soon enough for Melody. Things were getting harder in their relationship because of it. They found themselves fighting all the time. The stresses of being head of his department kept Nathan at work quite a bit.

Since he was on a salary he never seemed to be bringing home
quite enough money for the time he spent away. Since home life was becoming increasingly confrontational, he delayed coming home longer and longer each day; which only made it worse.

Melody knew she didn't want to have anymore children and grew cold and scared of making love to Nathan for fear she'd get pregnant again.

Nathan finally got tired of sharing the bed with Clarity (Maia was already sleeping in her own room) and getting snubbed or pushed away every time he tried to get close to Melody. He started sleeping on the futon in the spare bedroom.

They both felt anxious and unfulfilled. They made it through 2007 together and in 2008 Melody started asking Nathan to go to marriage counseling with her.

"We don't need that," he said. "The girls are getting older. In two years Clarity will start school, too, and then we'll have time for ourselves again. We just need to make it over this hump."

Melody felt it was more than just a hump. She had fallen in love with Nathan because of his lust for freedom and willingness to take chances. All he did anymore was work and play it safe. They didn't even go to local shows and never spoke of going on tour at all.

"That was fun when we were younger, but we've

got kids and responsibilities now. I want to establish some credit and buy a house," he said. She couldn't believe these words were coming out of his mouth.

The thought of it all frightened Melody. Here she was, getting trapped with someone who swore he would never be trapped again. Finally, something happened to change things.

For New Year's Eve 2008 into 2009, Widespread Panic announced they would finally play somewhere besides Atlanta for New Years.

For New Year's into 2009 they decided to play the Pepsi Center in Denver. Sensing the imminent destruction of his marriage, Nathan bought tickets the minute they went on sale, booked a flight, and called his mom to come watch the kids.

On the winter solstice, Melody did something that took Nathan by surprise. He came home from work to find that she had cut off her dreadlocks.

He was taken aback, confused, and unsure of what it meant for him.

"I still love you," she promised. "It's just hair."

Nathan's mom arrived at their house on time and the two parents flew off together to a Widespread Panic show together for the first time in six years. Maia was about to turn 6 and Clarity was 3. Melody and Nathan were both pushing 30.

Jessica's cell phone was ringing as soon as she turned it on after the plane landed. Her ring tone was Widespread Panic doing "Arlene." She answered the phone.

"Hello?"

"Hey Jess, it's me." It was Kale. No matter how many years passed, or how far away he was, she would always recognize his voice. "I heard you were gonna be in Denver for New Year's. Got any plans?"

Jessica had come on a whim. She had been missing her tour friends and reminiscing about the old days. All she had were tickets to the show and no plans. However, she was making enough money that she could pretty much do whatever she wanted to. Her career was taking off.

"Not really."

"Well, there's this after party thing at the Crowne Plaza Hotel downtown. I booked a room there next to Melody and Natron. The whole hotel is full of Panic kids and there's gonna be bands late night."

"Melody and Natron are actually coming to a show? I heard they had two kids now."

"They do, but Natron's mom is watching them for the shows."

There was a pause in the conversation as they both thought about what might have happened if the two of them had decided to raise children together. But however much of a free-spirited hippie Jessica had been in her youth, she was always religious about her birth-control pills.

"I really want to see you," Kale said.

"I don't know where I'm staying yet. I just landed. I've got to get my luggage and take a cab downtown. Wanna meet for lunch? I'm starving."

"If you want, I could just pick you up at the airport."

Melody thought about for just a second. She went with her feeling.

"That would be great."

"I'll be there in about half an hour."

Kale sped to the airport and made it in twenty minutes. Jessica was waiting out front with her suitcase. Kale couldn't believe how good she looked. Over the years a few girls had come in and out of his life, but none of them compared to Jessica. She was the love of his life and he hoped he had this one chance to redeem himself to her.

She got in his car and smiled at him.

"Hi," she said.

"You look great," he said.

"You, too. When did you cut your locks?" she asked.

"It's been a few years now."

They went to lunch at the Watercourse, a fancy vegetarian restaurant near downtown Denver. They laughed and talked over lunch and it was like old times. Jessica went with Kale to check into the Crowne Plaza. She followed him to his room and on the elevator they kissed again for the first time in years.

Jessica had missed Kale, too. Every man she had dated since him was either too much or not enough. She hadn't felt anything like this until she kissed him again.

Melody and Nathan checked into their room, unaware that Kale and Jessica were making love next door. Nathan knocked, but there was no answer.

"I guess Kale's not here yet," he said.

Two hours later there was a knock on Melody and Nathan's door. When Melody opened the door her brain did a back flip. Was that really Jessica who Kale had his arm around?

"Jess?"

"Melody!"

"Oh shit, it is you!" There was some screaming and hugging while Nathan gave Kale a quizzical look. Kale just nodded and smiled. Nathan shook his head in amazement.

Everything seemed right in the world. The four of them took a cab together to the Pepsi Center. In the cab ride Nathan realized he was the only one of them who still had his dreadlocks.

"Damn, things sure change over the years," he said.

"Yeah, but a lot of things stay the same," Jessica said, looking over at Kale.

"I'm just glad we're all here together again," Melody said.

"Absolutely," Kale finished the thought.

That night was exquisite musically. Jimmy Herring certainly isn't Michael Houser, but he can play the guitar and is a better fit for Panic than George McConnell. There were so many new songs, for everyone except Kale (who had seen the evolution firsthand) it seemed like a new band.

There will still moments that sent them back through the years and memories of their lives. During "Genesis," Melody and Nathan held each other close and fell in love all over again. The whole night had a kind of Grateful Dead feel to the air, with a sick "Other One" Jam in the middle of "Pigeons."

That night at the hotel they skipped the after party and went to bed early. They were part of the older crowd now.

No one slept alone that night.

For New Year's Eve, everyone was dressed to the nines. Jessica brought a special red dress she had made just for the occasion. Melody was in a tight little black thing that accentuated curves that seemed too smooth for a mother of two approaching thirty. Kale had a black suit and Nathan wore a forest green one.

Kale broke out a stash of molly he had been hanging onto and dispersed it amongst the group. Jessica and Melody quickly ate their dose right there in the hotel room. Nathan hesitated. It had been so long and he had become so responsible over the years. Melody saw his hesitation.

"You sure you want to?" she asked him expectantly.

"Yeah." He'd go anywhere with her.

They got to the show and had just enough time to go the bathroom and get a beer before Panic took the stage. There had been an opening band, Yonder Mountain String Band, but this group was here strictly for the Panic. The first set was completely familiar to everyone. It was a rundown of their first album, "Space Wrangler," originally released in 1988.

The songs are timeless. It was the album that had turned Kale onto Widespread Panic. Before he went on tour, back in high school, it was his bluest tape. He would lock his car and listen to it in the parking lot before school.

Somehow, it made it possible for him to face the containment of the public education system, and still feel free inside. He followed that music out the door and into a world that he fit right into. The No Deals Café of Panic and Phish lot was a thing of the past. He had a setup inside Bonnaroo, Coachella, Wakarusa, and several other festivals across America during the summer. He hired a crew and rang numbers in the tens of thousands at each show, even crossing $100,000 at places like Bonnaroo and IT up in Maine.

He had found his niche, but there was something missing. He always knew exactly what it was. She was finally dancing next to him again. Jessica couldn't believe it herself. One thing that had always bothered her about Kale was an apparent lack of ambition. All he ever wanted to do was go to the next show.

Jessica loved it at first, but eventually wanted to grow her life in a different direction. The very reasons she fell in love with Kale were the same reasons that eventually distanced her from him. He always told her to hang on just a little longer and things were going to change and get better. But they seemed to keep ending up in another dark parking lot trying to hustle just enough money to get out of town.

After Jessica left, Kale changed that. He continued to be himself, but he looked for more in himself than he ever had. He struggled, and eventually took his tour kitchen to the next level. It was a major operation now. He was a success. He still had to work, but had found a way to make a living that he enjoyed and felt served a kind of greater purpose. He was providing food to people he knew were seeking something more out of life. He knew why he first came to the shows, and he saw the same questing search in the eyes of the young people buying his quesadillas.

Somehow, it all made perfect sense to him again, with Jessica dancing by his side. Melody looked over at the two of them and thought about her own situation. She'd been seriously thinking of leaving Nathan, it had gotten that bad. Maybe she didn't have to. Maybe they could find their way back to the place of acceptance they'd known so well during their years on tour together.

The music reminded her of that love they used to feel. She didn't want it to be over. She wanted to dance like this forever.

~40~

During the set break, the lights came up and images from the year on tour were flashing on the jumbo-tron. Someone came out onstage and started going over the highlights of the year. 2008 was coming to an end. Nostalgia flowed through Melody, Nathan, Jessica, and Kale.

Melody was filled with a wistfulness, wishing she were still on tour. The announcer confirmed that Panic sold-out Red Rocks that year for the 30th, 31st, and 32nd time in a row. Nathan felt like he had missed out on something that could have been very important to his life. Jessica had enough memories from years past, that the nostalgia she felt wasn't one of missing something. Kale, likewise, felt complete. He had been at most of those shows.

Then, Jojo, the keyboard player came out and the countdown began. Melody wrapped her arm around Nathan, who leaned into her. Kale and Jessica looked at each other and smiled, mouthing the numbers to each other as they counted down to one.

At the second the horn blew and the confetti came streaming down, everyone kissed. "Auld Lange Syne," that traditional New Year's song, played over the house speakers. Kale chose that moment to do something he had been waiting to do for years.

"Jessica," he pulled a small black felt box from his pocket.

"I've had this ring for years, back when we were on tour together, but I never got up the nerve until now. Will you marry me?"

She didn't even have to think about. She grabbed Kale and kissed him again, "Of course I will."

Kale and Jessica were beaming smiles to everyone around them and especially to each other. Jessica finally looked at the engagement ring she wore on her finger. The diamond glittered in the lights.

Then JB came onto the stage and sang a Frank Sinatra song, "As Time Goes By." Even though this

song came from the 1950s, a love song, it held the
tones of Widespread Panic beneath it's surface:

You must remember this
A kiss is still a kiss
A sigh is just a sigh
The fundamental rules apply
As time goes by
It's still the same old story
A fight for love and glory
A case of do or die
The world will always welcome lovers
As time goes by.

The lovers intertwined with each other and
danced and kissed. Everything was right with the
world. Then all of sudden it was really Panic again,
and Jojo was hammering out the opening licks to
"Tallboy." Jimmy Herring picked up the signature
guitar line originally laid down by Michael Houser.
It was good.
Kale passed around some more molly, and
everyone was soon shedding their skin, hoping to
carry this feeling into the morning. The rest of the set
was an awakening for Natron. He felt who he was on
the inside again, and saw himself in the music. He
looked at Jessica and Kale, happily dancing in love,
and could tell they were people of higher quality and
character than most of the people a person meets in
their lifetime.
He could tell this even though they didn't have
dreadlocks anymore.
He looked to Melody dancing at his left and saw
the same glow emanating from her beyond her new
chopped-short haircut.
After "Tall Boy," they went into a brand new song.
Kale was the only one who had heard it before and
explained the song to the other three.
"It's a new one, 'Walk on the Flood.' They started
playing it this spring."

After the new song there was a short break as two of the guys from Yonder Mountain joined Panic on stage. With the addition of a mandolin and a banjo, Panic reached back to their roots and a country feel permeated the air. "Ain't Life Grand", "Who Do You Belong To", and "Fixin' To Die," were all thrown together into an outpouring of music that had everyone remembering Mikey again.

After the country jam, they dropped their electric instruments, picked up acoustic ones, and played Mikey's quintessential song: "Vacation."

Nathan couldn't believe how in love he felt with everyone, himself, the situation, and especially Melody. Watching her dance he felt his heart soar higher and higher. Why had he ever doubted that this woman was the woman meant for him?

"I love you so much, Melody."

"I love you too, Nathan."

She wrapped her arms around him and they kissed as passionately as two people can kiss. After some more great music, that was made all the better with Kale's generous offerings of molly, they found themselves at the encore.

JB came out and mumbled something into the microphone, "Well thank you for hosting this little shindig, Denver, Colorado. And a very, very happy New Year. Now let's get it on."

The song was "Up All Night." It was relatively new, but had been in rotation for two years. Melody, Nathan, and Jessica had never heard it. Still, the song played right to their very souls. Singing about New Years and how they would, indeed, be up all night. There was a jamming "Disco", a "Love Tractor," and then the show was over.

With the end of the music, and the lights coming up, other things were about to surface.

They went back to the hotel with every intention of staying up all night, watching some of the late-night music that was included with their wristbands, and taking a complimentary shuttle in the morning to a Bloody Mary breakfast at Quixote's that was also included in the hotel package.

They went to the after show in the hotel for about twelve minutes before they knew they were done with loud music for the evening. They ended up in the room, packing a bowl, cracking open some beers, and all four laughing together. They told stories, talked about each other's lives, and were in love with each other all evening. At some point around 4:30 in the morning, Kale and Jessica went to their room and crawled into bed together. Melody and Nathan did the same.

No one slept.

At 6:15 Kale was banging on Nathan and Melody's door.

"Get up! We gotta go to the Bloody Mary breakfast!"

Nathan disentangled himself from the lovely woman in bed with him, put on some pants, and opened the door. Kale was bleary eyed but smiling.

"Come on. You know you want a Bloody Mary. Jessica said she wouldn't go unless you guys come."

"Alright, we'll go," Melody called from the bed. She knew this was a temporary existence. Soon she'd have to go back home to Nathan going to work and her being at home with their two daughters. She needed to pack as much into this trip as possible. The long night of making love had to end with the Bloody Mary breakfast.

They boarded a shuttle provided by the promoter. It was operated by a Rastafarian puffing on a joint. He shook his head at all the crazy white kids on board and dropped them at the warehouse bar of Quixote's just north of downtown Denver.

The place was crowded. People poured in and out. The group of friends exited the shuttle and entered the bar.

"Four Bloody Mary's," Nathan said to the bartender.

"Sorry, we're all out of Bloody Mary's."

"What? It's only just now 7 am? On New Year's Day?"

"Well, we're out."

"But, I want a Bloody Mary."

"Too bad."

Nathan walked away from the bar and joined his friends.

"Where's the bloodies?" Jessica asked.

"Uh, yeah. They don't have any."

"What?"

"Exactly. I want a Bloody Mary," Nathan said. "Let's go."

They left in a cab. There was vodka in the room. Nathan had the driver stop at Walgreen's, where he got Bloody Mary mix, olives, pickles, celery, A-1 steak sauce, and some Tabasco. He also bought a comb, a brush, and a pair of scissors and hid them in his pocket.

Back at the room, Jessica mixed Bloodies for everyone. They relaxed with their drinks and Nathan pulled the scissors from his pocket.

"It's time," he said, and handed the scissors to Melody.

"Time for what?" she said, baffled.

"Time to cut these locks off."

"Really?" Melody said.

"I love you," Nathan said. "Watching you and Jessica and Kale last night, I realized it doesn't take dreadlocks to make a person glow. You all stand out, even without your locks. I don't need 'em anymore. I'm almost thirty."

Melody cut the first one off, then they passed the scissors around the room and took turns cutting the ropes from off of Nathan's head. When it was finished, they brushed out what remained and Nathan's new hair stood straight up.

He ran his hands through his hair, feeling his scalp for the first time in years. The sensation tingled his whole body.

Melody curled up next to him and brushed her fingers through his hair.

"I love you, so much," she said. "I'm so happy we came here together. I feel like we're really ready to grow together and move to the next stage of our relationship."

"I never want to be with anyone else besides you for the rest of my life," Nathan said to Melody. They meant every word of it

Part 3:

The Feeling I Forgot

~42~

There is a point, in some people, when the illusions of modern life become completely intolerable. Once past that point, panic becomes the only appropriate response. People will destroy their own lives and those around them just to interject some chaos into the regulated existence they feel they've been forced into.

In the early months of 2009, Melody and Nathan were in love. They came home from the New Years show basking in the glow of each other. Nathan's mother recognized it instantly when they walked through the door. She smiled and clapped for his haircut and went home thinking everything would be alright for a good, long while.

They came home from New Years in love, but they came home to the very same cage. The afterglow lasted only a few short weeks. Soon, everything was back to normal. They tried to translate their transcendental feelings from the music and the ecstasy back into their everyday life, but fell short. That was always the struggle.

It's easy to experience divine bliss and love while the music is playing, the hard part is in hearing that music everyday.

Nathan was still working more than he needed to, being gone for what seemed like days at a time. Melody was desperately lonely. All she wanted was for that bright-eyed boy she had fallen in love with to come back. Instead, she was partnered with an overworked, borderline alcoholic who took her for granted.

Melody was tired of life falling short of her

expectations. She was tired of struggling. She was tired of Nathan. Near the middle of April, she carried through on a threat she had been making for a year now.

"I'm leaving you," she said to Nathan.

He fell to his knees. He cried and begged her to stay.

"Where are you going?" he asked. "Don't go," he pleaded through a fountain of tears.

"I'm going," she said emphatically, crying just as much herself. "I don't know where yet. Nowhere at first. I just know I can't be with you anymore. We're never going to grow together. It's just going to be the same shit over and over again."

"So are you moving out?"

"I don't have a place yet."

"So, then I'm leaving?"

"I didn't say that, either."

Nathan was confused, hurt, and instantly destroyed. Years ago he had set aside his dreams of freedom and replaced them with dreams of a stable family. Now he was losing that, too. "What am I supposed to do?" He had nothing left to dream.

"I don't know. Can you stay with some friends? Or go camping or something?"

He exploded into tears again. This was hitting him harder than she thought it would. She thought he would be relieved.

"I gotta go," Nathan said. He staggered out the door, sobbing. "I don't know when I'll be back. I can't just sit here and watch you leave."

The girls were crying as he drove away. There had been yelling and tears flowing through their home all day. The girls didn't know how to feel, or what was happening, but they knew it was bad. They missed their father the instant he drove away.

Their cries cut Melody like a knife. What had she done?

Nathan drove away, tears obscuring his vision. He ran his fingers through his hair and wished he still had his dreadlocks. At least then there would still be something constant in his life.

He felt like his life was over. He had been on his hands and knees, crying for her to stay, promising anything. It didn't matter that they had both been dissatisfied and fighting for months; maybe even years. He honestly loved her with everything he had to give. Everything he'd ever been told was that this deep, all-encompassing love would be enough to get them through anything together. It wasn't enough for her anymore. He had promised things would get better. Things stayed the same. She was through with his promises.

He felt scared and hollow as he drove away alone. Why was this happening? Wasn't he supposed to be a husband and a father? Hadn't he tried? He gave her his heart and soul and she destroyed it all. He drove aimlessly until he ended up far from the city on some shady dirt road. Suddenly there was something in front of him. He slammed on the brakes and a cloud of dust kicked up.

When the dust settled, he saw it in the middle of the road.

A coyote was sitting on it's haunches, examining Nathan with a quizzical expression. The beast cocked it's head. With a feeling of wonder, the tears stopped flowing from Nathan's eyes. He was entranced by this wild animal who sat in the road before him. For a full minute Nathan sat behind the wheel of his car, gazing into the eyes of this animal that had stopped to examine this man.

Coyote holds connotations of magic and trickery in the culture of most of the indigenous tribes of North America. He is like a god and a demon at the same time. On the most basic level of reality, coyotes are the only large mammal native to North America that have actually increased in number since civilization began overrunning the continent.

With an intelligence emanating from his animal eyes, the coyote continued to sit on his haunches and examine Nathan from the middle of the road. Finally, the coyote gave a slight bark that could only be perceived as laughter. Grinning from ear to ear, the mystical animal trotted out of the road and gave Nathan a final, mischievous glance behind.

Nathan was dumbfounded.

"What the hell was that supposed to mean?" He yelled to no one in particular. No one in particular answered with only a gentle breeze.

43

The girls were crying. They were always crying; always needing something. Everyone needed something from Melody. She was the finder of lost shoes, misplaced wallets and car keys. She treated minor injuries, bruised egos, and tired feet. She bought groceries, cooked breakfast, lunch, and dinner. Everything she did was about making someone else's life easier.

When was it her turn to need something?

She was breaking apart inside.

"Be there in a minute girls. It's going to be okay," she said from the driveway, the dust from Nathan leaving mingling with the tears on her cheeks to muddy her face.

Then she broke down crying and washed the mud away. It was awful, what she was doing. It was awful to break everything apart like this. There had once been such love in their house and now it was filled with tears.

She had to end it.

Her heart had been aching far worse than it was right now for so long. They were going nowhere and nothing else was going to change that. The steady misery of a wasted life was far worse than this specific, and intense pain.

At least life would become memorable again. No more would her days blend into one another. Everything was going to be new again. She was free again. Nathan couldn't understand how trapped she felt. She had given it her all, it wasn't enough. Nathan would fade away in ambivalence when she tried to tell him how trapped she felt. She'd been his girl for the best years of her young life.

Then these kids had been inside of her and clung to her body for years, draining her. She certainly loved the girls, but they were so much work. She hadn't been anyone except mom for so long. Her life had been a balancing act through a cluttered room.

She needed out into the open. Now. Not next week and certainly not next year. Now. Now Nathan was gone. She had honestly thought they would last forever. But she told herself that nothing lasts forever. The man she sat next to watching movies every night wasn't the adventurous man she had originally fallen in love with.

But then again, she thought, was he even really a man when she met him? Wasn't he just a boy? She had been only eighteen years old and he was just nineteen. They thought they knew so much about themselves and how they were going to live their life together. They had been so sure, but none of it had worked out like they planned. Melody wasn't sure of anything anymore, except that she needed drastic change in her life.

She knew this would do it.

The day passed in the familiar miserable drudgery of domestic tasks, but everything was different. Melody was numb with the transpirings. When she had told Nathan of her intentions to leave, she had thought in the back of her head that there were some things she wanted to accomplish by herself, some things he needed to do, and they would probably, eventually, come back together with a fresh perspective on life and their love together.

She hadn't expected him to completely fall apart like he had. She had wanted him to understand where she was coming from but he couldn't. He was prepared to drag out their minimal existence indefinitely, going to work everyday without complaint and coming home stoic and tired. She would do the dishes and cook the meals. Where was it going? It was a bland existence and there was nothing on the horizon that foretold any change.

She had wished to see some kind of emotion in him for so long but had seem nothing but ambivalence. Until now, when he crumbled into a heap of emotion beneath her ending their mundane existence together.

There was some satisfaction in this, in seeing him squirm at her will. He was always so sure of himself. It hurt her deeply, but she felt a great weight lifted from her shoulders. She had discovered the bars of her prison, and it was Nathan. He never listened to her anymore, ignored what she had to say, and was now physically gone from her life instead of nearby but absent.

She dried her tears and went looking for her cell phone. She'd found some old friends on Facebook and was wondering what Lucy was up to these days?

44

We are born into these bodies with a certain temperament that maintains a fairly constant setting throughout our lives. Sometimes, we're thrown off balance by life-changing events, but for the most part, we think and behave along the same lines since we first began thinking and behaving. This is part of who we are, but doesn't completely establish an individual's character.

Character is developed through responsibility. Personal responsibility is only part of who we are and who we become. There is a collective, societal responsibility we owe to each other. Our temperament may remain constant, but the destiny of character walks upon a razor's edge based on the care and love we're given from other people.

Small decisions made in instances provided by the circumstance of life become pivotal moments that define the eventual outcome of who each of us is destined to become. Just because we don't recognize these moments as they happen doesn't make them any less important.

Many moments had come and gone for Lucy. She had made decisions and Melody could tell that Lucy was obliviously content in her little world in Northern California. She had a dance performance the night before, and was taking care of some chores tonight associated with her grow operation. Earlier today she had gone out to buy some hydroponic chemicals and another grow light. Now it was time to fill the reservoirs and hook up the new light.

She was just about to get started for the evening when her phone rang. It was Melody, the girls were in bed and she had some things she needed to get off her chest with an old friend. Lucy was excited to hear her voice.

"Melody! I haven't talked to you in so long. How are things going?"

"Awful. I'm leaving Nathan. I told him and he just

blew up and left."

"Really? Why? I'm so sorry, honey. Tell me what happened?"

"Just the same things that have been happening for years. Nothing. He's not who he used to be and neither am I. It's like we don't have any dreams together or any fun anymore. I'm not even sure I ever really wanted to have a family, but here I am. I mean, I love my girls, but I just don't feel like I got to do everything I wanted to do before I had kids."

They talked for nearly an hour about everything they had both been through in their lives.

"You know, I never told anyone this," Lucy said. "But I was pregnant once. I had an abortion. I just couldn't see myself as a mother. When I look at my life now, it's a decision I never regret."

Melody, felt a tangible weight on her shoulders pressing down from the decisions she had made and the decisions she had neglected to make. What would've happened if they hadn't had Maia? Would they still be in love? Would they have separated much sooner and with less heartache? Melody felt like her life had carried her along for the ride. She was always waiting for things to come to her.

It was time to go out and take from life what she needed.

Talking to Lucy was actually very depressing for Melody. Lucy was so happy and jubilant about everything it began to sting Melody with an envy for a life she had neglected to live. Maybe if she had just stayed in Oregon all those years ago, and not gone on Panic tour she could've been a part of Lucy's fire dancing troupe. Maybe she would have a new name as melodic as Gypsy Moon Angel.

She could've been Autumn Lilly, instead of just Mom.

When she hung up the phone with Lucy, Melody knew what she had to do. She had to seize control of her life again. If she didn't actively pursue her destiny, then it would be decided for her in ways she didn't necessarily want.

Phish was back on tour, and from what Melody had heard, the shows were sounding better than ever.

She knew it was time to see Phish again, no matter what.

~45~

Phillip was pulling through the drive-up window at Burger King. He was feasting on his lunch of a Whopper with cheese, French fries, and a Dr. Pepper. "Fuck it," he thought as the greasy meat found it's way into his stomach. It didn't matter anymore. Nothing really mattered to Phillip anymore. He'd cut his locks off months ago and started eating the same shit as everybody else.

What use was it in this fucked-up world anyway?

For years his life had been a roller-coaster ride of pharmaceuticals, grow rooms, drug deals, concerts, and late nights in expensive hotel rooms with lots of powder to eat and snort. He could hardly remember what it was he had set out to accomplish, if anything, and focused on hiding away as much cash as he could accumulate. His interest in it was waning, but he kept on just to have something to occupy his time.

His operation was somewhat legal now, with California's relaxed medical marijuana laws, and he thought nothing of the ten pounds he had in his trunk. He was making a delivery to a marijuana dispensary and picking up a $38,000 paycheck.

Business as usual.

Sure, he still lived in Eugene and had transported his weed across state lines from Oregon to California, but he held a card in California and honestly, didn't care or have a single concern to the legalities of the situation. He was just doing what he always did.

He pulled up to the dispensary, which looked like a normal storefront with a large picture of the medical insignia painted on the window. The snakes coiled around the staff, however, were painted as green vines with the conspicuous five-fingered leaf of the marijuana plant. Phillip grabbed the duffel bag in the seat behind him and strutted into the building.

"What the fuck is up, man?" The heavily-tattooed fellow with a shaved head and monstrous red beard behind the counter said when Phillip walked in the door.

"How you doin' Jake?" Phillip replied.

They pounded their fists together and Phillip threw the duffel bag on the counter.

"Got your shipment for this week. It's all mine this time. You got some Durban Poison in there, some Northern Lights, Strawberry Kush, Master Kush, White Widow, Sour Diesel, and Purple Haze. I loaded up on the Durban Poison and the Sour Diesel, since everyone's nuts for that shit right now."

"Nice work man. Hey, I got a proposition for you."

"What you got, Jake?"

"You like that band Phish, right?"

"Yeah, they're alright."

"Check it out Phillip. I'm flooded with product right now. Everyone is coming in at the same time. I'll still buy your weed at $3,800 a pound, as usual, but how would you like to make an extra 12 G's and get to see Phish in the process."

"I'm listening."

"They just changed the medicinal marijuana laws in Colorado and my cousin is opening a dispensary out there. He's short on product. You take your ten pounds out there, plus another 20 I need to unload, and I'll give you $50,000 for your 10 pounds."

"Sounds good so far. What's Phish got to do with it?"

"They're playing at Red Rocks in July. Tickets sold out instantly. They haven't played there since 1996. But my cousin's got a friend who works for Red Rocks. He's already got two tickets for each night. He wanted me to send someone out to stay with him until then to help him get his grow operation going. He figured the Phish tickets might be a nice little bonus to throw on top of the regular pay. No one knows how to grow weed better than you. Plus, I can get him to pay you another ten G's just to help him get started, and then he'll buy clones off of you and maybe fold you into the operation, if you want."

"I don't know man, I had some plans for this

spring. Can I think about it?"

"Yeah, we got some time, but I'm gonna give you $50,000 for this ten pack anyway. When my cousin asked me to bring him some weed and get him started, I knew I couldn't leave. But I thought of you instantly, man."

Phillip walked out of the door with a duffel bag $12,000 heavier than he expected. On the drive home, he decided he might as well go to Colorado for a minute. He was completely harvested, and it wouldn't be hard to get rid of the clones he had started. Plus, Phish hadn't played Red Rocks in 13 years. Phillip had been there the first time, in 1996 when the nonsense had gone down in Morrison. He was in the show, so he missed all of that. It was the grubby kids stuck outside without tickets who got in trouble.

About a thousand or so kids without tickets crowded the streets of Morrison. When the cops asked them to "move along," someone threw a beer bottle. The ensuing riot landed 9 people in jail and three injured. Phish was banned from Red Rocks indefinitely.

In the summer of 2009, the ban was lifted, and Phish would play Red Rocks again for another four nights

46

Melody was packing. What do you do with the articles of a shared life when that life is no longer shared? Melody couldn't bring herself to throw anything away. Let Nathan sort through the detritus. He had finally called. He was staying with some friends until she was gone from the house. He agreed to keep up the rent, give her the money for an apartment, and sort out the details later. He said she could take all that shit in the house she wanted and burn whatever was left, for all he cared. This made her cry. He wasn't supposed to completely cut everything instantly. He was supposed to leave a door open for her to come back.

Nathan's emotions took him for a dizzying ride. Sometimes he was glad she was gone, and anger rolled through his body like a tornado. However, there wasn't a day that went by that he didn't miss her intensely at some point.

He left the door open in his heart, but slammed it in Melody's face. For some reason, he deluded himself into believing she might want to come back if she saw that he didn't care she was gone. He spent his days off with the girls visiting parks while Melody looked for an apartment and a job. He stayed out of the house they had shared for so many years, avoiding it like the plague.

She eventually found a decent apartment and got a job at a bar as a waitress all on the same day.

Would she file for divorce? Would she try and get custody of the girls and child support? She didn't know. Everything was up in the air. The girls were playing happily in their room while Melody packed the kitchen. She took half the plates, half the silverware, half the coffee cups and put them in a box, wrapped neatly in newspaper.

She went through the house, taking what she wanted and leaving some things where they stood. Nathan said he would go through it when he got back.

Eventually, she found that box of pictures in the back of the closet every family invariably collects. She tortured herself by trying to go through them. Finally, soaked in tears, she gave up. So much had gone wrong. This was never what she wanted.

Soon, everything she thought she needed from this failure of a life was packed in the van. She would be back for the furniture. The girls were buckled into their car seats as Melody watched their former lives blink slowly away in the fading horizon of the rearview mirror.

47

Life was moving by in vignettes. There was no consistency to anything. Melody was pacing the apartment while Maia and Clarity slept; walking on eggshells around her packed boxes, waiting for some other foot to fall and destroy her completely. For years she had been living in default mode, just going through the motions without feeling anything.

Now, she woke up every morning at the mercy of her mood. She woke up missing Nathan and the day was awful, because she knew she really didn't want to be with him anymore. It was just the comfort of what she had always known. However, on some days she woke up excited about the prospects of her new life.

Things were moving along for her. She made friends through her job at the bar and they helped her with watching the girls while she worked. It amazed her how many single mothers were coming out to the bar on the nights the kids were with their fathers. It was a late night job, but the pay was pretty good when the tips were up.

She was having fun. Being a single, attractive woman has its advantages. There was this one guy, Brian, who had been coming in every night since she started working. He eyed her from across the bar and bought her drinks when her shift was over. He was funny and attractive; and most important, completely different from Nathan.

Where Nathan had become responsible and reserved, Brian didn't think too much about anything and often got drunk out of control. He made Melody laugh with his antics. She'd slept with him a few nights ago, and after years of obligatory sex with the same person it was exciting and different. Thinking about it aroused her even now.

She was certain she'd see him tomorrow at work, but there was a problem. Sure, she liked him, but she didn't have the ability to fall in love with him, or anyone right now. She wanted to be single and responsible only for herself and her children.

She was learning that life wasn't something that happened to you, rather something crafted with skill and intention. Sure, there was much that couldn't be controlled, but there was certainly a part to play in how everything evolved. She was trying to make some plans, but they all seemed to stop with getting to a Phish show soon. She'd figure it out from there.

She had to do that first. She had to reconnect with the girl inside of her who had left everything searching for freedom. Here she was, leaving everything again.

Brian was at the bar waiting for her again that night. He bought her drinks and told her he wanted to go places with her. This made her nervous, as she was only interested in going to his house after work and fucking him before picking up the kids from the babysitter. He was a generous lover and did whatever Melody told him to.

She felt pampered in his presence. He was different from Nathan in every way. Sex with Nathan had become something that lasted about two minutes and was done with impatience. He had gotten so eager to make love to her that she just wasn't interested anymore.

Brian, on the other hand, was new and moved in ways Melody hadn't experienced. He touched off a spark inside of her that she had forgotten existed. Her sexuality bloomed again under his hands and now she was sizing up every man she saw as a potential lover. She watched them drinking their drinks in the bar and wondered about their ability in the bedroom and the size of their penis. Trying some of them out was bound to happen. Brian would be upset, but she didn't care. She didn't owe him anything.

In fact, that very night she had found herself on the dance floor with a cute Hispanic guy and his blonde friend home from the Marines. The Hispanic guy was looking into her eyes as she rubbed up against him and back against the Marine behind her. She could feel both of the erections hidden in their pants and it nearly drove her wild.

She fucked Brian that night like it was an Olympic event. She wasn't particularly attached to him, but he served her purposes for now. She wanted escape, and being with Brian offered that, if nothing else.

She made sure to keep their conversations superficial and she didn't concern him with her problems or concern herself with his. His biggest problem was that he was lonely and wanted Melody around more. She refused to introduce him to the girls, not wanting to complicate their lives any further.

The next night Melody ditched Brian for the cute Hispanic guy. She kind of liked his moustache. He came back to the bar without his Marine buddy, specifically looking for Melody. They ended up on the dance floor when she got off work. The place was empty except for Brian pouting in the corner and the music was horrible. It was the kind of DJ who gets gigs at bar mitzvahs and bad weddings. It didn't matter to Melody. She shook her ass at Paul (she thought that was his name) while the DJ blared House of Pain's only hit song from fifteen years ago.

A few more shots, and they did the Electric Slide together. Brian slipped out alone.

Later that night, she really got off. Robert (that's what his name turned out to be) had the body of an athlete. She ran her hands over his muscled stomach and felt a certain hunger overwhelm her. It was an explicit evening.

The more sex she had, the more she wanted. It seemed she was living her life bouncing from one sensual pleasure to another. She drank and smoked constantly, sometimes dabbling in a bump of cocaine or molly in the girl's room at the bar with some of her new girlfriends.

She hadn't spent hardly a night alone since she told Nathan to leave. She was telling herself that she was embarking on a new adventure, but actually she was still waiting in the gate of distraction.

Maia and Clarity spent a lot of nights alone with a

babysitter.

When she finally got home (after removing herself from Robert's bed) at four in the morning, the babysitter was passed out on the couch and the girls were in their beds. The babysitter was a pretty young girl of 17, making extra money babysitting before she graduated high school in a few months. Her name was Ava, and Melody had met her through an ad Ava had placed in the paper offering babysitting services. Melody liked her instantly. She was young, blonde, beautiful, and smart. Her whole life was ahead of her and Melody looked at her sleeping on the couch and felt envious. She had been just like Ava once, long ago.

Ava was planning on leaving Asheville after she graduated high school. She was going to New York City, where she planned on checking out the city, maybe trying to find an apartment and a job before starting school at NYU in the fall. She had gotten a partial scholarship and her parents had enough money to cover the rest.

Ava was excited about the future.

Melody was avoiding the future. The dreams she once had, whatever they were, certainly weren't to be a divorced cocktail waitress in a seedy bar. She never dreamed she'd find herself here. Since she couldn't alter her situation, she altered her mind with whatever came by.

The beautiful young girl on the couch stirred in her sleep and breathed a sigh. Melody just stared at her sleeping, while swaying back and forth from a night of working, drinking, and sex. She realized how much she actually hated herself and broke out in tears.

She ran to her bedroom, afraid she would wake Ava or the girls and crawled under the sheets. She was crying so hard her body shook in spasms.

She spent the next day in the park with Maia and Clarity. Soon Maia would start school and these carefree days of play would be replaced by hurried mornings of packing lunches and rushing off.

While they were at the park Brian drove by and saw them. He pulled his car to the side of the road and got out. "Hey Melody!" He waved.

"Hi girls," he said to Maia and Clarity.

"Mommy, who's that?" Maia wanted to know.

"My friend, Brian."

He walked over and gave Melody a hug. She was disturbed by the familiar touch in front of her daughters.

He made himself welcome at the park, introduced himself to the girls, and joined them in their make-believe mermaid game. He was a pirate.

She watched Brian playing with her daughters. It made her feel sick inside. Brian came over and put his arm around her.

"Those are beautiful girls you have," he said and smiled at her.

It almost made her vomit. This wasn't what she wanted at all. For years she had been Nathan's girl. Now all she had to do was relax and she could fall into being someone else's accessory. Brian had a good job working for the forest service. He had an actual career, made decent money, and was paying the mortgage for the house he lived in instead of just the rent.

It could be so easy.

And it would turn out just the same.

She rolled out from under his arm. "I've got to go," she said. Then, without hesitating she took off in the direction of her children. "Come on girls, we've got to go."

They were ready and bounded off to the car. Brian was left standing there wondering what he had done wrong. He had played everything just like he was supposed to. He had been nice, not too intrusive, and she was on the rebound and ripe for the picking.

It didn't make sense.

He shook his head as she walked away, fully aware of the level of rejection he had just received.

What was wrong with him that he couldn't find a decent woman? All he wanted was a wife and some children. The doctors had told him he couldn't have kids of his own, so he was continually attracted to women who already had kids.

None of them had seemed to be willing to try raising their family with him, not yet. Surely, there was some gullible woman out there willing to play house. It wasn't going to be Melody.

Phillip's drive from California to Colorado with 38 pounds of weed stuffed in the trunk of a rental car with Arizona plates was uneventful. When he got to Denver, he realized that Jake's cousin was a fucking moron. His name was Charlie and he didn't know the first thing about growing weed.

He was, however, loaded with money he made selling his father's ranch on the plains east of Denver. There were almost six-hundred houses on the acreage his father and grandfather had ranched cattle. Charlie figured he'd put his family fortune into the budding weed business in Colorado. He handed Phillip a $5,000 tip as soon as he pulled up, whether Phillip planned on staying or not.

"Look, I got you a nice hotel room downtown at the Monaco. You can stay there as long as you want. It's a nice place. Tomorrow I'll show you the dispensary and the warehouse. Jake said you'd need a big place with lots of power. We got it. All the legalities are handled, at least as much as they can be. We've got enough licenses to start growing a thousand plants and we should be able to expand from there."

Phillip shook his head. "Let's talk about all that tomorrow. Call me a cab and get this rental car returned."

The Monaco is the only place to stay in Denver, as far as Phillip was concerned. The suites are named after rock stars and it seems like the staff kind of looks the other way when underground rock stars like Phillip show up. Extensive cash tips always help. A hundred dollar bill left on the bedside table with a little note that says, "Thanks, gracias," can go a long way in helping the low wage maid overlook the fact that the mirror has been taken off the wall and there's a peculiar powdery residue all over it.

Phillip felt like he was at home when he walked in. The guy at the front desk waved in recognition.

"Mr. Johnson, nice to have you back with us. I see you'll be staying for an extended period this time. The room is booked up until the first of August. Let me know if there's anything I can do to accommodate you."

Phillip liked being treated like this. He deserved respect, and when people gave it to him he responded accordingly. He handed the guy a C-note in exchange for his room key.

Another thing he really liked about the Monaco was that each room had it's own programmable safe. Phillip locked away thirty thousand dollars in that safe. It was a duffel bag full of hundred dollar bills and it was his insurance.

He ate a handful of pills and collapsed into the soft bed. It had been a long drive straight through, and he had needed some help staying awake. Now he needed some help going to sleep. He popped a few pills and lied on the bed. It was seven o'clock in the evening and he slept for fourteen hours straight, until 9 a.m. the next morning.

Phillip woke up feeling different. He felt refreshed and balanced from the long night of sleep and was thinking along different lines than he had been. No matter how much success he achieved in his underworld operations, he always felt like a defeatist. At some point he was sure he would go to prison, piss off the wrong person and get shot, or just overdose on something. He fully expected his life to end while he was still young, like so many other people he had known. But he kept dodging bullets and kept staying alive. He wasn't even really young anymore.

It just happened.

Life always seemed filthy to him, and his perspective had gotten worse as he got older. Steadily, he gave up everything clean and pure he had ever known in himself. He snorted coke and smoked heroin and kept a religious pill habit. He ate

Burger King twice a week. From time to time he picked up a hooker, but mostly he got his sex for free picking up girls at the bar or at some party. He especially preyed on the young, unwitting college students from the University of Oregon. All he had to do was flash some cash or some coke and those girls were his.

He kicked them out in the morning, if he hadn't been able to the night before, and picked up where he left off on his pills. He was consciously trying to kill himself or just move onto the next real adventure.

Did he finally hit his rock bottom on the drive out to Colorado? Maybe he did. Maybe he could start all over again. Maybe this was his time and these mountains were his place.

The medical marijuana boom had just started. Thousands of people were signing up to get their cards every month. There would be countless people trying to cash in and get rich growing and selling weed that had never grown or sold weed before. Phillip had a head start. He could really come up and do it clean
and legal.

He called room service first and planned on calling Charlie after breakfast.

Before his breakfast even arrived, he had already decided to devote his energy, and his resources, into making this venture a success. More importantly, he was going to be cleaning himself up at the same time.

It was going to be hard work, and Phillip knew it. If he really hit the ground running, then maybe he could do it. He looked at the plate of bacon and eggs in front of him. He had ordered it and it cost $22. All he had eaten were the potatoes. He couldn't bring himself to eat the dead animals. He drank the organic orange juice and shook his head thinking of how dirty he had let his life become.

It was time to start something fresh.

He called Charlie, "I appreciate you letting me sleep in."

"Not a problem man," Charlie answered in a friendly and respectful voice. "You wanna get together soon?"

Phillip checked the clock on the wall, "Give me an hour or so to take a shower and let's meet up for lunch. You know the Water Course?"

"That nice vegetarian restaurant uptown? Yeah, I know the place."

"Yeah, I feel like eating something healthy. Meet me there around noon."

After he hung up the phone Phillip went to the bathroom. He opened his medicine kit, as he called it, and pulled out various bottles of pills and little bindles of powder. He looked at them all lined out on the counter, knowing exactly what each one was for and when he would usually take it. He fondled the little baggie of cocaine, knowing that generally he would begin the day with a bump and a Valium. It took the edge off.

He looked at himself in the mirror. He had his mother's brown eyes. They were sunken deep into hollow eye sockets.

Nothing had meant much to Phillip in a long time, especially himself. He had once been proud of his ability to move through his pathetic life and only put healthy food into his body. In a way, it balanced out how he felt about himself versus his lifestyle.

It made him feel better than the shady characters he was forced to deal with, and more like the people he really respected.

People like Nathan and Kale. Nathan was raising a family and Kale was a legitimate businessman. They were certainly doing better at life than he was. He hadn't seen them in a long, long time, it seemed.

Now, Phillip was here in Colorado, starting over again. He knew a few people and had connections scattered about the state, but it was nothing like the organization he had become intimately involved with in Oregon and California. He could start something fresh here, just for himself, using what he knew and still be true to himself.

He stopped just thinking about it and finally threw the pills and powders into the toilet and flushed. He closed his eyes and thought of himself and the power he had inside.

When he opened his eyes again, breathing felt like something new.

~49~

Women's brains are wired differently than men's. As humans, our brains are divided into two hemispheres. One side controls logic and reasoning, while the other dominates emotions. Women have a neural pathway connecting the two sides men do not share.

What this means for a woman is that she has the ability to logically examine her emotions. However, this also inhibits her from acting based on a completely logical foundation. Feelings are always tied into a woman's behavior. Whether something makes perfect sense or not can be completely usurped by how a woman feels about it. This may be the biological explanation for women's intuition.

Men, while being able to completely put aside feelings in favor of sound reasoning, become completely unreasonable when thrown into an emotional state. Nathan's emotions were dominating his life. Nothing made sense. There was no reason to anything. There was just this overwhelming feeling of wrongness permeating everything he did.

It came and went in waves, but it was always there. Sometimes the tide would come in so strong he would collapse where he stood. Other times it was just a faint swooshing in the background. It was always there. He was barely able to work.

There was this endless back and forth in his head. He hated her and was glad she was gone. He loved her more than anything and wanted her back.

He finally came to the empty house he had once shared with his family. There was still stuff in it, but everything was gone. Melody had taken what she wanted: most of the dishes, the good furniture, some tour memorabilia, the kids clothes, and her clothes. The house they had shared was a disheveled mess of broken dreams and unfulfilled expectations.

He knew he couldn't stay here.

He tossed his clothes into a box with a few other random things and then borrowed a friend's trailer. It took three trips to the landfill before everything was finally gone. He didn't feel any better. Nothing seemed to make him feel better.

He got an apartment of his own and went back to work.

No matter what happened he was determined to remain a good father to his girls. They were the most important thing in his life.

Melody and Nathan traded the girls back and forth, mostly on a week-to-week basis, but hardly spoke a word to each other. They both silently agreed to keep the courts out of their life and it was okay if they were still married on paper. It was just easier that way.

The last months of spring dripped away and summer began. Melody was still out partying constantly and Nathan got reports from their mutual friends that tore him up inside. She was giving herself away for free to random men who could in no way appreciate and love her the way Nathan did. It was cheap and she was so valuable.

Through many nights of anguish he finally came to the conclusion his heart demanded. He loved her, no matter what. It didn't matter if she slept with a hundred different men in one night, he would be there to hold her in the morning. He would love Melody for the rest of his life. There was nothing either of them could do to change that.

His mistakes haunted him. Why hadn't he listened? She had been on the edge, but still in love with him, when she asked him to go to counseling. Why hadn't he gone? He was too arrogant, too sure of himself, and so certain that the deep love they shared was enough to keep them together.

He didn't know just how far gone she was. It seemed sudden at the time, but with the perspective of hindsight he should've seen it coming. He should've done something to keep her. She was gone and he was empty.

If ever he got the chance, he would rebuild his family with her, but different. He would make sure she got enough time to herself. He would pay attention to her and what she wanted. He would tell her the truth about everything, even that fateful night in Tucson so long ago. There would be nothing that could separate them. If he ever got the chance.

They had shared so much together, so many stories, so many adventures, not to mention the births of their children. They had been so close. There was only one woman who could be the mother of his children and only one woman who he had traveled the country with when he was younger. He would do anything and forgive anything if only she would come back.

He found himself recalling those happier times with a nostalgic grin and no one to share it with. There were stories he couldn't share with anyone, like the time they'd snuck into the hotel pool somewhere on tour and made love in the shower. They laughed about that every time they took a shower together. He found himself thinking of that time whenever he showered, now by himself. It didn't help. So many mornings he woke from his dreams with the notion that she was lying beside him. The emptiness of the bed nearly destroyed him.

He was working steady and paying dear attention to those little girls because that was all he could do. Maia and Clarity came back to Melody's apartment telling stories of how much fun they had with their father. It made Melody happy to know that even though she had dismissed her husband she hadn't also gotten rid of Maia and Clarity's father.

They needed him. She certainly wasn't in any position to pay them the kind of attention they deserved. The years of being a stay at home mom had worn on her. Even though she loved her daughters deeply, she couldn't deal with being a mother. Not right now. Right now she needed to be simply Melody, the girl who had left her boring life behind in search of something more fulfilling. The last few years had been anything but fulfilling.

Nathan saw and quietly understood. He had assumed she'd made the same decision as he had when the girls were born. She hadn't. She was always going to be the same little girl who had expected a parade to go by everyday. No amount of added responsibility or external pressure could change that.

50

To dance is to be free of the normal constraints on the body. To truly dance is to also be free of the normal constraints on the mind. There was nothing Lucy loved more in life than dancing. She loved it so much that she approached her everyday life as a dance.

Life is hard. Lucy's life was hard. It started early. She never told anyone how her father sexually abused her as a child. From the time she was ten years old until her parents divorced four years later every day was nightmare. He would rape her, but say vile things about what a good father he was. It took years for her to come to terms with this. She had lost her virginity to her own father.

Maybe that was why she was always looking for love without the weight of sex. But those men that she truly loved, and never slept with, invariably disappeared. All she was left with were the ones she had sex with just because she could or maybe she thought it would make someone love her. Maybe she was trying to fix something.

Maybe some things remain forever broken.

However there were times in her life that were truly exquisite. She glided around her house some mornings, dancing while she fixed breakfast and tea for herself. Too often her days began with quickly getting dressed and rushing out the door to be a part of the dance she had created for herself in Humboldt, Northern California. She had a life here, between her many friends, her ganja business, and her dance troupe.

The dance of her life consumed so much of her time that her actual dance was suffering. She missed practices and rehearsals because she had to water, or meet somebody somewhere. She only found time to really dance at performances, and the last one the girls played a song she'd never heard and preformed a routine without her. Dancing with her troupe was the only thing she truly loved, but it also wasn't the same spontaneous dance that had moved her so long ago.

She needed to get back to something she had lost. For a minute she thought of Phish and how she had felt dancing at the shows. She was driving to her grow house with nothing on the radio. She thumbed through her iPod and put on a bootleg from '99. As always, the music transported her to a different time within herself.

She needed to get back to something and she knew it. Lucy wasn't one to avoid acting on impulses and she mentally started planning a trip to see Phish. She was smiling as she pulled into the driveway of the country house she rented but didn't live in. It was the home to hundreds of marijuana plants in varying stages of development, and lots of electric lights, fans, and water pumps. It had taken her years to get the place flowing smoothly. The hard work had paid off and she had twenty thousand dollars in cash she didn't need to touch to continue her operation.

Her mood instantly shifted when she saw the door to her house was kicked in and splintered where the deadbolt had been latched. A sinking feeling overwhelmed her as she walked in to see the devastation. Her mature plants in the flowering room were gone, hacked off at the stem. Some of her lights had been smashed in the process. The power was out in the veg room and the little girls were wilted and dying on themselves.

Everything was on timers and automated and Lucy hadn't been around since the day before yesterday. She was scared that whoever had done this would be back. They were probably dangerous and desperate people and she needed to get as far away from here as she could as swiftly as she could. She made a phone call to one of her friends in the business and offered him what was left of the equipment if he'd come and clean out the house. Then she stopped by her apartment in town, packed a small bag, and drove to the airport.

She needed so much more than a Phish concert and couldn't wait any longer for the summer dates. She was ready to explore something new and the death of her marijuana farm was the impetus she had been awaiting. Months ago she had gotten a passport, thinking it might be nice to get out of the country someday.

She booked a flight to India. There was a dance school outside of Mumbai she had been fascinated with for years. It was time to explore some serious depth to her dance and her life.

After she bought her ticket but before she could board the plane, her phone rang.

"Hey Moon. It's Phillip. How're you?"

Lucy laughed, "Funny you should call today. I just got everything ripped off and I'm leaving California."

Phillip lit up in expectation and hope, "You should come to Colorado. I got a real good thing going here and I could use your help. Also, I got tickets to Phish at Red Rocks this summer."

"Phish is playing Red Rocks?"

"Yeah, it's gonna be at the end of July, the first of August." He paused and listened to Lucy's breath on the far end of the receiver.

"Come with me," he said so firmly she almost melted. But Lucy had an excuse.

"I'm going to study dance in India." She choked back her desires and went with her original impulse. "I'm going to be gone for awhile. You should call Melody, she really wants to see Phish."

"Yeah, what about Natron? I only have one extra ticket for the first night."

"Her and Nathan split up, haven't you heard?"

" Really?" A sense of sadness; of expectation and hope came over him. "What's her number?"

Lucy passed along Melody's phone number to Phillip and then threw her cell in the trash.

She knew what she was doing.

She was living her own story.

51

Phillip looked at the slip of paper with Melody's number on it for a few days before he finally called her. It was around noon on Sunday and Melody was hungover.

Nathan was on his way to pick up the girls and Melody was tired of being a single parent. Their little voices always seemed to be pestering her for something. Their pleading for attention was an ice pick in her ears and her heart.

She loved her children, she really did, but sometimes she didn't have the patience for them. She felt guilty about it, lying in bed listening to Clarity wrecking the block castle Maia had built. They were both crying and she wished there were someone else around who loved them enough to intercede.

On top of it all, her phone was ringing.

She crawled out of bed and checked the number on her cell phone. It wasn't one she knew, but the 541 area code was familiar. Maybe it was Lucy.

"Hello," she finally answered on the fourth ring.

"Hi. Melody?"

"Yeah, who's this?"

"It's Phillip."

Phillip, the name took a minute to register.

"Like Phillip from Phish tour, Phillip?"

On the other end of the receiver he smiled at the tinge of excitement in her voice. He took a breath and smiled, resolving to be cool.

"One and the same. How you doin'?"

She audibly laughed, "Crazy, as usual. Just living, you know? What're you up to? Why are you calling me? How'd you get my number?"

"Lucy gave me your number. I called and invited her to come see Phish at Red Rocks with me. She couldn't come, but she said I should call you."

"Me? Are you serious?"

"Yeah, of course. I heard some shit went down with you and Nathan and I figured you could use some fun."

"You know I haven't seen Phish since '99. I don't have any money. I can't go."

"Then it's about time. You can come. I've got plenty of money. Have you heard any of the shows?"

"No, I've been living in a kind of dead zone as far as music is concerned."

"You should come check it out. I'll get your flight and everything. Just come. I want an old friend to hang out with. The band sounds better than they ever have. Trey's happy again and sober, too. The whole scene is wicked cool."

She smiled when he said "wicked." It made her think of home.

"Of course I'll come with you," she said happily.

At the sound of their mother's happy voice, Maia and Clarity sorted things out in the other room and went about playing together. This gave Melody a chance to focus on her conversation with Phillip.

"Wow it's great to hear your voice again," she said. "It takes me back. So much has happened since we all lived together."

"Tell me about it," Phillip spouted. "I've been a success and a fucking mess all at the same time."

"Weren't you always a fucking mess of a success?" She laughed.

He laughed with her.

"Yeah, and little-miss-too-good-to-sell-nitrous is divorced with two kids and working in a bar from what I hear."

There was a silence. The ice was broken.

"So, what happened?" Phillip asked.

"You mean, between me and Nathan?"

"Yeah. I mean, you guys were great together."

"We were great together. But then we weren't. People change. Things change. It got to the point where being around him just made me feel awful. It was like we were opposing forces and anytime we got near each other we either treated each other like shit or just ignored each other. He wasn't even sleeping in the same bed with me for the last year."

"So you left him."

"I did, but he gave up long ago."

"How'd he take it?"

"He fell apart, actually. I was surprised. I thought he'd be happy."

"Why would he be happy losing a woman like you," Phillip dropped the first hint of what he intended.

"I'm not the same woman I used to be."

"Oh yeah? Are you a bad girl now? Wanna come hang out with a bad boy?"

"I've got a few bad boys to hang out with already." Melody always did know how to deflate Phillip's ego.

"Well, I'm not trying to be a bad boy anymore. I'm cleaning it up, going legal."

"Yeah?"

"Sure, why not. I mean, I should probably be dead or in prison by now, but I'm still going."

"Still going," Melody repeated.

"Still going," Phillip said again. "It's hard to believe sometimes."

"I know," Melody said. "It's like I just keep waiting for some other catastrophe to happen."

"See, I think that's some kind of fucked-up implanting that's happened to almost everyone. We're supposed to believe the whole world is going to end so we keep manifesting it in our own little worlds."

"Right. We had our own Armageddon over here a few weeks ago, but then it just keeps on going. Nathan keeps saying he can't live without me, but he's not dead yet. It's like tour, you just keep going to the next show."

Phillip carried out her thought. "Of course, it's easy to get lost and lonely and confused between the shows."

"Oh God Phillip, I'm so lost and lonely and confused." Now Melody was crying again.

Phillip said the only thing that made sense to him.

"If you get confused, just listen to the music play."

She laughed through her tears.

Melody was excited at the prospect of what Phillip was offering. Her life, as she saw it, was just about to start again. Two more months. Two more months and she would get to see Phish again. She would get to dance again. She would get to be free and happy again, even if it was only for four days.

"What are you thinking about?" Phillip said from the other end of the line.

"I'm just imagining what it's like to dance at a Phish show again and to feel free and happy. I've felt trapped and sad for so long."

"Yeah, there's nothing like going to a show." Phillip said, "Sometimes I feel like it's the only reason I'm still alive. It's like my life is just a constant struggle between those moments when I'm at a show and the music just lifts me to that other place. I can't seem to find that any other way."

"Right," Melody certainly understood what he was saying. "I tried doing Yoga, and it's fun, but it doesn't get me to that same place the music sometimes can. It's like the only time everything seems right in the world."

They talked until the doorbell rang. It was Nathan. Melody didn't tell him she had just been talking to their old friend.

52

The end of July finally rolled around and Melody boarded a plane bound for Colorado. She kissed her daughters goodbye and dropped them at Nathan's house. She waited just long enough to see him open the door and drove off before she had to see the forlorn look in his eyes.

While she was on the plane, Phillip was suddenly met with a kink in his plans.

"Fuck," Phillip said over the telephone. "Are you serious?"

"Yeah, I'm serious," Charlie said. "What can I say, those tickets are like gold. People are trying to trade their children or a kidney to get one. I was lucky to get you and me a whole set."

"Yeah, but I got this girl coming up and she was expecting to get to go to all the shows. It means a lot to her."

"Sorry, man. My hands are tied. I'm not giving up my tickets, but you can give her yours if you want."

Phillip laughed. He was still Phillip. "Shit man. This girl is old school family and hasn't been to a show since '99."

Charlie thought about it. Phillip had helped him out a lot, and done so without being an asshole. Charlie knew his business wouldn't be succeeding if it weren't for Phillip. When medicinal marijuana caught on in Colorado, dispensaries opened everywhere and grow operations doubled or tripled in volume. No one knew what they were doing or what the laws were. Charlie had learned a lot about law in general from his real estate lawyers and knew there had to be loopholes to this whole medical marijuana thing that could make him some more money. The same firm had no problem backing him in this venture by outlining the grey areas he could operate in.

Everything was quasi-legal, profitable, and expanding.

"I tell you what," Charlie said. "I've got some other things I should be working on tonight anyway, so I'll hook you up with my ticket for tonight. How's that?"

"That's awesome, man. I can work with that. How about that molly? Were you able to score any?"

"Of course. Who do you think you're talking to."

"Thanks, man. I just gotta say, things have been working out so amazingly well between us. I really appreciate you."

"I really appreciate you, too. That's why I'm doing this. I'll drop off tonight's ticket and some molly in about an hour."

There was a knock on the door.

"Gotta go," Phillip said.

She was standing there. She was really standing there. Her sandy hair had grown out to her chin since she cut her locks off. Her deep-green eyes were glowing with happiness at seeing Phillip. It made him feel ten feet tall.

"Come in," he said.

She bounced into the room, simply oozing joyful exuberance. She hadn't felt like this in years. "Hi!" She exclaimed and gave him a big hug. The bellhop came in behind her with a small bag and set it in the closet. Phillip tipped him a twenty.

He couldn't start in right away with the bad news about the tickets. Instead, he gave her another hug and felt her soft, warm body next to his.

Melody was equally enthused with the contact. There was nothing behind it. No dreadful history of bad feelings and mistakes, just a warm shared past and an understanding that neither of them were perfect. Being with Phillip was already shaping up to be the naughty adventure she had dreamed of.

"Did you get the molly?" she asked.

"Of course. It's on the way."

"Wee-hee!" she said, clapping her hands. "This is going to the best show ever. The best shows ever!" She emphasized the plural and Phillip winced inwardly. He still wasn't prepared to tell her. Maybe he could just score some tickets on the side and she'd be none the wiser.

They sat on the couch in Phillip's plush suite rehashing over past times and recalling their favorite Phish moments. Phillip had a lot to tell Melody. So much had happened in the ten years she missed. There were as many highlights as there was darkness. Some of the music had been pretty bad, and the scene had decayed as the band was getting sick of playing. The breakup and the last major festival, Coventry, were both a messy, muddy, fiasco.

"But there were some sick shows along the way. You should've been there."

Melody shook her head, a smirking smile on her face, "I'm here now."

Eventually Charlie showed up. Phillip introduced him to Melody with no reference. "This is Charlie," he said. Charlie shook hands with Melody and they nodded at each other. Then Phillip and Charlie went into the other room. They were in there for a few minutes of hushed conversation. Then Charlie came out, told Melody "bye," and left.

"Come in here," Phillip called from the other room. He was sitting on the bed with a baggie of white powder. "This is the shit," he said. "Graphite. Ecstasy as pure as it gets."

"Well, let's do some then," Melody laughed. "Just a little, though."

Phillip licked his finger, dipped it lightly in the molly, and offered it up to Melody. She laughed and licked the ecstasy off his finger. Then Phillip took his own. It had been a long time since he had tasted that lovely metallic tinge of good drugs. It set his mouth to watering. He took another dip.

"Let's smoke a bowl," Melody said. "Then I wanna go to the lot. It's already almost five-thirty. When's showtime? Can I see my ticket?"

Phillip was reeling from the molly, just from the taste of it, since it certainly couldn't have already kicked in. He was glad to be able to produce her

Thursday night ticket without thinking.

"We've still got time," Phillip said and patted the bed next to him. "They won't go on until just before sundown."

Melody shook her head. She certainly didn't want to jump into bed with Phillip within the first half-hour of seeing him. "I really wanna go to the lot," she smiled and he couldn't resist. He phoned the front desk and told them to send for a cab.

By the time the cab came, the molly was starting to kick in. Melody's mouth was slightly dry, her stomach was starting to tingle, and her arms and legs felt like they were floating. Phillip put his arm around her and sighed, leaning back in the seat next to her.

"Whew," he said. "I'm starting to feel really good." It had been months since Phillip had been high like this. He was already thinking about being higher. He pulled out the baggie, took another dip and offered it to Melody. She turned him down, "I don't want to get too wasted right away."

He was already thinking of finding some cocaine on lot and maybe a couple Valium or a Xanex or something for later. They arrived on lot and Phillip fell out of the cab after Melody. She was smiling and clapping and jumping up and down. Phillip put his sunglasses on and concentrated on his wavering equilibrium.

They strolled through the lot, Phillip saying ,"What's up," to a number of people he knew, or thought he knew. He was talking business with a dread from Boulder when Melody started screaming. Phillip jumped and turned around. Then he smiled. Sure enough, Melody was locked in a deep and meaningful embrace with Jessica.

"I've been wondering about you so much," Jessica said as she held Melody by the shoulders, looking her over. "You look good," she said.

"I feel good," Melody said.

Jessica smiled, "That's good," she giggled. They hugged again.

"Oh momma, it's been so long," Jessica said. "I wasn't sure I'd ever see you on a Phish lot again."

"I didn't think I'd ever be here."

"You have tickets, right?" Jessica asked.

"Yeah, totally."

"That's good, because I've never seen anything like this before. People are selling tickets for like $300 or more, and getting it. Plus, there's hardly any extras floating around at all. How did you get tickets?"

"Phillip got them for me."

"No shit, where is that fucking dirt bag."

Phillip told the dread he'd see him around and stalked over towards the ladies. He adjusted his flat-bill cap and pushed his shades up.

"How you doing, Jessica?" He crooned.

"Amazingly good, Phillip," she said as she gave him a hug. "You got any more of that molly you're ridiculously high on?" They all laughed and he pulled his baggie out.

"For you, gorgeous? Anything."

"Aww, your so sweet," she said as she took a dip of the ecstasy. Phillip took another and offered it to Melody.

"I'm alright," she said. "Wanna go for a walk?"

"I'm stuck here." Jessica said as she waved her hand over the articles of clothing she had hung on the back of her Forerunner for sale. "Give me your cell number and I'll call you in a minute. I gotta wrap some things up here. I'm gonna try to sell some of these clothes, but I wanna dance with you guys tonight. Kale's not here."

"Really," Phillip was disappointed. "Why?"

"Well, not everyone's a big-time baller like you Phillip. We didn't have enough money and we could only find one set of tickets anyway. I'm selling clothes so it doesn't cost too much. Anyway, he got to go to New Orleans by himself back in the Spring for Jazzfest, so this is my trip."

"Hey, you got any of those sick hoodies you were making before?" Phillip asked.

"Not the patchwork ones anymore, "Jessica laughed, "But I got some nice stuff. I got a black hoodie with this sick Carini stencil on it that would fit you perfectly."

"I'm gonna hang with Jessica for a minute," Phillip said. "You'll be back, right?"

"That's cool," Melody said. "I wanna get some water, go pee, and walk around for a minute. You guys will still be here, right Jess?"

"Right here," she said.

"Cool, I'm just gonna walk up to the Trading Post. I'll meet you down here in a little bit or I'll call and we'll definitely all dance together tonight."

They traded numbers and went their separate ways. Melody pushed uphill on her gelatin legs, just high enough to be feeling really good, but not so high as to be outside of herself. It was a wonderful summer day and the hot mountain sun was occasionally shaded by white, fluffy clouds.

The lot was different than Melody remembered it. Hardly anyone was set up selling anything and the crowd didn't appear as disheveled as she remembered it. There weren't as many dreadlocks and there was only one loud young hippie wearing patchwork and a tie-dye. People steered clear of him. He was handing out pamphlets for something called "The Twelve Tribes," and inviting people to come check out their bus.

Melody laughed to herself. All the tour kids were in their thirties, had cut their locks off, and probably gotten involved in something else for most of their time. Just like she had. The tour kids had grown up, sort of, she giggled.

At the top of the path that leads from the bottom lot of Red Rocks to the Trading Post, Melody spied a young family working with a cooler of water.

"Ice cold water. One dollar," the dusty little boy happily called while his dreadlocked mother and father looked on with a smile.

"I'll take one," Melody said and the boy's mother

took her dollar, smiled, and handed her a cold bottle of water.

Melody cracked into the plastic container and felt the cold water wash through her sticky mouth. "It's hot out," she said to the young family.

They all three nodded in unison. The little boy went back to advertising the family business. Melody walked on, unable to shake the comparison of that family to her and Nathan in their best days. Why hadn't they just taken the girls on tour? She sighed. Would that young family still be happy and free in five years? Ten?

Maybe so. Maybe not.

As soon as Melody stepped away from the family, they were accosted by some cops who confiscated their cooler of water and told them to "Get lost." Melody couldn't believe it. She knew they were hard on vending at Red Rocks, but this was too much. She watched, entranced by the sickening drama as the cops confiscated the entire cooler of water, but at least they sent the family walking away.

Melody strolled over to the Trading Post shaking her head. A group of people were gathering around and she wondered what was happening. When she came out of the porta-pottie, a slim guy with a neatly-trimmed dark beard was standing on a big rock overlooking the small gathering of people.

"Can everyone hear me?" He asked.

Most of the crowded nodded.

"Okay, so this is the first meeting for the green crew this weekend. If you're not on green crew, you need to leave."

A few people straggled away, but Melody decided to stick around. She had been involved with the green crew some on Panic tour. They stuck around and helped pick up the mess in the parking lot afterwards. She'd done it before and gotten free tickets out of the deal.

"Okay, the rest of you. We've only got a limited number of tickets, so not all of you will be getting in every night. Tonight's list is as follows. When I call your name, come and get your ticket." He called a list of about a dozen names and happy people danced through the crowd to get their magic piece of paper.

"So listen, if you got a ticket that means I expect you to show up tonight and pick up garbage. If you didn't get a ticket, then show up tonight and maybe tomorrow will be your night. Meet right here about thirty minutes after the show. If you're here, and you pick up garbage, you're going to be much more likely to get a ticket the next night. I'm paying attention. Everyone have a good show."

"Hey Melody, is that you?"

She turned to see who was calling her name. It was an old acquaintance from Panic tour, Half-Moon. He had cut his locks off like everyone else and had his arm around a very attractive dark-haired girl. Melody also noticed he was wearing a backstage laminate.

"Half-Moon, good to see you." They gave each other a hug.

"Are you doing the green crew?" Half-Moon asked.

"I don't know. Maybe. I already have tickets, but I don't know what to do with myself at a show when I'm not vending. I was just checking out the meeting." She laughed.

"Where's Natron?" Half-Moon asked.

Melody felt a pang in her chest, "Oh, we split up."

"Are you serious?" Half-Moon was baffled. "What the hell for? I always thought you guys were perfect together."

"Well, things change," Melody stumbled over her usual defense to this all-to-common statement made by her friends.

"It's none of my business anyway," Half-Moon said. "It's great to see you." Melody could tell Half-Moon was distracted and wanted to get going.

"It's good to see you, too," She said and he let go of the attractive woman on his arm long enough to give Melody a hug. Just then, the guy with the neat beard from up on the rock was walking by and Half-Moon flagged him down.

"Hey Craig," Half-Moon waved the guy over as he was making his way through the crowd.

"Half-Moon, what's up, man?"

They slapped hands together.

"Not much. I want you to meet my friend Melody."

"Hi," Melody said shyly and waved. Why was she here? She wanted to get back to Jessica and Phillip, and go to the show.

"Are you part of the green crew?" Craig asked. "I've never met you."

"No, I was just walking by and heard the meeting."

Half-Moon chimed in. "She used to do green crew for Panic back in the day. Hey, I gotta run." The introduction accomplished, Half-Moon strolled off again with his arm around the pretty, dark-haired girl.

"Well, if you want to help out, you could show up here after the show. There's always a lot of people at the meeting, when we give out tickets, and not so many when it comes to actually picking up trash after the show."

"Thanks," Melody said. "Maybe I'll see you later."

"I hope so, " Craig smiled as Melody flitted into the crowd.

53

"What a bunch of assholes!" Jessica was yelling to a group of cops walking away from her as Melody was walking up.

One cop in the group turned around and stalked back over to Jessica. "Excuse me, miss." His voice dripping with disdain. "Would you like to go to jail, next?"

"No sir," Jessica quoted, her head down.

"Good, now maybe you should go into the show. If you have tickets. You do you have tickets don't you?"

"Yes sir," she mumbled.

"Then I suggest you enjoy the show."

Melody held back for a minute, watching Jessica stomp around. Phillip was high. He was leaning against the back of Jessica's car with arms crossed, hat low, and sunglasses dark. "Fuck those pigs," Melody heard him mutter as she walked up.

"You can keep the money, Jess," Phillip said.

"What happened?" Melody asked.

"Those fucking pigs just took my brand-new 'Carini' hoodie," Phillip spat.

"They were being cool, and letting me set out some of my clothes way down here," she was hysterical. "But I had all the stuff with Phish lyrics or something on it in my car. They're mostly like gifts, or shit I could sell in the hotel or something. I needed to make some money on the lot with my other stuff. But that's it. I'm shut down for the weekend. They just happened to be walking by when I got Phillip's hoodie out of the car."

"That shit was tight, Jess. Totally worth $200. I probably would've paid $300 if you asked."

"I spent a long time on that thing. I kept thinking someone really cool would get it. Now, I'm fucking pissed those bitch-ass cops are walking away with it." Her eyes were watering and her fists were shaking.

Melody couldn't tell if she was about to cry or fight someone.

They all looked down the aisle at the group of cops harassing some kids with a cooler. One of the younger deputies looked back at them and smiled.

"Fucking bitches," Phillip muttered again.

Then he shook himself out of it.

"Fuck it. Let's eat some more molly and go to the show."

Melody and Jessica were both feeling their ecstasy just fine, but they took a little more at Phillip's insistence. Phillip took a little more than they did.

The hike up from the bottom lot took almost an hour. As the hill got steeper, they got higher. There were lots of stops to laugh and talk to people. They huffed and puffed their way to the upper lot and hung out at the bottom of the entrance ramp to catch their breathe.

"Shit, I'm ready to go in. I wanna see me some Phish," Phillip said and started walking again.

"Maybe we can still get a good seat," Jessica smiled.

It was a giggling parade of hilarity as Melody and Jessica weaved their way through the terraced seating of the lower aisles of Red Rocks. Phillip drifted along in their wake. Eventually they found a spot complete with satisfactory views of the stage and ample dancing space.

Without bravado or introduction the band made their way onto a stage they had been banned from for close to fifteen years. The opening notes floated through the mountain sky, divided by the massive rocks on either side of what may be the greatest concert venue in America, and maybe even the planet.

After Trey's first mellow solo, the band paused to soak up applause and to give everyone the opportunity to appreciate their surroundings in the setting sun. Melody couldn't believed how polished the band sounded. As she danced to that familiar guitar sound she felt herself jumping off the rocks and into space. The band really came in, and she turned to Jessica and smiled. Jessica reached over and hugged her. They hollered as they danced together. Phillip nodded along to the rhythm behind his sunglasses and the glaze of ecstasy over his eyes. All he knew was that this felt good.

The whole crowd was moving. Phillip looked first at Melody and Jessica dancing, then turned to take in the crowd behind him. He nodded approvingly and shook hands with the man directly behind him. This was something everyone hed needed for a long time. It was clean, open, and bright. There had been too much darkness in Phish's recent past.

They went into a new song and Phillip was sure they were saying, "Don't be the only one left on the lot."

Phillip shook his head and returned to the present. There was an ocean flowing in his veins and salt in his tears. He was still alive and two beautiful women were dancing next to him and singing along with the band. He dipped into his pocket, felt his stash, then felt his stomach turn. He left the baggie there and kept bobbing on the surface with the music.

The evening went spectacularly. During the first set Melody had her poor heart stolen once again and felt winds blowing differently than ever before. The feeling of being connected and disconnected to everything at the same time coursed through her as she danced.

She had found her voice again, singing along as it always had behind everything she did. Song after song was vibrating through her heart and tearing away the clouds that blocked her understanding.

Why did hearing this music do this for her? It made no sense, but she was sure of it. She was relaxing into her subconscious.

"Hey guys, we're gonna be back in about fifteen minutes. Thank you."

Melody jumped up and down screaming, Jessica alongside her. Phillip clapped and smiled. What a set.

"Whew," Melody exclaimed and looked around, rubbing her hands together and checking out the joyous expressions on the nine thousand faces around her. Melody could think of only one place where it was possible to be surrounded by so many people filled with such carefree happiness. No matter what was wrong with life or the world, everything was always alright during the show.

She looked down at Phillip who was reclined on the rigid concrete and lumber benches. He looked as comfortable as a person could be, smiling and nodding his head along to the beat of the set break music.

Melody tapped Jessica on the shoulder and directed her gaze towards the lounging Phillip. Jessica laughed and nodded at Melody. An understanding was passed between them. They each sidled up to Phillip, Melody on his left and Jessica on his right. They put their arms around him and rubbed his back. His already manic grin exploded to such an extent that Melody and Jessica burst out laughing.

"This sucks so bad," he said with sarcasm dripping from each word. "I fucking hate Phish."

"They're lyrics don't make any sense," Jessica joined in smiling.

"None of them can sing," Melody giggled.

"And they just noodle away on their instruments." Phillip stated, flatly.

"The only reason anyone goes is for the drugs," Jessica raised her eyebrows at Phillip. He smiled, dipped into his tunic, and dangled his stash.

After taking a little more ecstasy, they made their way to the little-used public bathrooms and the concession stand at the very bottom of the venue. Phillip bought everyone a few beers and a few bottles of water to share, and the little troop of three marched their way back to their seats. The molly was really kicking in now.

In the dark night, under the lights, everything was starting to look like fractals. The house lights went down and the stage lights came up.

"Ladies and gentleman, Mike Gordon." Trey introduced the bass player to the audience. Then he did it again, as Mike left the stage for a moment.

"You gotta love a guy who walks back off stage so he can be introduced again," Trey said to all of their friends in the audience.

Then the familiar opening riffs of "Mike's Song" rained into the audience. Melody, Jessica, and Phillip entered into a familiar space again. Their sarcasm from earlier seemed to carry on as they looked at each other and sang the first refrain.

"Trapped in time, and I don't know what to do. These friends of mine I can see right through."

And Melody could see right through herself as well. She walked through the hallways in her mind and discovered that she didn't really want a nice guy. She wanted a selfish asshole. Her gaze drifted back over to Phillip again.

She really didn't want a guy at all, that's what made a selfish asshole appealing. She didn't want a guy to look at her and think, "There's my girl." She wanted to be her own girl. She needed to, and that's what the voice inside of her was singing.

She looked at Phillip and thought about her silly fantasies of the two of them. She desperately needed to fall in love, but not with anyone else. She needed to fall in love with herself and her life again.

Trey took an extended solo on the guitar and Melody drifted into the sound. It was nostalgic and progressive at the same time. Phish was still intact, while Panic had lost Mikey and their music just hadn't been the same since. Panic's guitar sound was different and Melody had found herself barely able to fly in those later years of tour; all except that last New Year's show.

This guitar sound, as Trey led the audience through a sonic journey, was reminiscent of what she had known, would know, and how she would get there. She lost herself in the music and the lights. Everything around her was in tune with this triumphant song. There wasn't a shade of darkness to any of it.

Everything was bright, and happy. Melody drifted on the sweet, subtle notes of "I Am Hydrogen." Phillip passed her a water bottle. She drank and they smiled at each other. The bass led them into "Weekapaug Groove" while Phillip danced with Melody, singing along the words, "Try to make a woman, that's your move."

They shared the groove together.

Part of what makes a Phish show meaningful is the acknowledgment of the darker side of the universe. Life isn't all sunshine and gumdrops, and neither is the music of Phish. After the fervent jam of "Weekapaug Groove," they settled into a slinking, familiar groove.

"What song is this?" She asked Phillip.

"Ghost," he replied ominously.

The ghost for Melody was Nathan. She could feel his silhouette as she danced along to the funky song. This was her big secret. Maybe she just stopped needing him as much as once before. But maybe, he was still with her.

Looking at Phillip dancing next to her and she knew she hadn't told him everything. There was a story to this ghost that would haunt her forever. She had really loved Nathan, at one time. She had given him every little piece of her heart and now she didn't. It was a strange thing, to have loved someone so intensely and to now feel hardly anything for them. It made her feel hollow. The music reverberated through her emptiness. Phish got spooky and held onto it for an almost twenty minute rendition of "Ghost."

Melody was disconnected from herself now. She floated through her memories, led by the guiding light of the music. Was this really worth it? She had torn apart her family, made her children cry, and broken the heart of the one man who she had ever really loved just to be here unfettered. How selfish was that?

Near the end of "Ghost," she was ready to run and hide and never come out again. Somehow, she just kept dancing and worked through her fear. She was on her own now, there was no other option. She couldn't go back. She didn't love Nathan anymore. Near the end, Phish got silly with it. Paige assaulted them with whatever strange noises he could find in the database of his keyboard. Melody found herself laughing at her own seriousness. This was supposed to be just fun, right?

The song morphed and suddenly they were on to the next thing. A chinsy "Wolfman's Brother" broke the spell and Melody was able to stagger away on her own and find the bathroom again. When she came back, they were still chugging through the same number. Finally it came to an end and there was space in the music.

Then the sweet and subtle sounds of one of Melody's favorite songs drifted through the air. Sometimes, Phish can be truly beautiful.

"The shoulder that I leaned on was carved out of stone. But when I'm done freezing I wanna be alone." Melody tearfully sang along with, then closed her eyes and disappeared into the odd time signature of "Limb by Limb."

They were singing directly to her. "Left the route my walking takes. Left alone with my mistakes. Up against a person who up 'til now I never knew."

The person Melody hadn't known up 'til now was herself.

"Up and down, it's up to you."

She would decide where she would go from here.
"Up from hell the answer blew."

She knew that very soon she would be taken far away. There was a song being sung off in the distance, if she could just become a part of it. She could feel the awful weight she had collected, and all of it washed away. Lingering slowly, then melting away.

The song ended and there was a pause. When the next song began, it was with the same earnest grace that flowed through "Limb By Limb," only more heartfelt.

"Softly sing sweet songs."

Now she found herself swaying back and forth, one arm around Phillip and the other around Jessica. The anxiety of leaving her family melted away with the honest notes of the song. She was exactly where she was supposed to be. Phillip chose this time for another dose of molly. He offered some to Melody and Jessica, who waved it away and continued swaying with the music. They were as high as they needed to be.

Phillip took a little and melted further into himself. While Melody was on a journey of introspection, Phillip was avoiding any pressing issues on himself. He had quit using everything, but here he was again on familiar high ground. Why was he so entranced with using drugs? Why couldn't he moderate himself?

The next tune began after a small pause and a wash of applause. Jessica looked over at Melody and smiled. "This is our song, " Jessica whispered into her ear.

Melody looked at her quizzically, "I don't remember."

By now Trey was through the first verse and into the chorus. Jessica looked Melody in the eyes and mouthed the words to her, "It got away."

There was a flash and then Melody remembered. "I don't think I'd even know you if it weren't for this song," she smiled at Jessica.

"That's probably true"

The tempo picked up and the girls joined into a dance. There was genuine love between them. Melody was reaching out to her strongest female friend.

Jessica felt sorry for Melody. She knew, from firsthand experience, how fragile Melody was at that point. Stepping away from a familiar reality is a difficult task to begin and one that isn't completed in one step. Melody had left Nathan, but Jessica knew that was just the beginning. Soon, if she hadn't already, Jessica was sure Melody would be offered traps to fall into that appeared like the easy way out.

Finding direction is one of the hardest things in life to accomplish, especially for people who spent their formative years in a directionless quest across America in search of something they weren't even sure existed.

As the elusive sounds of the "Squirming Coil" drifted into the cool night air the band stomped into an old song with only four words separating it from being an instrumental. Melody, Phillip, and Jessica pounded their fists and sang along. "David Bowie," was their chant to accompany the strange mix of emotions floating through the air: elation, sorrow, acceptance, and gratitude.

Melody felt oddly at home within herself. In spite of everything that had gone so wrong with her family, her prospects for making a livelihood, and her ambitions for herself and her children, she was somehow at peace with herself. She had been here before. It had been too long.

As she danced, she swore to herself to never go so long without indulging in the selfish act of letting everything go for an evening to dance with the honest woman that lived inside of her. She shook off her outer skin and Phillip couldn't help from eyeing her and seeing how beautiful the years had made her.

She wasn't the doe-eyed little girl he had met so long ago. This was a woman to be reckoned with and Phillip was a little scared of her.

While Melody exited the situation by immersing herself completely in the present moment, Phillip was fretting over how he would tell her about the tomorrow's tickets.

As suddenly as it began, the music was over. An empty space hung in the air that begged to be filled with the screaming voices of the nine-thousand civilian casualties in the audience. After a few minutes of reverie, the band returned for another song.

The Rolling Stones are sometimes credited with giving birth to rock and roll as we know it. They may have been the first suburban white kids who felt bonded into slavery enough to express the same kind of musical frustration as their darker-skinned counterparts from the ghettos of the world. Their music is still immediate and relevant today.

When Trey sang the first refrain to Loving Cup, "I'm the man from the mountain," it was as if the song were meant just for this band, in this place, at this time. Melody let go for one more time, content in the knowledge she had tickets to cover three more nights of this enjoyment.

54

Melody came to a decision before the encore ended. She didn't want to rely on Phillip for her tickets. She didn't want to rely on anyone other than herself. The house lights came on after the band left the stage and the small group of friends mingled with the crowd around them for a minute. Everyone was very pleased with the show.

Phillip was high as a kite. Melody looked at him, saw him fumbling around, and even though she felt a definite attraction for him, she didn't want to be in his pocket, either.

"Hey Phillip," she said. "I just want to thank you for the ticket tonight, but I'm going to take care of myself for the rest of the nights."

"How're you going to do that?" Even though he didn't have the tickets he'd promised her, he still wanted to comply. He wanted to bring her back to the Monaco and see what she looked like naked in his bed.

"Green crew," she answered flatly. "I don't want to feel like I owe you anything."

Jessica nodded in agreement, "That's cool. It feels good to be in charge of yourself."

Phillip just shrugged, "Whatever. You can stay here and pick up trash if you want, but I'm heading back to the Monaco to eat the rest of this molly and maybe find some coke. You sure you don't wanna come with me?"

"Maybe I'll meet you later," Melody said.

"I've got a room at the Motel 6," Jessica informed her. "There's two beds and no one is staying with me."

"Maybe," Melody said. She was high, and felt there was something else she needed to do. "I'm gonna head down and meet the rest of the crew. I'll catch up with you guys later."

She hugged her friends, congratulated them on a good show, and then made her way down to the

Trading Post. The parking lots were already starting to filter out and a small gathering had collected near the rock Craig had given his speech from.

Some of the people gathered to help pick up trash had the same wide-eyed stare that Melody had. They were pretty high. Finally Craig showed up and started handing out trash bags, explaining the procedure. He nodded at Melody, acknowledging her presence.

"Okay, so obviously there's not as many people here now as there were at the meeting earlier. We're going to have to make it work. We'll split up into different groups and we'll all tackle a different lot."

Melody joined the group destined for the bottom lot. They fanned out at the top of the lot, per Craig's instruction, and made their way as a group downhill. Everyone carried a bag and picked up the trash within ten yards of the swath they chose to cover. By the bottom, Melody had collected about half a bag worth of trash, also finding an abandoned sleeping bag amongst the rubbish. She decided to keep that. Looking behind her, the lot was now surprisingly clear. It took about 45 minutes in all. They threw their bags in the dumpster and then Melody found herself alone on the lot.

She thought about her next move. She could call Phillip and join him in his debauchery at the Monaco. She could call Jessica and sleep on the available bed in her room. There was also a third option, and it was the one she chose to exercise. She grabbed the sleeping bag she had found and trekked off into the park, looking for a suitable place to spend the night.

Camping is illegal in Red Rocks Park, but without a car or a tent Melody was able to seclude herself amongst some bushes and standing rocks. She spent the night beneath the stars, watching them on their steady march across the night sky.

For some time she lie in the sleeping bag, still feeling the ecstasy and the reverberations of the music and understandings she had experienced that night. There was something genuinely right about where she was. She thought of Nathan and the girls and it made her sad, but she also felt a kind of acceptance that this was what she needed to be doing. She thought of Nathan's disdain for Phish, and though she had always silently agreed with him, she felt something different now.

The fact was that the first hiatus hadn't been the kind of break they needed. When they disbanded after Coventry, the whole thing was over. It took completely losing what they had to realize how precious it was and how badly they needed it.

From where Melody was lying, looking up at the stars, that made perfect sense. They wouldn't be here now, as happy and in the moment as they were, if they hadn't completely divorced themselves from being Phish for awhile.

Eventually she drifted into sleep, snug against the cold night air in the ground-scored sleeping bag. The morning came early and she made her way down a narrow foot trail that led to the town of Morrison, leaving the bag stashed amongst the rocks. Along the path she passed a water tower covered with the graffiti of hundreds of people who had been this way before. In town she had eggs Benedict with smoked salmon instead of ham.

Jessica also had a mellow evening after the show. She waited in her room for Melody to call and ended up talking to Kale on the phone for hours. She was upset at having lost the ability to make any money at the show, but Kale convinced her to not worry about it and to just enjoy herself.

Phillip, on the other hand, had the opposite of a mellow evening. He wandered around the hotel hallways, high on ecstasy, until he found some other kids who had rented a room and brought a lot of cocaine along. He threw money at them and they took the mirror off the wall and partied well past sunrise.

He felt a conflict of emotions at Melody not being there. Part of him was forever sad and lonely, but he was very capable of drowning that part beneath a mountain of drugs. He was glad he didn't have to share his cocaine with her, or bother with finding her tickets. The internal conflict of wanting to take care of someone and not caring about anyone besides himself could have rendered him some enlightenment if he could find a resolution, but the battle remained undecided as cocaine won the evening.

He staggered onto the lot a few minutes before showtime, alone and coming down fast. He was able to score some more cocaine on the lot as well as some LSD that would surely keep him up. He ingested the two reality-altering agents and made his way up the steep climb, fingering the ticket in his pocket.

Melody's contribution to the green crew the night before didn't go unnoticed. When Craig was passing out tickets that day, Melody was overjoyed to hear her name called. She had found a miracle in a lot full of scalped tickets. She looked around for Jessica and Phillip before the show, but never found them. Her cell phone was dead so she made her way into the venue alone and drifted near the same spot they had occupied the night before.

She kept scanning the crowd for her friends, but couldn't see them. One thing she noticed was a lack of really young people in the audience. Everyone seemed to be at least in their late-twenties, though most were in their thirties or older. It didn't seem to be such a young person's sport anymore and the thought of it made Melody a little sad. With some effort she finally spotted a couple under twenty.

She waved to them through the crowd. They saw her and waved back, their enthusiasm obvious. That made her feel a little better. This scene, and this music shouldn't end with Phish and Widespread Panic, like it didn't end with the Grateful Dead. Since the dawn of civilization there have been traveling gypsies making a circuit through the sedentary people. As usual, those stable people are baffled, excited, and a little scared by the nomads who roam the countryside.

Under the pretext of rock and roll, the people who needed this lifestyle had still found a way to make it happen. The thought of it not being available to the next generation made her sad. How long before another internal strife split Phish apart permanently? How long before the hardworking members of Widespread Panic just couldn't do it anymore?

There had to be another band on the horizon. People talked about STS9 like they might be it, but how could someone find the same kind of understanding in strictly instrumental music? Umphrey's McGee was also in line, but it seemed they were attracting the same older crowd as Phish and Panic. Maybe there was another band out there, playing dirty, empty bars and not being understood yet.

Finally, in the late afternoon, Phish took the stage. They settled into their places and without a word delved into the evening's festivities. Melody was instantly on her feet. They were playing her song, "Runaway Jim." There was a cool breeze whipping through the Rocks that distorted the sound some. Melody advanced on the stage, drifting through the crowd like only a person with no one in tow can maneuver.

The first set started off strong. Phillip was at the top of the venue, seated on the lumber and concrete, but still drifting through the air due to the combination of drugs, music, and ambiance. Jessica was dancing alone on the stairs, the only place with enough room to move as much as she needed to.

Melody stayed immersed in the crowd for the first three songs of the night. After a sick "Bathtub Gin," they devoted the sunset spot of the first set to a new song, "Time Turns Elastic." As soon as they began this song, Melody found herself looking around to gauge people's reactions. Phillip, sitting at the top chose this time to go to the bathroom and get a beer.

He tried to choke down a burrito from one of the venue operated food vendors, but found he couldn't get more than half of it into his stomach before it became completely unappetizing. It was the first thing he had tried to eat in twenty-four hours that wasn't a drug.

For more than 15 minutes the band trudged through their new song. Jessica stopped dancing and kind of felt bad for the band. Some kids next to her started laughing, calling the song "Time Turns Molasses." She could tell the band really wanted this song to work, but it just didn't seem to be the kind of thing that would ever untangle itself properly.

It was a noble effort, but it fell short. That's the problem with experimental music. Sometimes it fails. At least they were willing to try.

Finally the song was over and everyone found their way back during "Lawn Boy." The sky was glowing in the colors of sunset spiced with the pollution of Denver down in the flats below them. Clouds continued to gather and Melody was certain they were going to get rained on soon when Phish undertook "Water in the Sky."

It was enough to finally make her forget about the drudgery a few songs before. She danced under the clouds, in the wind, and a sprinkling of mist glistened on her as the water in the sky made it's way down to Earth.

By the time they got to "Split Open and Melt" the clouds split open and a downpour ensued. The song started in its usual vein of happiness. Friends scattered around the venue tried to dance in spite of the increasing rain. Halfway through the song, the rain became a torrential downpour. Phish tapped into the desperation the crowd was experiencing. The song entered into a darkness that it doesn't usually find.

Phillip was disoriented by the rain and the dissonance raging from the stage. He was extremely high and the water was very, very cold. Before the song and the first set were finished, he hightailed it down into the new visitor's center built just a few years ago. There's pictures and memorabilia down there from previous performances. There's a bathroom, a bar and grill that closed for the evening, and a small theater where a movie about the construction and history of Red Rocks played on repeat. It was heated shelter. There was also already half the audience squeezed into this ever-shrinking space.

The band screamed as the rain poured down. Jessica and Melody, in their respective spaces, focused all of their energy into dancing through the downpour. It was insanity. Phillip was feeling terribly claustrophobic packed so tightly into the underground structure with so many people.

Finally, "Split Open and Melt" came to an eerily dissonant ending and Melody and Jessica remembered the Visitor's Center at the same time. They made their way up to the top of the venue, scrambling in the chilling rain to find some shelter. Inevitably they made it. Jessica entered about two minutes before Melody.

There was a locomotive of voices echoing through the downstairs chamber where everyone crowded to get out of the rain. Melody jumped right in line for the restroom. Jessica was coming out and saw Melody standing there.

They were instantly laughing and talking and making plans to not get separated again tonight.

"I can wait for you to finish the green crew thing and give you a ride out of here," Jessica offered. "I got kind of lonely last night and I want to hang out tonight for sure."

The girls continued their conversation above the rising din of the crowd packed into such close quarters. More and more people were piling in.

Phillip had found a refuge. There was a handicap elevator that went between the landing where the entrance was and the lower level. He crawled into the elevator and thankfully shut the doors against the merciless roar of the wet crowd in such a tight space.

As the elevator drifted back and forth between the two floors, Phillip relaxed on the floor and pulled another bump of cocaine out of his stash. The next time the doors opened on the lower level, there was Melody and Jessica.

"Hey girls," he called to them.

They turned and saw him sprawled on the floor with white powder dripping feloniously from his face. His eyes were swollen red and bloodshot with a gigantic vortex for a pupil.

"Oh my," Jessica said. "Phillip, are you ok?"

"Excellent. Step into my office."

The girls joined him in the elevator and relaxed a little when the doors shut out the deafening noise.

"This is nice in here," Melody smiled at him.

Phillip rose (with obvious effort) from the floor of the elevator and gave both girls a hug.

"I'm sorry about last night. I don't know what happened," he said. "I just know I want to hang out with you two tonight." He held his arms out for a hug.

The three of them formed a huddle and Melody smiled to her friends, "I love you both and I'm so glad were here together."

Jessica shared her sentiments. "Some people, you just know are going to be friends for the rest of your life. I love you, too."

"You girls are awesome," Phillip mumbled.

They rode the elevator up and down a few times, finally noticing at the top that the rain had started to let up. The three friends made their way, arm-in-arm into the cold drizzle.

"I wish I had my hoodie," Phillip stated, frowning at Jessica.

"I wish you had it, too," Jessica frowned back.

The second set started with a very appropriate Phish song, "Drowned," which they often played after rain had passed. The rest of the set was pretty good, with a sick "Crosseyed and Painless," "Tweezer," and "Fluffhead." However, the show didn't seem quite as good as the previous night.

Melody, Jessica, and Phillip danced together for the rest of the show Phillip and Jessica waited for Melody to finish with the green crew. They were some of the last people off the lot that night. Jessica drove to the Monaco and they all three headed up to Phillip's room. The previous days exertion had finally caught up to Phillip. He needed help from Jessica's Forerunner into the hotel. Once in his room he removed his shoes, staggered over to his bed, and passed out.

Melody frowned, "I think at least one of us should stay with him tonight."

"He's probably fine, but you're right. Sleepover in Phillip's swanky room."

The girls stayed up laughing while Phillip snored in his bed. They pulled out the couch and found it quite comfortable. Melody was more than happy to be sleeping next to Jessica for the evening. In the morning the girls were awake before Phillip.

"I've got to get back to my room and get a change of clothes," Jessica said.

"Wanna get breakfast, first?" Melody asked her.

"I'd like to, but I need to save my money," Jessica reminded herself. "I'll call you before I head out to the show and see if you guys need a ride."

The girls parted ways and Melody watched TV and dozed until Phillip grumbled awake. He was hungover. His head hurt and his mouth was a desert. "Breakfast," the word crawled out of his throbbing head.

Melody laughed to see him in such a state. "On the phone you told me you were cleaning yourself up. You don't look cleaned up to me."

"Oh, I guess this was a reminder why I haven't been partying like that anymore. Hand me the room service menu. You want anything?"

"Sure."

Phillip ordered Melody a plate of bacon, eggs, and potatoes. He also got himself a full order of pancakes, a pot of coffee, and a half-gallon of orange juice. He ate Melody's potatoes as well as his own and some of the pancakes. Afterwards he felt kind of like a person again. He sat up in his bed and cleared the plates away.

"It's good to see you." He said to Melody.

She smiled back at him," It's good to see you, too."

"I feel like I haven't even been here this weekend," Phillip shook his head. "For some reason I thought I had to party just because it was Phish."

"I know what you mean." Melody smiled at him. "Sometimes I remember all the great times I had at Phish or Panic shows all fucked up on molly or something. But I also had some really great times completely sober. When Nathan and I used to do the kitchen," she winced at the memory. "I had to stay sober. There was no way to work the parking lot when we did too many drugs."

"There's a fine line," Phillip stated. "I've learned so much from my experiences with drugs, but I also use them to forget myself."

"Why are you trying to forget yourself?" Melody asked.

"I'm nervous about being with you. I haven't felt nervous about a girl since I was a kid. It's silly."

"Why would you be nervous about me?"

"Cause I really like you. I've had a crush on you since we first met, but I was with Lucy then. Also, I lied to you."

"What did you lie about?"

"I don't have your tickets."

"Really?" she smiled at him, her eyes lighting up. "That's crazy." She felt a tingling sensation thinking about discovering the green crew and the miracle of being able to get in the shows every night. It was destiny. There was no denying she had made the right decision to be here, and therefore been correctly on her path from the moment she left Nathan. This was supposed to happen.

"I don't need you to take care of me," Melody said, dripping with happiness at her own self-confidence. "And I don't really need to take care of anyone besides myself."

Phillip cocked his head at her, raising his eyebrows. "Damn, momma."

"What? I always thought I needed someone to be with me. I don't know, to justify my existence or something. I've never really been on my own. I mean, I've always had someone else's best interests in mind. First it was my mom and my sister, then Nathan and the kids. For the first time in my life I'm actually on my own."

" Are you really on your own?" Phillip asked. "I mean, how is Nathan doing with the girls?"

"Nathan's doing good. He was always a good father. I guess I'm lucky for that. He's not gonna disappear and leave the girls with me."

Phillip felt a stinging guilt as she spoke about his old friend Natron.

"Are you sure you're ready to give up your family?" Phillip asked.

"I'm not thinking in terms of giving up my family. I'm thinking in terms of gaining my sanity again and meeting myself as an adult for the first time. I mean, I can't really be a good mother if I'm always resenting them for not getting to be myself. I've got to figure out how to be myself first and I'm sure I'll be a better mother. Until then, Nathan's doing a great job taking care of the girls. They're better off with him right now, anyway."

It was somewhat disconcerting for Phillip to see this woman, who had always been a model mother in his judgment, suddenly seem willing to forsake everything she had once been to pursue some vague ambition.

It was a fascinating morning. Phillip told her about his business, his partners, and even his family. He told her about his wasted years and the feeling of worthlessness he had worked so hard to make a permanent part of his personality.

Melody told him about the duties forced on her as a wife and a mother. She reminisced back to her time on tour and wished she had been able to explore herself more, instead of instantly assuming the role of Nathan's partner. They both felt like they had missed opportunities and blown chances in their lives that they were facing again in the here and now.

It was inevitable that they would sleep together. There was no stopping it at this point. It wasn't desire that led Melody into Phillip's hotel bed, but more of a sense of taking chances. She'd always kind of wondered about Phillip and too many conversations with Lucy had left her with the sense that he was an excellent lover.

He didn't disappoint. The forbidden nature of what they were doing added a level of excitement. But it also added a level of guilt. Even though he was hundreds of miles away, Nathan was certainly in the room with them. Neither of them could forget him and they knew that what they were doing would tear him up inside if he ever found out.

They were taking the path of least resistance, experimenting with each other's bodies. Phillip had fantasized about Melody since they'd first met. Maybe it was the drugs, or Nathan's ghost, but for some reason Phillip couldn't finish.

They had sex for over an hour until he just stopped. There was no release for him. Melody, on the other hand, had been able to guide him to exactly the right spots. She did her own version of "Split Open and Melt."

Eventually, after another round of room service, Jessica called Melody's cell phone and plans were made to finally leave the comfort of the hotel room. Melody sighed. She knew instinctively that the surreal morning she had shared with Phillip would have trouble translating into the bright sunshine streaming through the curtains.

It was excruciatingly hot outside as Phillip and

Melody waited on the curb for Jessica.

"So what have you two been up to all day," she asked, nonchalantly.

"Not much," Melody said. "Just talking, hanging out. You know."

"You didn't!" Jessica whirled on them with such ferocity Melody instantly began blushing. "We're adults," she said in defense.

They all silently agreed to change the subject.

"Got any more of that molly?" Jessica asked Phillip. "I think I'm ready for a little more after last night."

"Sure," he passed her what was left of the bag. It was still a decent amount, enough for two (or maybe three) people to have a real good time.

Jessica took a little as she headed towards the highway bound for Red Rocks then passed the bag to Melody. Melody took a little, smiled at Phillip, and handed him the bag. He put it away without dipping into it at all.

The lot was scorching hot. Melody met the green crew again by the Trading Post. "Tonight's going to be a little different," Craig said. "You guys have been doing such an awesome job that there weren't enough tickets for everyone who deserved one. I've got a few here," and he called about six names. Melody's wasn't among them.

"The rest of you, we're going to walk in the stage door." This time he called Melody's name.

It was Saturday night and expectations were high. There was enough energy amongst the green crew that a foot race ensued up the mountain. Most gave out huffing and puffing early on, but Melody and some guy pushed themselves to the end. Melody came out ahead.

The guy who had given her the most competition managed to breathe out a question. "Damn, I jog every morning. How did you beat me?"

"Where are you from?" Melody asked, grinning.

"Cleveland."

"It's the elevation," she smiled.

They laughed as Craig and the rest of the crew caught up with them. They were escorted in the back door and turned loose into the audience. Melody met Phillip and Jessica right away, where they had planned on meeting.

Right off the bat, Phish threw down for this Saturday night at Red Rocks. A rocking "AC/DC Bag" was the opener and Melody and Jessica helped themselves again to Phillip's ecstasy. Phillip abstained. The music was enough for him tonight. It had been a long time, if ever, since he had been to a Phish show without the aid of some substance.

A scorching "Curtain" followed and Melody felt herself being taken away again as she sang along, "Please, we have no regrets." She was one of the thousands running along, chanting words from the song. Her life had run away from her and there was no getting it back. All she had was the insanity of the present.

After "Curtain," Phillip got to experience something he had been waiting on for years. They finally pulled "Mound" out of their pockets and dusted it off.

The tempo knocked back into as easy rhythm and the girls danced along to the nonsensical, easy feelings of "Gotta Jibboo." "Guyute" followed and everyone sang along as loudly as they could, "I hope this happens once again."

The rest of the set was relentless, culminating in an amazing "Run Like An Antelope" with the darkness of the mountains lit up by the fountain of music and lights flowing from between the rocks. Melody was exhausted by the end. She almost couldn't believe there was another set on the way.

She slumped into the chair and found that if she sat backwards, with her feet in the air, she was amazingly comfortable. Jessica fell into her and they laughed until their sides split.

"I'm having the best time with you," Melody smiled

at Jessica. Phillip watched approvingly from just slightly beyond the girls. They were the embodiment of happiness and innocence, both of which had been strangers to him for so long. Now they were here, next to him, and he was filled with a sense of glee. Nothing could be better than what he was experiencing with these two amazing women.

"Can we have some more drugs, Phillip?" Jessica asked.

He laughed, "Of course."

"You're not high at all, are you?" Melody asked.

"Nope," Phillip stated with a smile. "Not tonight."

"That's a first," Jessica giggled as he handed her the bag of ecstasy. They finished it off. "Do you think we could get some coke for tonight?" Jessica asked. "I wanna stay up late and come to the Sunday show hungover."

"I bet that can be arranged," Phillip chuckled. "And I'll probably join you on that adventure. I just don't think I can handle any hallucinogens right now."

They milled around, making plans for later, and then the band took the stage again.

Without a word Phish delved into history and came up with a cover of a Velvet Underground song. Despite all the complications, Melody found herself dancing to the rock and roll. This was the parade she had been looking for her whole life. This was the meaning, undiluted. She could dance to the music and it was alright.

Nothing else could have helped her at all. If it weren't for this fine, fine music she might have found herself on some other path, exactly like the path her mother had been on. She might feel lost and confused right now, but it was far better than being trapped. This was the way out. She could see herself clearly now, and knew what she had to do. After a ten minute instrumental jam that had Melody soaring through the stratosphere, she came down to sample something dirty again.

What she wanted was selfish and didn't take into

account the structures she had been building to encase her life. No one could responsibly support her in listening to the demons that were dancing in her head. She had been waiting too long for the time when she could finally say, "This has all been wonderful, but now I'm on my way."

Now, she was on her way.

Phish was the vehicle transporting her to this remembered freedom. She soared higher and higher through the jam on "Down With Disease" and found herself in another place when they finally landed. It was a funky acceptance of a new situation. After a long time on the funk riff, the band slowly drifted into a nothingness that flowed into the next song.

Melody found her peak for the weekend during the next moments. It was during "Free" that she finally found the feeling she had forgotten, the same feeling she had first discovered at Oswego all those years ago.

After that, it had been easy to disconnect herself from having expectations for an outcome to her life. She'd been able to look no further than the next show or even the next song. Her young life had been lived truly in the moment.

But as those moments piled up on her life, so had her expectations for where those moments would lead. She'd forgotten, and now she was remembering again. Expectation fell away and she was the same little girl she had always been, looking out the window for a parade. It was like swimming weightless in the womb of the world.

She left her body dancing in the stands and joined the greater consciousness that listens when we sing our songs. It had been too long since she had been there. Thursday night, she had knocked on the door, but tonight she broke through. Jessica, dancing next to her, could tell something was happening inside her friend. It wasn't a hard stretch for Jessica to understand, with Phish going off on "Free," that Melody was finally coming to terms with the extent of her personal freedom.

To lighten the mood, Phish returned to their slapstick humor and regaled the audience with the twisted tale of "Ester" and her evil puppet. Melody couldn't help but to laugh at the organ grinder's song.

However, in stark contrast to "Ester," the next one made her cry. She felt it coming with the opening whistle. When Trey sang the first words, "I'd like to live beneath the dirt," tears were already streaming down her cheeks. She was thinking of Nathan, and the push and shove they had been dealing with for so many years.

It made her sad and lonely to imagine what life might have been like if they'd just been able to stay true to each other and themselves at the same time. It made her sad and lonely to think of Nathan all alone in his apartment with the girls. Then she thought of her daughters and the unconditional love she felt for them. Hopefully, when they were older, they would understand why their mother had to leave.

She still had more leaving to do.

The tears washed her clean. She needed to cry like this, from the very depths of her soul. "Dirt" was the catalyst. As the guitar sailed through the wind, Melody found herself subliminally shouting her own name into the wind. From somewhere she felt a sense of peace and approval. She was living her own life now.

The ecstasy was flowing through her veins as Phish returned to a song Melody hadn't heard in years, but had once meant so much to her. "Harry Hood" carried flashes of previous songs from the evening. Trey slipped in the guitar riffs for "Dirt" and "Free" and Melody laughed when he did it.

Soon the music was flowing, the lights were just right, and Melody was feeling good. It was still okay just to feel good. All the responsibilities and weight of her life slipped away without effort as she danced. For fifteen minutes she was entirely in every second of her life. There was no desire to be anywhere else or with anyone else. There was only thanks for this joy and this moment.

Eventually, after touching on the darker side of things for a moment in the jam, Phish left the stage to a resounding applause. Melody and many others cheered completely through the break until they returned for an encore. To lighten the mood, John Fishman took the lead vocals and entertained the crowd with a song supposedly about his inability to perform sexually with a previous girlfriend. Poor John Fishman and his "Sleeping Monkey" got him sent home on the train.

The show ended with a bang. "First Tube" is one of Phish's most energetic instrumentals. For one last time that evening Melody let herself transcend what any words could possibly say. The rising crescendo and thundering rhythm of the song drove her to new heights.

Phillip watched her without looking away. She kept her eyes closed and flailed about to the dancer in her soul. As far as she was concerned, no one was watching. But someone was watching and he found himself falling in love with her.

55

"I've come to a decision," Melody said as they sat at some random bar in downtown Denver, trying to ride the high they had developed during the show.

"What's that?" Jessica asked over her cocktail.

"I'm going on Phish tour. After this is a show at Shoreline, two at The Gorge, one in Chicago, then four in the Northeast. I'll get a chance to see some shows and make my way back home at the same time. I haven't seen my family since grandma and grandpa died."

Phillip sipped on his beer, "How are you going to afford that? What are you going to do for work?" He smiled, "You could sell nitrous."

"I don't know yet. Not that. I'll probably get a cooler and some water to start. As long as I'm careful with my money I should have enough to make it to The Gorge even if I don't make anything at Shoreline."

"What about a ride? I mean, you don't have a car out here or anything?"

"I'll find a ride to the next show. That's not too hard."

"Well, Best of luck to you," Phillip raised his glass in a sarcastic salute.

Jessica laughed, "It sounds like a great idea. Have you talked to Nathan about it at all?"

"I haven't spoken to him since he picked the girls up before the shows. He left me a few messages. I just can't talk to him anymore. I suppose I'll call him in the morning."

"Are you sure about this?" Jessica asked.

"As sure as I've ever been about anything. I need more of this. I'm starting to feel like a whole person again, but one more show won't be enough. I need to know that I can do this by myself. I've never been on tour by myself."

She pointed at Phillip, "I was always riding with you or Nathan. I've never been my own person in control of myself. I need to know I can do it."

"You're capable of anything," Phillip said. "You just have to make it happen."

"Well, I'm going to make this happen." She took another drink from her cocktail.

"Well, I'm going to manifest some cocaine, then we should head back to the Monaco for the evening."

"I'm gonna head back to the Motel 6 and leave you two alone for the rest of the night," Jessica said as Phillip began his search amongst the crowd gathered at the bar.

"You can come with us," Melody offered.

"Nah, I just wanna get some sleep and get ready for the show tomorrow. I have to leave right after and start driving back to Chicago. If you do go on tour, make sure you call me before the show in Chicago. Kale and I already have tickets and if you're there, you better come out with us." Jessica gave Melody a hug and headed out to her car. When Phillip returned with a smile on his face he asked where Jessica had disappeared to.

"She just wanted to go to her hotel."

"Really? I thought it was her idea to stay up all night doing blow and go to the show hungover? Whatever. Let's get a cab and head back to the Monaco."

"Did you find some blow?" Melody asked.

"Of course. We can go back to the room, get high as kites and fuck all night long." He smiled but Melody winced. She really didn't want to get anything started with him, but the sex had been fun. What had happened earlier today may have been born of loneliness, but it had felt really good, physically. She was excited to do that again, but in his eyes she could tell he was hinging some sort of future expectations on her. She wasn't ready for anyone to expect anything from her.

"Maybe I'll go on tour with you," he added.

She wanted to scream, "No, you can't. This has to be me on my own," but she couldn't find the words.

She just nodded as they got into the cab.

They were dropped off at the doorstep of the Monaco. Phillip was giddy with excitement. He'd been sober all night and now he was hoping to indulge in two of his favorite things: cocaine and wild sex with a beautiful woman. He was walking backwards so he could talk to Melody, gesturing wildly as he explained to her how he felt during the show tonight. She was paying attention to him and didn't notice what was about to happen.

As Phillip was backing towards the hotel, two police officers were exiting the door. Phillip backed right into them. They were already angry about something and instantly sprang on Phillip. They held him to the ground, paying no attention to Melody who slipped by and watched from the lobby with a dozen other people.

The cops pulled the eight-ball of cocaine out of Phillip's pocket and slapped handcuffs on him. Melody slipped out the door again to hear them reading Phillip his rights. He did not choose to remain silent. Instead, he made eye contact with Melody and starting repeating four numbers over and over.

"Two, nine, one, four," he said. "Two, nine, one, four."

"Shut the fuck up," one of the cops said as he slammed him into the back of the cruiser. In tears of exasperation, Melody made her way into the hotel. She alternately fingered her cell phone and the room key to Phillip's suite. She called Jessica just as she got off the elevator on their floor and explained what had happened.

"They're going to come back and search the hotel room. Get all your stuff out of there, now! If you've got time, ditch any drugs Phillip has stashed in there. I'm on my way to get you. Meet me in front of the hotel down the street."

Melody tore into the room they had left in such a lithe mood that afternoon. She wanted to curl up on the bed and cry, but she knew she couldn't. Quickly, she tossed clothes into her bag, pausing only briefly to gauge if they were hers or Phillip's.

She riffled through the bathroom, carelessly shoving her toothpaste, toothbrush, hairbrush, deodorant, razor, and other toiletries into her pack. She had to get out. She could feel time ticking away. If she didn't get out soon, she would be joining Phillip in jail. She flushed his bag of weed and some pills down the toilet.

She was almost out the door before she noticed the closet. In haste, she flung open the door just to see what was in there. A few of Phillip's nicer clothes were on the hangers, but nothing incriminating. The door was almost closed before she noticed the safe on the floor. It had a digital keypad for a locking mechanism.

"Two, nine, one, four."

She pressed the corresponding buttons and heard the tumblers give way inside the lock. The door hinged open to reveal a blue duffel bag. Melody yanked it from the safe and tore back the zipper, not knowing what to expect.

She let out a squeal of surprise when she saw what was in the bag. A neat pile of bundled hundred dollar bills and Phillip's Sunday ticket waited patiently inside the bag, unconcerned by all the ruckus Melody was creating. She quickly zipped the bag closed and clutched it close to her. She half-ran down the hallway to the elevators.

She was going to make it.

On the bottom floor her elevator opened in time for her to see six police officers with their back to her standing at the front desk and questioning the night clerk. The clerk gave her a grave look, but didn't indicate to the cops she was there. All those tips Phillip had been so generous with paid off in giving Melody a few extra seconds. She quickly punched another button on the elevator and went back upstairs again.

She was carrying too much stuff in the middle of

the night to walk past those cops. She got off on the third floor, formulating a plan. She ran down the hallways, her heavy backpack slowing her down considerably as she also dealt with the clumsy weight of the duffel bag full of money.

She made it to her destination and entered the stairwell that led to the parking garage. The cold Denver night greeted her with the whirring of motors and the flashing of police lights out on the street. Three patrol cars were parked in front of the Monaco.

Just down the street she could see a worried Jessica sitting in front of the Residence Inn. "I'm going to make it," Melody said to herself and began to flow nonchalantly towards Jessica's Forerunner. Jessica spotted her emerging from the shadows and felt her heart flip-flop inside her chest. In true Jedi fashion, Melody sauntered deliberately over to Jessica's waiting vehicle. She opened the door, settled her pack into place, and took her seat. She looked at Jessica. Both girls were wide awake and scared.

Due to the one-way street they were on, they would have to drive by the police cars on their way out.

"Just fucking go," Melody whispered.

Jessica put the truck into gear and let the idle speed of the engine carry them slowly past the flickering lights. Phillip was still there. He was in the backseat of one of the cruisers and he gazed out at the girls as they drove past. He didn't say a word and the police missed the girls rolling by. Within minutes they were just another rolling box lost amongst thousands of others on the Interstate.

They made it to Jessica's hotel room, fully expecting every cop they passed on the interstate to pull them over and take them to jail. Neither of them could sleep. They were both just bundles on nerves. They fidgeted on the beds or paced the room, crying to each other.

At four-thirty in the morning Melody's cell phone rang. The number came up as unlisted and she debated whether or not to answer it. She finally did, on the fifth ring, just before her message picked up. She answered hesitantly while Jessica watched on expectantly.

"I just called to give you a message," she recognized the voice. It was Charlie. "A friend wanted me to let you know that he hopes you got everything for your trip. If there's anything of his you need to use, there's no obligation to return it. It'll be awhile, but plan on visiting again. In the meantime, you enjoy yourself."

And then Charlie hung up. She wanted to call him back and find out something about Phillip, but she couldn't. She didn't have his number. She thought about calling the police station, but decided she better not. It was best not to get too involved in the situation

"Who was that? What did they say?" Jessica held her hands together and stared intently at Melody.

"It was Phillip's business partner. I think he said I could keep the money."

56

"Hello?" Nathan answered the phone expectantly. It was Sunday morning and the voice he had waited so long to hear was finally speaking to him again.

"Hello," she said.

The silence was uncomfortable. Neither of them were willing to begin this conversation. A sense of dread filled Nathan as he waited for her to find some words.

"Are you alright?" He finally asked.

"Yeah. I'm fine. Everything's fine. It's just..." she trailed off. How could she do this? How could she leave her family? She was an adult, with responsibilities and people who depended on her.

"How are the girls?" Melody asked.

"They're good. They miss their mother. They miss their family."

She felt it welling up inside of her again. Could she really do this? How was it worth it? But the way he had said "family" made her cringe. He was talking about a prison, not about freedom.

It wasn't forever. Nothing was forever. This was just the next moment in her dance. Tour was going to be over in two weeks. She'd spend another week or two in the Northeast, then probably head back to Asheville. Probably, if that's where her path led her.

Maybe so. Maybe not.

"I'm not coming back," she finally stated.

"What? Where are you going?" Nathan asked, trying his best not to sound upset or confused, even though these were his two prevailing emotions.

"California, Washington, Chicago, and the northeast. I need to see my family again. I haven't seen them in so long."

She was being purposefully vague with him. She didn't need to explain herself to him anymore. She didn't even need to explain herself to herself. This is what she felt and she felt it so persistently, even in this morning after, that she had to act on it. This is

what felt right and the universe had given her everything
she needed to continue.

"Are you going on tour?" Nathan finally asked. He knew the Phish dates. She was quiet, but he knew.

"How?" He finally asked.

"I just am."

"Did you find another man?"

"No. That doesn't matter. Let me talk to the girls."

When she was done, both Maia and Clarity were crying and the only sound from the other end of the line when Nathan got the phone back was a dial tone.

57

Sunday's show was very muted for Melody. She wasn't sure of herself at all. She was still clinging to this feeling that everything would be all right. She just wasn't so sure. Was leaving her family in search of something that maybe couldn't be found anymore really the thing to do? Maybe there was never really such a thing as freedom. Maybe the music was just music, or just the noise so many people said it was.

She was certain of nothing.

Melody and Jessica slipped quietly into the venue together. They didn't have much to say to one another, the drama of last night still playing over and over in their minds. Somehow, they hoped Phillip would just be there and they could just go back to having fun, but of course he wasn't. He was surely languishing in a cell somewhere.

The girls stayed seated in the back while the first set seemed to just rumble on. It was an early show and the sunshine seemed too bright. During the set break they almost left.

Then Mike kicked off the bass line to "Boogie on Reggae Woman," an old Stevie Wonder tune. They stood up and Melody tapped her foot along with the beat. Jessica started to move just a little bit and the motion infected Melody. Suddenly they were both dancing like they had been.

The girls couldn't help themselves. It took this kind of dance to shake off the weight of all the conflicting emotions they felt.

Trey sang, "I'd like to see both of you fall deeply in love."

The women looked at each other and understanding passed between them. No matter what happened, this music and this friendship would always be here. The strange energy that flowed into Melody was forever available, if only she could tap into it. The music helped, but it wasn't responsible for anything. Melody controlled the power to feel good about herself, her situation, and to connect to the spirit moving in all things. Whether she found it through Widespread Panic, Phish, or somewhere else, it was always there.

It didn't matter who she was dancing next to, where she was, or what drugs she was on. Completely sober, she felt as if she were leaving her body when in reality she was just finding the unwavering truth that was always present in her as it was in everyone and everything.

Certainly there were pitfalls along the way. Darkness threatened to overtake her on all sides. It was a crazy, mixed up world she was traveling through. It only made sense that she should feel mixed up and lost. Somewhere, beneath it all, this wonderful song was always being sung, if only she had the ears to listen.

For now, the best thing she could do was to live her life in love with every minute she had. She was merely a note in the entire symphony of existence. She danced, and in the music, she let go of her concerns for Phillip. He drifted off in the wailing notes of the guitar, and away went the despair she felt for Nathan and her daughters.

She loved each of them dearly, but couldn't be responsible for what they felt. The only person she had any power over was herself. She was through putting herself and her own desires behind anyone else.

For the encore Phish mirrored her sentiments with a heartfelt rendition of "Bittersweet Motel". Trey let the audience know his daughter had been pestering him to play it all weekend. Melody found herself in tears again. The music had moved her life physically and emotionally for so long. It was all she knew. It certainly wasn't all she cared about, but it was a method for discovering and rediscovering herself again and again.

None of us are ever completely at home in our bodies. We're just passing through and everyone knows it on some level. Trials and turmoil are the darkness that allow us to appreciate the light of love and laughter; and friendship. Melody gazed over at Jessica and felt intimately connected to her dearest friend. Years may have passed between them but Melody was aware now that nothing would ever separate them.

She scanned the crowd and felt the same interconnectedness to all of them. When these bodies finally stopped dancing, and the rhythm of these hearts stopped beating for good, everyone was going back to the same place.

The songs of our individual lives will rejoin the symphony playing through everything. We will all fade away into the collective consciousness that embodies everything. When we sing songs of rain, the rain might fall. When we remember our dearly departed friends, their fire shines in ten thousand flickering lights carried by the hands of the loved ones.

Everyday, there is a parade, whether we notice it or not. Every moment our life is a song, whether we choose to sing along with it or not. Dissonance or harmony can envelop us. It is our choice.

There were still many choices to be made for Melody. Would she eventually go back to Nathan and her family? Maybe she'd meet up with Phillip when he got out of jail? No matter what, she was certain that she could never mute the song in her heart and be happy with her life. She was going to be the Melody of herself. A Melody in motion, changing and growing with each passing day and each circumstances she encountered.

It had taken ten years of hearing the same songs over and over again to finally realize that these songs were constantly playing, not in the background, but in the forefront of life. A layer of skin had been shed on these magnificent rocks and she was fresh and new. She no longer felt anxious about the journey she would undertake or what she would leave behind. Nothing is really left behind.

In a final farewell to a life she had lived without ambition for far too long, Melody was cascaded with the flowing notes of "Slave To The Traffic Light." She danced, and felt the years of servitude to expectations of who she was supposed to be washed away again. Life is an adventure, just waiting to happen, and Melody wasn't going to let it pass her by anymore.

In the lot afterwards she and Jessica both hung around to help the green crew with their final cleanup. Jessica was willing to do anything not to have to leave Melody yet.

"I'm worried about you," Jessica said.

"Don't be," Melody firmly assured her. Melody was clear and focused on her personal journey. She was going to undertake an adventure, and the music of her own soul would be the soundtrack. "I've got to do this."

"What are you going to do with yourself on tour? Are you just going to blow all that money?" Jessica didn't want to sound motherly, but she felt a certain sense of duty to Melody.

Melody reached out and held Jessica's hand. "I want you to sell me all the clothes you brought to work here. Have some more ready when I get to Chicago, and I'll buy them, too. However much you can make. Maybe I'll open a shop in Asheville when tour is over."

"Of course," Jessica was overjoyed. Suddenly this trip wasn't a complete bust. She had almost five thousand dollars worth of clothes at retail price. She sold it all to Melody for $3,000.

Jessica gave Melody a ride to a used car dealership, where she bought a Chevy van with cash and outfitted it for tour.

In the morning sunlight Jessica was heading east, back to Chicago and Kale.

Melody was heading west, pursuing a destiny that could never be fully explained.

Epilogue:

Was It For This My Life I Sought?

Nathan was amazed at his own sense of acceptance and peace with it all. He knew exactly what Melody was doing and why. He even supported her. For too many years she'd been a quiet servant to his needs. Now her needs were calling and he completely understood. In some ways, he wanted to be doing it himself. Jealousy flickered into his heart thinking of Melody and the adventure she was allowing herself to undertake. The flicker of jealousy haunted him for the rest of the evening.

He'd been doing his best to be zen-like about this situation. Anything else just left him feeling heartsick. He was just as powerless to change anything she was feeling as he was to stop his own heart from still loving her.

The girls required only the briefest of explanation that their mother was okay, still loved them, and would be back in a few weeks, then Maia and Clarity ceased their terrible wailing and returned to their play. Nathan was always astounded by the resilience of children. Less than half an hour passed between them believing their mother had left their world forever before they were happily playing again.

He knew the empty space in his own heart would take a lot longer to go away.

He walked his daughters through their regular nighttime ritual. They took a bath, brushed their teeth, and curled into their beds while he read them a story. Nathan gave each of them a goodnight kiss and Maia and Clarity went to sleep muttering, "I love you daddy."

Nathan retired to his own bed. He was exhausted from the events of the past few days. He lied there, examining that small flicker of jealousy. Did he really want to be on tour again?

Certainly he missed feeling that overwhelming connection he could experience at the shows. He could still feel that whenever he listened to Phish and especially Panic. Excitement bubbled inside of him when he heard those familiar songs.

He listened to the music in his head until he thought of his daughters and the sweet little voices that said, "I love you daddy," and was overwhelmed with a feeling of love akin to what he'd experience dancing at so many shows.

His memories traveled through the years and he saw the faces of his friends dancing in his mind's eye. Kale was perpetually on tour, but had found a way to make it work for him. Jessica could still be found at a show from time to time, but it wasn't her life anymore. Who could say what Phillip or Lucy were doing?

Then there was Melody, back out there in the mix, forsaking the stable family life Nathan had tried so hard to build.

Who could say what was right? If this was what she needed in her life now, he could he deny it? If he really loved her without condition, then he had to accept this. There was freedom in knowing that he would always love her, no matter what, and that there was nothing that could be done to change that.

He let his mind travel back down the roads of his life. In some ways he was lucky to be alive and well after everything tour took out of him. Natron could easily have been one of those random kids overdosing in the parking lot or a hotel room. It happened frequently enough that he'd known a few of the kids who died along the way.

But no one called him Natron anymore.

The love he felt for his children had supplanted his need to seek out anything else. The only thing missing was Melody, and maybe she'd come back one day. The door would forever be open to her.

Until then, he had a purpose and a reason, and they called him "daddy," and depended on him to be present. Certainly those years on tour had introduced him to the unconditional love ever present in the universe and taught him how to tap into it.

It was because he knew that this love was always there, permeating everything and singing in the background, that he was able to be the father he'd become. The basic reason he went on tour was to find some meaning to life. He'd found it, as had so many of his friends. He learned that happiness isn't a destination, rather a method of travel.

But some were still searching. How could he criticize anyone for undertaking the same journey he had been on? How could he judge Melody? At least she was trying to become the best person she could be. At least she was doing what she felt necessary for the evolution of her soul. All he could do was wish her well in her journey.

Nathan had learned that neither Phish or Widespread Panic held the answers. They could offer insight, but in the end each individual at the show chose what they took home. Some found nothing at all. Others got a taste of something and went to another show and another show after that, perpetually. Maybe they would find that elusive meaning they had been seeking in the first place and maybe they wouldn't.

For himself, Nathan had found what he needed. Sure, he'd still go see Panic when they came to Asheville; and maybe Phish if they ever came close enough and he could actually get a ticket. But the drive to keep seeking it out was gone.

He couldn't imagine waking up every morning contemplating how to get to the next show. He'd made it to the end of that road. He still listened to the music and it still inspired him. It was great music, extolling a great philosophy, but in the end the greatest music isn't formed by musicians. It is being played everyday on the stages of our lives.

The small flame of jealously that had been burning in his mind slowly flickered away. The fire of longing replaced it. His heart reached out to Melody, wherever she was on her journey, and wished her back home. It didn't matter the miles she covered, the men she slept with along the way, or the drugs she took. She would forever be the true and honest love of his life. If she was gone forever, then he would still be glad to have known her and spent so many joyous years with such a vibrant woman.

He was destined to live a long and lucky life. Now, he had two young lives to apply this great love, understanding, and acceptance to. A person could go to a million shows, traverse their own mental landscape with the aid of every available substance out there, and never discover the meaning of their own life. Then again, they might find it hidden in one note of the encore at their first show.

However, if the search just keeps going and going and the wisdom found along the way never gets put into practical use, then the meaning becomes meaningless. Nathan was certain that life isn't about searching and never finding out anything. Life is a journey to be undertaken with no destination.

Unable to sleep, he stirred from his bed and wandered into the girls' room.

Under the glow of their night light he watched them breathing. The emotions they created in him were unlike anything he ever thought life could contain. This was more than enough meaning to last him far beyond the next show.

Somewhere in the night their mother was dancing.

Nathan instinctively knew she was dancing her way home, just as he was.

-THE END-

Acknowledgments:

This book wouldn't be possible without the help of many people. However, there were two women, in particular, without whom this just wouldn't have happened at all. They deserve much more from me than a few words at the end of a book, but it's all I've got. Much thanks to Melody Dawn Gentry and Lauren McFarlane for taking the time to read along as I struggled to write. Without their advice and constant support this would be just another unfinished project.

Thanks to everydaycompanion.com and phantasytour.com for information and setlists.

Thanks to Panicstream.com and LivePhish.com for providing tunes.

Endless thanks to Phish and Widespread Panic.

An extra special thank you to my family, especially my mom Gwynn Busby, for the constant support, no matter what I've been doing with my life.

Daniel Quinn also deserves as much praise as I can possibly give for basically nurturing the writer inside of me, but also for reading an earlier draft of this book, letting me know what was wrong, and offering suggestions on how to fix it…and also for being my friend.

READ ISHMAEL

Thanks to Hillary for the inspiration.

• See you at the next show •

About the Author:

I was born in the dusty flats of West Texas and escaped shortly after graduating high school in 1997. Instead of college, I opted to travel America, having now visited or lived in 47 states at the time of this writing.

It was during the early days of life on the road that I met the best-selling author of *Ishmael,* Daniel Quinn. Quinn became my writing mentor and friend, inspiring my first book, *Feasting on the Breeze*, which was originally published in sections on Ishmael.com beginning on 1/1/2000.

In the Spring of 1997 I made it to my first Phish concert in Austin and shortly afterwards my first Widespread Panic show in Dallas. I was hooked. From 1999-2005 I was on tour like it was my job. Illegally vending quesadillas and fajitas across the country. I managed to support myself and discovered a way to slip through the cracks of modern civilization.

After my boys, Travel and Noble, were born, I settled in the remote village of Crestone, Colorado. I'm still trying to discover some way in which my art can support us.

I know that creating art isn't about creating a means to an end. The creation itself satisfies me so I keep writing and performing music with my band, Stimulus, occasionally slipping out for a show or a whole tour with either my band or another.

In the meantime I hustle up whatever work I can to pay the rent and feed the kids. So if you need an ordained minister for your wedding, a band for your house party, a waterfall, patio, or rock wall in your landscaping, new carpet laid, your house painted…etc.

Also, I've got a school bus retrofitted to be a fully functioning motor home complete with stove, sink, shower, fridge, & toilet. If you would be interested in hiring me and my bus to chaperone you through a tour or a leg of tour, that can be arranged.

You could go on tour like the band goes on tour, with a sober driver, a king size bed to sleep in between shows, and a guide who wrote the book on tour.

You can buy my books here: www.lulu.com/spotlight/carlcole

Check out the band here: www.stimulusmusic.com

Connect on FaceBook here: www.facebook.com/carl.cole.50